TREACHEROUS MAGIC

MODERN MAGIC - BOOK THREE

NICOLE HALL

To Amy and Kelly, here's the magic stuff

PROLOGUE

MADDIE

WHEN MADDIE THOMAS IMAGINED DREAMWALKING, she pictured a tropical island with beautiful shirtless cabana boys bringing her fruity umbrella drinks. Instead, she blinked at the glare of neon beer signs in an unfamiliar bar that smelled of whiskey and regret.

Dark wood paneling and dim lights cast shadows across most of the booths. The giant Texas flag hanging on the wall told her she'd traveled a long way from the little room in Wales where she'd fallen asleep. She looked down, unsurprised to see the leggings and tank top she'd gone to sleep in, but her knee-high boots were a new addition to the outfit.

Maddie shrugged. Strange occurrences happened every day for her. None of the patrons paid her any mind, and the bartender ignored her when she settled onto a cracked vinyl barstool. Country music played from the speakers, and Maddie winced at the twangy noise. She'd never liked the sound, despite growing up in a tiny town in East Texas.

There was no one else sitting at the bar, so she cleared her throat. The guy with the big belly drying glasses didn't look up. Maddie sighed and glanced around. What had brought her here?

Her eyes skipped past a familiar face in the far back booth, then jumped back with a shiver. He was looking down at a phone, so she couldn't be sure, but his profile seemed right. Maddie suddenly felt very exposed by the lights over the bar. The stool squeaked as she slid off of it, and the bartender finally looked up. His brow furrowed as he stared at the seat where she'd been, then he went back to drying.

He hadn't seen Maddie. Yep, dreamwalking. Too bad she'd been unceremoniously yanked into a nightmare.

Despite her throat closing up, she calmly walked to the shadowy corner on the far side of the room and leaned back against the wall with a good view of the booths. The man glanced up at the door, and she had her confirmation. Torix was in the bar with her. Or she was in the bar with him. Her heart sped up with fear, but he ignored her just like the bartender.

The door opened with a rush of cold air, and a disheveled man in a topcoat came in. Maddie had seen him before too, but it took a moment for her to place him. Sera's ex-husband. The creepy one who'd followed her to Mulligan last year. The last time she'd seen him, he'd looked like a movie star, but since then, he'd lost weight and grown a ratty beard. There was no doubt in her mind why he'd shown up, and after a quick survey of the room, he made a beeline to Torix's table.

The mild annoyance on Torix's face transformed into a welcoming smile. Maddie couldn't hear what he said, so she chose a booth closer to theirs—behind Torix's line of sight —that allowed her to see his profile and listen in.

"I'm glad you could make it, Will. We have much to discuss."

"You said you had a solution to my problems." Will looked around the bar and frowned. "This place is a dump."

A muscled ticked in Torix's jaw, but Will didn't seem to notice. "A temporary meeting place, nothing more. You wish to take revenge on Sera and her ilk for what they've done to you."

Will's eyes shot back to Torix. "What do you know about that?"

Torix tilted his head. "I know a great many things. You were once successful, powerful, the master of your world."

Torix's smooth voice coated her nerves in a hypnotizing calmness. Her fight or flight response worked overtime to convince her she needed to leave. Now. Nothing good could come from Torix and Will working together.

Will sat up a little straighter at each of Torix's words. "Yes. I was the master, and that bitch, Sera, took it all from me. They did something to me. Made it hard to think." He shook his head roughly for a second. "I see things that weren't there before."

"I can help you. You can be powerful again."

Maddie didn't know Will, but she wanted to tell him to run far away from that offer. Memories tried to blind her from her own time with Torix, but Maddie pushed them away to focus. Sera had taken all of Torix's power over a year ago, so Maddie wanted to know how Torix planned to fulfill his end of the bargain.

Will nodded, greed in his eyes. "What do I need to do?"

Maddie closed her eyes and shook her head for a moment. The idiot didn't even ask any basic questions. She opened them again in time to see Torix pull a pouch and a tiny knife from a bag sitting next to him on the bench. "We share blood. Like unto like. Only a few drops into the pouch and we'll work together to destroy Sera and her mate."

Will's hand clenched into a fist when Torix mentioned Sera's mate, and a new fear filled Maddie. She loved Jake more than anyone. Her brother had saved her last year while helping Sera stop Torix, and mate was definitely the right term for his and Sera's relationship now. In all the time that had passed since then, Maddie hadn't considered that Jake might be in danger.

Her fingers tapped silently on the table. She wanted to stop the ceremony, but she wasn't really there. Knowing Torix, these events had already happened.

Torix sliced a shallow cut across his own palm with the knife and raised his brow. Will didn't hesitate. He extended his own hand, palm up, and Torix made a matching slash. He held both their hands over the open pouch so the blood could drip into it. Maddie's nose wrinkled as the smell of sulfur drifted to her, but no one else seemed to notice.

Will gasped, and a wave of magic shot out from the booth. Maddie couldn't see it, but she felt it like electric tingles covering her body. She shuddered. Years ago, she'd felt the same tingles, but this time, she experienced the sensation from the outside. Will didn't know it, but he'd doomed himself.

"It's done. You'll return to your room with the bird to await further orders."

Maddie's eyebrows winged up as a pretty little songbird hopped out of the bag and flapped up to land on Will's shoulder. He didn't react to the new addition. In fact, all the personality had drained from Will's face, like he'd been replaced by a mannequin. Man and bird got up from the booth without a goodbye and headed for the door. Torix watched Will walk out of the bar and smiled. Maddie considered trying to follow him to see what would happen, but to her surprise, Torix turned and offered her a slow appraisal.

"You look well, my dear."

Maddie's breath caught in her throat. He shouldn't be able to see her, unless she'd been in his head the whole time. Her heartbeat pounded in her chest. She got a stranglehold on her panic and shoved it down hard. "What do you want?"

He tsked and sent her a charming smile. "That's no way to greet an old friend."

"You were never my friend." She spit the last word at him, and his smile dimmed a bit.

"It seems we remember things differently. All that time spent together, causing mayhem." Torix leaned toward her, and his tongue snaked across his lips. "I've missed the taste of your fear."

A cold chill skittered up her back, but Maddie refused to retreat. "Leave me alone."

His eyes sharpened, and his nostrils flared. "I'm afraid that's not possible. You've hidden yourself well, but the time for patience is over. It seems you have something of mine."

Maddie reminded herself that Torix was powerless. He couldn't touch her, but with what she'd just witnessed, she had trouble believing the adage. "How did you trap Will?"

He tilted his head at her like he was studying an interesting bug. "I don't believe I'll tell you that." He closed the pouch and tucked it in the bag.

Torix had pulled her in for a reason, ostensibly to show her he'd made a Will-zombie, but why would he want her to know that? Maddie wondered about the bird as well, but other aspects of this little visit took precedence. "You're back in Mulligan."

He nodded once. "You'll come to me, but will it be too late to save your brother?" He shrugged as his smile grew. "Perhaps I'll come to you instead. Wales, is it?"

Maggie snapped her shields closed tightly, cursing herself for reverting back to a scared little girl and forgetting her training. He'd been manipulating her, as usual. Misdirecting her, providing irresistible bait, and using her distraction to fish for information on her location. Maddie frowned when Torix didn't disappear. As long as her shields were closed, he shouldn't have had access to her mind.

Fine. She'd separate them the old-fashioned way. Torix may have been controlling things until now, but it was *her* dream. She straightened her shoulders and stood. When he would have followed suit, a low growl from beside her had him narrowing his eyes instead.

A speckled, grey and white wolf had appeared next to her. His huge body came up to her waist, and his lip curled back revealing very sharp teeth pointed at Torix. Maddie spread her fingers in the coarse fur along his back, glad to have backup, no matter how unexpected.

Torix raised a brow and disappeared. The bar began to slowly fade around her, and Maddie took a full breath for the first time since she'd seen him. Seventeen months. She'd been hiding for seventeen months. Training, yes, and reading every scrap of magical information she could get her hands on, but in the end, her fear had trumped all.

The wolf stopped growling as soon as Torix disappeared. He settled back on his haunches and stared at the now empty booth. The two of them together might have scared Torix off, but she didn't think that was the case. Either way, she could have handled it herself.

Maddie crouched down in front of the gorgeous animal, meeting his golden eyes.

"I know you're not a wolf," she said quietly.

He held her gaze for a moment, then she woke up in her bed in Wales. Maddie sat up and ran her hand through her long, tangled hair, pulling it away from her face. The weak predawn light of the room revealed her backpack and little else. In those seventeen months, she'd learned to travel light and always be prepared. When Jake and Sera had told her Torix had escaped, she'd known the danger would return. Fear and resolution fought for dominance, but Maddie refused to let fear win again. She threw the thin blanket off and began collecting her belongings.

Torix had threatened Jake to force her back to Mulligan, and she'd do anything to protect Jake. Even deplete her savings. Maddie slung her pack over her shoulder and pulled out her phone. The international airline booked her on a flight that day for the cost of a small car. Without more information about the setting of the dream, she couldn't afford to wait for a better deal.

With trepidation fluttering in her chest, Maddie left her boarding house and waited for the bus to Cardiff. She'd wasted enough time hiding.

1

MADDIE

Maddie hadn't seen her family in almost a year. To be fair, her family hadn't really seen *her* in much longer than that. She stood down the street from the house that she'd grown up in, which like Mulligan, had changed very little. Cars lined the street, and people gathered outside despite the chill in the air. She'd known about Jake and Sera's christening party, but as usual, she'd declined the invitation. As far as her family knew, she had no plans to leave Europe. A visit from Torix provided great motivation.

Her dad had the grill going in the back, and Maddie could smell the brisket from where she'd stopped walking. The scent urged her forward, making her mouth water. She hadn't had a good brisket in months. The party made her nervous, but it also probably meant Torix hadn't made his move against Jake yet.

The bright sun made up for the fog and rain she'd left in Wales. She slid her sunglasses into her hair and squinted at the party. Jake and Sera would be there with baby Amber. It was their house after all, but so would Ryan and Zee. Her steps faltered. She hadn't had much dealing with Zee, a few conversations after the events of last year, at Sera's insistence, but if her experience had taught her anything, it was that Fae couldn't be trusted.

A cold gust of wind made Maddie shiver in her thin sweater. Her pack slapped against her back as she abruptly stopped in front of Sera's old house next door. Maddie hadn't been spotted yet. She ducked into the side yard between the properties and settled behind a couple of leafless trees. Her dark clothes blended with the shadows, and she crouched down to make herself smaller.

Laughter drifted to Maddie, and she felt a pang of longing. She wanted to be there with her brother and her parents. Her niece was five months old, and Maddie'd never met her. Jake and Sera emailed her pictures, but it wasn't the same. They treated Maddie as if the events last Halloween hadn't happened, and the guilt nearly drowned her.

Wisps of blond hair escaped her braid and blew into her eyes with the next breeze. She tucked them away and watched Jake come out the back door with Amber on his hip. Her shoulders sagged in relief at the proof that she wasn't too late. Torix knew exactly what to say to get her to act, but after seven years, she'd gotten good at reading between his half-truths. He intended to kill her brother, but he wanted her first. And he wanted her in Mulligan.

Jake had a beer in one hand and a huge smile on his face. He stopped at the grill to talk to their dad, then strapped the baby into a swing set up in the yard. Amber smiled big, like her dad, and kicked her legs at anyone who walked by. Sera came out of the house next, and Jake pulled her close. He said something to her that made her shake her head and dropped a kiss on her forehead.

The whole exchange was exactly how she imagined their life. Easy and wonderful now that she couldn't cause trouble. Maddie rubbed her chest where an ache spread. They'd tried to incorporate her after Halloween, but it had quickly become clear that she needed distance. The things she'd done for Torix, as Torix, haunted her. She couldn't forget when every time she saw Jake the images of him unconscious on the forest floor flooded her. Maddie didn't fool herself that she deserved the happy ending.

Jake said something to make Sera laugh, then went back into the house. A couple of people stopped to chat with Sera as she made her way to the baby, and Maddie wondered what would happen if she crashed the party and announced Torix was back.

Probably everyone would welcome her with open arms and patronize her while they tried to handle it. As if Torix were a minor annoyance or something. They'd more than likely get themselves killed. Maddie shook her head and adjusted to a more comfortable position. She'd gotten bitter, but then, she had a pretty good excuse. Seven years of servitude would do that. Apparently, a year of freedom didn't provide a better mindset. Still, she should be thanking Sera instead of watching in the shadows like a creeper.

Even now, Maddie couldn't make herself walk over to her family and warn them. She'd come back for that express purpose, but crossing the distance proved harder than she'd thought it would be. Maddie considered emailing Sera the information to avoid any questions, but she didn't want them searching out Torix. He may have lost his own power, but he'd clearly found another source.

The baby waved her arms, but all Sera did was rub her little tummy and say something to Maddie's dad. He nodded, and Sera turned to look directly at Maddie.

The trees and shadows hid her well, but Sera was half-Fae. Maddie was surprised her hiding spot had lasted this long. Sera strolled through the brush at the property line and came to lean against a tree with her back to Maddie.

"Why are you hiding in the yard?"

"It seemed like as good a place as any."

Sera sighed. "There's food and drinks in the house, and I know your mom would love to see you. Janet too."

"I know." Janet had sent her a healing crystal, though she hadn't known that Maddie even needed healing. It was strange and sweet, and nearly crushed Maddie with guilt for how she'd treated her former boss.

As for her mom, every day since leaving for Europe, Maddie got an email containing a run-down of anything that happened to anyone in Mulligan. Maddie knew her parents weren't planning to stay much longer, there were adventures to be had, but Amber was their first grandchild and they weren't going to miss the Fae naming. Maddie understood the sentiment.

"How did Mom take finding out about the Fae?"

Sera shrugged. "The usual, mostly. She skipped the denial phase and went straight to excitement. Did you know she'd always thought there was something strange about the Wood?"

Maddie chuckled. "Yeah. She's believed in the fantastic her whole life. Having a part-Fae grandchild must be the greatest thing that ever happened to her." She couldn't keep the sadness entirely out of her voice, and Sera picked up on it.

"She wishes you were there, Mad. Her greatest wish is to have her whole family together and safe...and for Thor to descend from the heavens in nothing but a kilt, but we're pretty sure that was the wine talking."

She snorted out another laugh. "That, I believe."

"Come to the party, Mad. Let us help you heal."

"I'm not interested in healing."

It was the wrong thing to say. Maddie couldn't see Sera's face, but the disapproval came through clearly in her stiffened shoulders. Years ago, *Sera* would have been the one hiding while Maddie coaxed her out. Coming into her magic had given Sera confidence that age hadn't. Maddie was only a year younger than her, but she felt much older.

"Jake looks happy." The subject change worked to get Sera's focus off of Maddie. "When are you two going to get married?"

Sera shrugged. "We're not in a hurry, but it would make things easier when we finally sell Evie's house."

"You know I'll be there, right?"

"I know. Jake knows too, but he'd be happier if his sister came home for good."

"I can't do that, Sera. I'm not sure I can ever move back to Mulligan. There are too many bad memories."

"I understand that. You know I do, more than anyone else, but running isn't the answer."

"I'm not running. I'm preparing. Torix will be back."

"He's powerless, Mad. He can't hurt you anymore."

Maddie shook her head, even though Sera couldn't see her. The moment had snuck up on her. All she had to say was *Torix is back, and he has a Will-zombie*, but the words were stuck in her throat. "Will was powerless. That didn't stop him from hurting you."

"That's true." She was silent for a moment. "We're worried about you and we miss you, but it's your life. You get to decide what you need out of it. Promise me you'll be careful?"

"I'm always careful now." Released from the pressure to

make an appearance, Maddie could breathe again. The baby
started to cry, but before Sera could push away from the
tree, Jake came out of the house to calm her down. "You
guys need to be careful too. Don't underestimate Torix and
Will."

Sera nodded, but the baby was distracting her. Maddie
needed to make her understand.

"I mean it, Sera. He's dangerous, even without his power,
and Will is under his thrall."

Sera spun around, and Maddie could feel the wave of
magic she used to check the area. "Are you sure?"

"Yes. I saw it in a dream."

Sera relaxed. "You had a lot of nightmares after we freed
you. Maybe something you were doing in Wales triggered
another one."

Maddie wanted to shake her. "It was real." She couldn't
claim any more than that because Torix could have been
manipulating the situation. At the very least, she knew for
certain that Torix had outside magic at his disposal somewhere near Mulligan.

Sera smiled and took her hand for a second. "Okay. We'll
keep our eyes open then. Maybe Evie or Lana have some
more information about Torix's whereabouts. I know where
Will is living. I'll go by and check on him."

Maddie gripped Sera's hand. "No. Please don't, Sera."
The whole situation suddenly felt like a trap. Could that
have been Torix's plan all along? Use Maddie to lure Sera
and Jake into danger? "Please promise me you'll stay away
from Will. Even if he calls you or something. I know you'll
keep it if you promise me."

Sera grimaced. "Okay, if it makes you feel better. It's not
like I hang out with him."

"I need you to say the words."

Maddie felt prickles of magic crawl up her arms as Sera met her eyes. "I promise to stay away from Will to the best of my abilities."

The prickles faded, and Maddie sighed in relief. "Thank you."

Sera glanced over her shoulder to Jake and the baby. "I have to get back."

"Don't tell them I was here. It'll just make everything worse."

Sera speared her with a look. "I won't lie to Jake. Besides, he knows I'm over here talking to you."

"I don't want you to lie. I just don't want you to bring it up."

She nodded and tilted her head. "Are you sure you don't want to come meet Amber?"

Maddie stared past her at the happy baby that Jake was bouncing around. She *did* want to come meet Amber, but too much darkness followed her. "I can't yet. I love you guys."

Her voice cracked at the end, and Sera pulled her into a quick hug. "Be safe."

Sera jogged across the yard toward Jake, who never took his eyes off of her. She said a few words, and his gaze shifted to Maddie's hiding place. He sent her a sad smile then gathered his family and went back into the house. A cloud drifted in front of the sun, and the breeze made Maddie shiver again. She had to stay as far away from them as possible. Torix enjoyed playing twisted games, and until Maddie knew the rules, she needed to take every precaution to keep them safe.

Maddie stayed in the shadows and circled the house until she was out of line of sight of Jake's place. The neighbors didn't worry her. Evie had left for the Glade months ago, and no one else would care that Maddie had returned. She'd spent a lot of time in the last few years severing connections. If she couldn't control her actions, she'd at least be able to limit the amount of people hurt by them. Torix had allowed it because it amused him to see her in pain.

The for-sale sign and the empty feel of the house made her sad. Even under Torix's influence, she'd spent a lot of good hours there practicing magic with Evie. Maddie hated what she'd done to her former teacher, and the time Evie had spent trapped ate at her. For a second, she considered going to the Glade and throwing herself on the mercy of the Fae, but they weren't well-known for their mercy. She'd heard Evie had tempered that a bit, but the idea of putting another person in charge of her fate again made her itch to run away as far and as fast as she could.

Maybe not the Glade, but the forest had always been her safe space. Maddie shouldered her pack and walked toward the trees across the street. She'd slept on the flight and the drive up from the airport, but she hadn't had a chance to stretch her muscles.

Maddie had taken worse strolls through the woods on a crisp January day. Her mind wandered as she wove between full pine trees and walked over crunchy leaves. Torix had engineered her presence in Mulligan. He'd known she wouldn't be able to ignore a threat to her family.

Torix said he'd been searching for her, and she wasn't ready for him to find her yet. Best case scenario, he'd get what he wanted and leave her more of a broken mess than she already was. Worst case, he killed her and everyone she loved. Maddie frowned. Mulligan was a small town, and by evening, everyone would know she was back. How could she keep away from Torix if they were both frequenting the same nine square miles?

She'd warned Sera and Jake; she could go back to Europe. An image of Amber kicking her feet in her swing popped into Maddie's head, and a fiery anger filled her. How much of her life was she willing to sacrifice for Torix? He'd stolen seven years. Was she going to give him another decade while she hid from him? She kicked a rock into the underbrush and looked up at the sliver of bright blue sky visible between the trees. He had to be stopped. *She* had to stop him. Everyone else had responsibilities, and none of them knew him as well as she did.

Fear threatened to overtake her, freezing her muscles and closing her throat, but she'd learned to move around it. Torix used fear to control, and she was done being controlled.

A clearing opened up ahead of her, and Maddie shook her head. She hadn't meant to walk there, but old habits died hard. It was bigger than she remembered, and full of tiny glowing balls of light. Sera had decimated the old dead oak, but the sprites and the circle of pines remained. She walked to the center and found the stone etched with ancient markings. Torix had called it a nexus. A place where several magics converged. And a place he'd spent several generations trapped in a tree.

She'd considered it the heart of the Wood, and considered the Fae stupid for trying to imprison a powerful force there. In the back of her mind, she'd always wondered if Torix hadn't manipulated that outcome as well.

A wind moved the tops of the trees, but the nexus stayed silent. The blue sky had faded as if the sun had gone down, but Maddie recognized the in-between space. At some point, she'd crossed from normal forest to magical trod. Maddie hadn't been able to make any paths since Sera had freed her. She'd tried. The trods hadn't responded before, but the Wood apparently wanted her here now.

Her stomach growled, and she remembered that she hadn't eaten anything since the questionable egg sandwich at the airport. Maddie cursed her issues for keeping her from the food at the party. She *really* missed brisket.

Maddie scrounged through her pack for a granola bar, but stopped when she felt someone watching her. She lifted her head and looked around. A quarter of the way around the clearing she spotted the wolf sitting in the brush. His dappled coat blended with the shadows. He looked relaxed, but his ears were perked up. She moved further into the circle, and his golden eyes followed her.

The last time she'd seen him, not counting the dream, he'd been as trapped as she'd been. Sera had removed Torix's hold and dismissed him as an errant wolf, but Maddie knew better. She dropped her gaze to her pack and pulled out her last two granola bars.

"You might as well join me. I have enough for both of us."

He didn't move right away, and when he slunk closer, he made no noise among the leaves. She sank to the ground and tore open one of the packages. He'd stopped a few feet away, and when she offered him the bar, he stayed where he was. It would be smart to fear him, but Maddie simply didn't. She sighed and tossed the food to him, then opened her own.

He ate the bar in three neat bites, but his eyes never left her.

Maddie tilted her head and stared back at him as she ate her late lunch. "Why do you stay in that form after everything he made you do?"

His ear twitched, but he didn't answer her. Not that she expected him to.

"You know he's back. That's why you're here. I get that part. What I don't get is if you're here to stop him or help him."

His shape blurred, and she felt magic dancing along her skin. Survival instinct said she should back away because if it was the latter, she was in trouble. Curiosity kept her still. His change fascinated Maddie, but watching him was probably rude. In all time she'd known him, she'd only seen the wolf. During the nearly instantaneous change, her eyes couldn't focus on him. One second a large wolf sat in front of her, the next, a large man crouched there.

He propped his arms on his knees, and Maddie raised a brow at his clothes. Honest to God leather pants tucked into high boots. At least they looked like leather pants, maybe suede, some kind of supple dark brown material. She had the urge to touch them and find out for herself. On top of that, his thigh muscles might have been bigger than her head.

He cleared his throat, and she realized she'd been basically staring at his crotch. A warm flush flooded her cheeks, and Maddie looked up. Broad shoulders, dark hair tied back from his face, a smirking mouth, and the same golden eyes. She'd expected him to look older, more grizzled, but the smooth angles of his face made her glad she'd been wrong. He couldn't have been much older than her. When had Torix had managed to capture him?

He quirked a brow, and Maddie was drawn back to his eyes. Wolf eyes, but not. He watched her like a predator, and a shiver went down her spine, but not from fear. If she ran, would he chase her? The thought sent a thrill through her, and she fought to shake off the effect. She had no time to be attracted to whatever he was.

Her mouth opened to question him, but her brain hadn't caught up with her common sense yet. "You look ridiculous."

He glanced down at himself. "How so?"

His rich, deep voice echoed inside her, and Maddie struggled to remember what she'd said a second ago. "No one wears leather pants unless they're going to a club."

"I'll keep that in mind the next time I'm in combat."

He didn't sound annoyed by her critique, which was fantastic because *Maddie* was annoyed with it. *What was wrong with her?* A sinful face and a sexy voice shouldn't be enough to completely shut off all rational thought.

She mentally shook herself and tried to focus on his relationship with Torix. The most likely scenario played out with him as a victim, like her, but people were crazy. Who knew what the effects of enslavement had been on him? "So, good guy or bad guy?"

"Neither." He didn't take his eyes off her, but he sat down in the pine straw, which made her feel a little better about his intentions. "But I'm not working with Torix. You?"

Considering her reaction to his human form, his response relieved her. She also appreciated having her instincts confirmed again. This time, they'd said he wasn't there to bring her back to Torix, and she'd learned the hard way to listen to herself first.

"No. I'm here for a different reason." She wasn't being coy; she wasn't sure why she'd ended up in the nexus.

He watched her a moment longer, then broke the tension by looking around the clearing. "Things have changed. I like it better this way."

She stifled a laugh. "You mean without the super powerful, psychopathic Fae controlling everything we did from inside a damn tree?"

His smile was quick, then it was gone. "Yeah, and being human again has its perks."

She sobered. "You couldn't change?"

"No. His hold was absolute, and he wanted the wolf."

Maddie nodded. She knew all about Torix's hold. "I'm Maddie Thomas."

"Aiden Morgan." He extended his hand, and she shook it. His warm, gentle contact settled her better than his words had.

Maddie drew her hand back reluctantly. "If you're not here to serve Torix, what *are* you doing here?"

"I'm here to kill him." The words were matter of fact, and Maddie respected his bluntness.

She nodded again. "Me too. You were in my dream."

He grabbed a handful of pine needles and stared weaving them together. "I was following Torix. He pulled you in; I pulled you out."

Maddie couldn't look away from his hands. The motions were delicate and precise. "How is that possible? I understand Torix and I are still connected, which theoretically lets him pop in, but how were you able to affect anything?"

He shrugged. "There must be more connecting us than indentured servitude."

Maddie wasn't so sure, but she didn't have a better idea. He worked a small circle in his hands, and she could see the beginnings of a tiny knot design forming. "You're not Fae."

"No." He didn't look up from his crafting.

He wasn't human. His magic felt like something...else. Not to mention she'd seen him shift from wolf to man. Most humans couldn't do that. "Werewolf?"

He chuckled. "You think the stories are true?"

"I think anything is possible at this point."

"Not a werewolf."

"Will you tell me if I guess it correctly?"

His eyes raised to hers, and she felt that tingle again. He fell quiet for a moment, intense, as if searching her for something. "I don't know."

At least he'd given an honest answer. "I'm going to keep asking."

His smile returned. "I know."

Maddie didn't usually go for the cryptic, know-it-all routine. She wanted direct answers to her questions, but she couldn't fault him for wanting to keep his secrets to himself. It's not like she was being all that forthcoming. Maybe she should ask a question that required a more complicated answer.

"Why a wolf?"

"Better than a dragon."

"I'm going to disagree with you on that one," she muttered.

A small crash and a thud came from the trees, interrupting their peaceful interlude. Both of them sprang to their feet. Aiden moved with an easy grace, despite being much taller than her. He scanned the area, turning in a slow circle, but didn't reach for any weapons. She didn't relish the idea of fighting side by side with Aiden in his human form. As a wolf, she knew what to expect from him, but men sometimes reacted in stupid ways.

He looked up at the darkening sky as if he'd seen something, and a flash of movement streaked out of the trees at them. Maddie didn't have time to think. She threw herself between Aiden and the creature. Her hands came up as if drawing a sword, and a blade of shimmering silver magic took shape.

She swung at what looked like a white lizard that was roughly the size of a cat. It dodged around the magic and leapt at them with bared fangs. Maddie jerked back and bumped into Aiden. One arm came around her waist from behind and spun her to the side. The lizard missed her face, but managed to sink its teeth into her shoulder.

Her breath hissed out between her teeth as fiery pain shot down her arm. Aiden grabbed the creature around its neck, and it disappeared in a puff of warm smoke. Blood trickled into her shirt as the trees started to slowly spin. She released the magic, and the blade disappeared, but she was having trouble keeping herself upright. Aiden's other arm slid under her knees, and he lifted her without much effort.

"Put me down. I'm fine." Maddie's weak voice embarrassed her as she tried to push against his chest. The guy was solid muscle.

"You're not fine, but you will be. It's okay. I'll take care of you."

She wanted to laugh at the idea, but her eyes drifted closed. He tightened his grip, which jostled her arm painfully. She must have made a noise because he shifted her until her head rested on his shoulder with her wound tucked between them. It should have been terrifying to let him handle it, but she was strangely okay with it. Her arm had gone numb, and instead of trying again to handle things on her own, she pressed her face into the softness of his shirt and marveled that he smelled like warm cotton instead of dog.

2

AIDEN

AIDEN HADN'T HELD a woman in his arms since before Torix. The last time hadn't ended well, so he pushed that old memory of Lexi aside. The present situation required his full attention. Maddie's weight concerned him. She felt light, even for someone small-boned and short, but she startled him by shifting around and whimpering. Her blond hair trailed over his forearm in a silky tail as she fought the effects of the poison. The last time he'd seen a salamander that big, it had bitten a cow and knocked it completely unconscious before dragging it off to the woods. He'd been a wolf at the time, so he'd let it have the cow in favor of watching from a tall tuft of wild grasses. Maddie should have succumbed to the effects almost immediately.

Instead, her face scrunched in pain, and her eyes moved wildly behind her closed lids. Aiden frowned. They needed to get to his cabin for the antidote, and her small frame meant he needed to hurry, movement or not. He snagged her bag with his fingers and called a trod. His house wasn't far outside the boundaries of the Wood, but the distance between here and there was fickle. Sometimes, it took him minutes to walk from one place to the next on the path, and sometimes, hours. He'd yet to figure out any kind of pattern for it.

He called his magic to hide his tracks as he walked. The salamander had left as soon as he'd grabbed it, but that didn't mean it wouldn't come back. Maddie pressed her face against his chest and mumbled something.

"Shh, *marenkya*. We'll be there soon."

Her lips parted, and she trailed her mouth across the bare skin at the base of his neck. Heat flashed directly to his cock. An image of her mouth on other parts of him popped into his head, and he groaned. She was going to be trouble.

"Take off your shirt." Her voice was muffled by the fabric, but he heard her clearly that time.

He looked down. Her eyes were closed, and long, dark lashes rested against her pale cheeks. She'd lost some color since she'd tossed him the granola bar earlier. The wound should have self-cauterized, but he could feel wetness along his side where she continued to bleed. He knew how to remove the poison and close the wound, but Maddie needed to be breathing in order for the process to work. His steps quickened, and he prodded the Wood to make this trip a short one.

To Aiden's surprise, it worked. Or the trip was already destined to be short. Either way, he was grateful to reach the end of the trod. Sprites floated past him out of the trees, but they did as they pleased.

He lived in a one-bedroom cabin that had been a vaca-tion rental at one point. For a moment, the setting sun reflecting off the large windows in the front blinded him. No matter. He knew his way. The rustic architecture included an A-frame roof and wood siding that made little sense in Texas' temperate climate. He released the wards surrounding it enough to get them both through, then raised them again. Nothing could find him if he had the wards up, so he never bothered locking his door.

Aiden left it open while he laid Maddie on the couch. After fighting the poison on the walk, her current silence worried him more with each passing second. He hurried to the locked cabinet in his bedroom and pulled out two vials labeled in neat handwriting. The first would rid her body of the poison, but he had to get her to drink it. The second would speed the healing of the wound, but it wouldn't do any good if she never woke up.

A breeze wafted in from the open window as he left the bedroom. He flicked his hand at the front door, and it closed with a push of his magic. Bugs flew rampant in Texas, even in January.

Maddie hadn't moved from where he'd put her. He knelt next to the couch and lifted her head and shoulders so she sat mostly upright. The next part was tricky. He woke his magic and let it sink into her until he hit her shields. The depth would have to be enough because her shields were extremely strong. He checked the label of the vial to be sure, then popped off the top. An ounce of dark green liquid sloshed inside, and he needed her to swallow all of it.

He opened her mouth and upended the vial in one quick motion, then used his magic to convince her the potion was something delicious. Apple juice flashed across his mind, and he filed that information away for later use. Maddie swallowed, and he breathed a sigh of relief.

She twitched and buried her nose against him again.

"Mmm... smell good," she slurred.

The potion need time to take full effect. He set her down

gently and pulled her shirt off her shoulder to expose the punctures. Blood sluggishly dripped from one of the holes. Both had angry red streaks radiating from them.

He opened the other vial and turned his face away from the strong antiseptic smell. Sludgy brown fluid oozed out when he dumped it over her shoulder. The second potion didn't go far beyond the wound, and a sizzling noise accompanied Maddie crying out in pain. Aiden winced, but smoothed stray tendrils of hair away from her sweaty forehead. Her body tensed for a second, then relaxed.

When he took another look at the punctures, they were already closing. Her restless movements slowed to a stop, and she settled into sleep. Aiden shook his head at the mess, both on his couch and in the last hour. He cleaned up the best he could and scooted a dining chair next to the couch to keep an eye on her.

What had she been thinking, jumping in front of him?

Salamanders could be deadly, and she'd had a strange reaction to the poison. Her sword, though, that had been new. As a wolf, many of his memories blurred together, but he'd thought she was powerless on her own. Torix had given her some of himself to allow her the use of his magic, and slowly, it had taken over.

As far as he knew, she shouldn't have retained any of it. He certainly hadn't, but then he'd never accepted Torix's magic inside of himself. Clearly, she had magic of some sort, but he'd never seen anyone wield it in quite that way. Where had she learned?

She sighed and shifted onto her uninjured side. Her shirt rode up, revealing a stretch of skin at her stomach. He almost reached out to see if it was as soft as the rest of her. The errant thought had him leaning back in the chair. Touching her had been necessary to administer the medicine, but she'd passed into a healing sleep. Any connection now would be motivated purely by desire. His attraction to her was inconvenient, but he'd deal with it. He had no intention of getting involved with someone he planned to use as bait.

She'd already been a distraction once. He should have sensed the salamander skulking around, but he'd let his attention linger on her too long. The salamander likely wouldn't have hurt him, but she hadn't known that. Her first reaction had been to protect him, despite the clear danger. And he shouldn't be moved by that.

Aiden scrubbed his face and stretched his legs out in front of him. What were the chances the creature had happened upon them by accident? Unlikely. In the nexus, surrounded by protective sprites? Slim. With Torix on the loose and pursuing Maddie? Zero. Salamanders were rare in this area, and that one had been hunting them in particular.

Maddie shifted again, trying to curl her leg out to the side, but the couch didn't provide enough room. Aiden hesitated, then picked her up and carried her to the bedroom. She'd gotten injured because of him; she deserved a comfortable place to rest while she finished healing.

He'd splurged on the bed while outfitting the cabin. The pillow-top mattress and soft flannel sheets made up for the years he'd spent sleeping with nothing but his fur for comfort. His feet had hung off the end of the one that came with the sale, so he'd upgraded it to the largest size he could find. Aiden loved that his whole body fit on the bed while he slept, despite his height. Maddie looked tiny tucked into it, but she immediately burrowed into the pillow and curled up.

The sun had set while he'd been dealing with her injuries, leaving the room dark. He pulled the curtain closed over the lone window anyway. If she slept through until morning, he didn't want the sun to wake her up early. Aiden reached into the bathroom on his way out and flipped on the light so Maddie wouldn't be totally disoriented when she woke up.

He closed the door most of the way behind him and shook his head at the couch. Maddie had fit on it fine, but he was in for a cramped night. The open concept main room contained a small kitchen against one wall and a fireplace against the other. The bedroom sat between the two. He'd inherited a simple table with four chairs and the couch from the previous owners. The cabin had electricity and hot water, so other than the bed, he hadn't cared about the sparse furniture. It made a difference now though.

Aiden lit the fire and ate a sandwich for dinner, then checked on Maddie every half hour or so. She'd most likely sleep well into the next day, but seeing evidence of the potions working relieved his mind. With Maddie there, he wasn't comfortable leaving to search for more information, so he settled in with a book he'd also inherited from the previous owner. The stories humans told about magic amused him.

The couch was as uncomfortable as he'd expected. After a restless hour, he tossed a blanket and a pillow onto the rug in front of the fire. At least he could stretch out. He'd slept in worse places.

Maddie was silent in the bedroom, and he considered joining her. There was plenty of space on the bed. The memory of her lips against his skin made him decide against it. He wanted more, and there could be no good outcome of being within arm's reach of her. She was a unique temptation that he wanted to steel himself against.

Something in her called to him. It was how he'd found

her in the first place. Thus far, he hadn't tried to resist. He'd
followed her scent in Wales, and again in the Wood, but the
draw told him where to start. The magic she kept shielded
explained part of the mystery. Their experiences with Torix
connected them, but he hadn't figured that out until she'd
revealed her power. She didn't know about the link, of that
much he was certain. Maddie's shields alone told him how
much she wanted to push the world away. Aiden also
suspected that he wasn't the only one who felt her uninten-
tional pull. Torix had found her too.

MADDIE

MADDIE WOKE up in a warm cocoon. It smelled familiar, like
leather and cotton and something else she couldn't pinpoint
but that made her feel safe. She opened her eyes to a giant
bed in a small room. Sunlight peeked around a dark curtain,
so she could only make out shadows at first. Her eyes felt
gritty and dry. Other than the window, there were two doors,
and a tall wooden armoire padlocked shut. She was alone in
the room, but quiet singing came from somewhere.

She stretched and winced at the pull in her shoulder.
The fight in the nexus came back to her in a rush. She'd
been bitten by the lizard thing. Aiden had picked her up,
and she'd passed out. He'd said something to her, but
Maddie didn't remember the words, only the rumble in his
chest against her cheek.

The bed was extremely comfortable, but also unfamiliar.
She had a policy of not spending the night in unfamiliar

places, so the morning wasn't starting off great. On the plus side, she'd finally recognized the scent in the bed as the same one from Aiden's shirt. His bed, his house, probably his locked wardrobe that she badly wanted to break into.

She sat up and looked around, but didn't see her pack.

Her ruined shirt was stiff with blood and had holes in it. She pulled the collar down to check her shoulder. It had two shiny new scars, but it didn't feel any worse than it normally did in the morning. The rest of her seemed to be in working order, so she shuffled out of the bed and into the bathroom. Aiden could wait a few more minutes.

She finger-combed her hair, peed, and considered chucking the shirt in the trash and having breakfast in her sports bra. As fun as it would be to see how Aiden reacted if she came out half-naked, she wasn't prepared to deal with the potential consequences. She liked his smile, when he shared it, but his eyes captured her. Seeing the wolf in the man's face was disconcerting, and he looked at her as if he knew all her secrets.

Maybe he did.

After waffling for several minutes, she left the bedroom in her bloody shirt to find the rest of the cabin empty. The singing drifted in through the open window from the yard. She skirted the couch and stood to one side to look out unobtrusively. Aiden sang under his breath as he worked in a neat kitchen garden. She recognized some of the plants as medicinal herbs she'd read about, but they weren't native to east Texas. They certainly shouldn't have been so bushy and green in January.

The sun shone on the tidy rows, and Aiden walked slowly between them crouching down to pull plants. He'd foregone the leather pants for grey sweats that rode low on his hips and a fitted long-sleeve shirt. His hair was shorter than she'd thought, not quite to his collar, but pulled back it looked longer. As if he could sense her watching him, he turned to the house and met her eyes.

Heat rushed through her for an unguarded moment, and she raised her hand in an awkward wave. He nodded and made his way around the house out of her sight. Maddie blew out a breath. She'd left her comfort zone far behind. Aiden was beautiful, and her brain couldn't handle it. She needed to get a grip and remember why she'd returned instead of staying secluded in a tiny village in Wales where she could practice and learn without hurting anyone.

Maddie was still standing by the window when Aiden came in the front door. The breeze felt good on her heated skin, but she couldn't figure out what to do with her hands. His eyes raked over her, lingering on her torn shirt.

"How do you feel?"

"My shoulder is fine. Is this your place?"

He nodded and went into the kitchen to pull out eggs and bread. "You need to eat. A salamander bite can take a lot out of you."

Maddie sat down at the table and watched him work. "Is that what it was? I've never seen anything like it."

"They're not particularly common. That one was smaller than usual, but I don't think it was meant to kill us."

Unease skittered up her spine. Smaller than usual? She raised her brows. "You think it was sent on purpose?"

He glanced at her. "Yes. Someone followed one of us, at least, to the Wood and set it on us. As I haven't made any enemies in the last year, I assume it was Torix."

Maddie shook her head. "He wouldn't do the work himself. It was Will."

"Either way. Salamander bites *can* be deadly, but mostly because the victim won't wake up without intervention."

She snorted. "Torix wants me unconscious?"

Aiden shrugged and turned the stove off. He slid a plate of scrambled eggs and toast in front of her, and her stomach growled.

"Thank you. For the food, and for helping me yesterday. It *was* yesterday, right?"

He joined her at the table. "Yes. You needed to sleep off the healing potion."

"Hmm, you know potions. Some kind of mage?"

A fleeting smile crossed his face. "No. The salamander disappeared after it bit you, but it's probably not gone. Certainly, Torix isn't. You need to be careful."

She shoveled in a mouthful of eggs and groaned. "This is good. Potions and cooking...alchemist?"

"No."

"What makes you think I was the target? It was heading for you when it came out of the trees."

"He has no interest in me. I've had no contact at all since we were released. Torix wants you."

It was a solid point, if she believed him, and she had no reason to doubt him yet. He'd had plenty of opportunity to take advantage of her, and as far as she could tell, he hadn't.

"Why help me?"

He was silent for a moment. "You tried to protect me."

"Tried, my ass. I succeeded," she muttered between bites.

"My hero," he said dryly.

She looked up to see the humor in his eyes. "Did I miss anything else while I was out?"

"You tried to lick me."

Her fork clattered to the table. "I did not."

"You did, and you said I smelled good. You also asked me to take my shirt off."

Maddie narrowed her eyes. He was enjoying this part. "What did you do about it?"

He leaned forward, and she found herself doing the same. "I carried you here, fixed your wounds, let you sleep in my bed, and made you lunch. With my shirt on." He pointed to her plate. "Eat. Then you can go home."

His easy dismissal disappointed Maddie just a smidge. She picked up her fork and finished her food. He'd been kind, and she needed to remember that, but she hadn't forgotten his words the day before.

I'm here to kill him.

They had the same mission. She'd been studying Torix and magic for years, waiting for her chance, but it seemed like he had knowledge she couldn't access. "We should team up."

"Team up?"

Maddie took the plate to the sink and rinsed it off. "We're both here to stop Torix. We're both skilled. We both like dogs. Besides, I could use a good sidekick." She purposely kept her eyes down, focused on washing her single dish and utensil. His chair scraped the wood floor, and Maddie waited. He'd either accept her offer or kick her out. The first choice would make her life easier, but either way, she'd already committed to her plan, sparse as it was.

Aiden came up close behind her, then reached around to turn the water off. He wasn't touching her, but she could feel his presence like a static charge. A brief memory of her lips against his skin flooded her with heat. She was thankful he couldn't see her face, even more so because the intensity his eyes caused all kinds of short circuits in her brain.

"I don't think that's a good idea." Despite his gruff words, he didn't immediately move away. Maddie stared out the window at the trees and got a strangle hold on her hormones. If he wasn't interested in sharing his information, she had no use for him.

He backed off before she could make a bad decision. "Can you find your way back on your own?"

Maddie turned to face him and quickly realized her mistake. He'd only moved a step, and she'd nearly run into him. His hands came up to steady her, but she shook them off. "I assume you mean through the trods?"

"It's the fastest way back to Mulligan."

"Then no. I can't call trods anymore."

His eyes narrowed. "You were in the nexus when we met. How could you get there without calling a trod?"

She shrugged and slipped past him toward the door. "I was walking in the woods, then I was walking in the *Wood*."

He picked up on her emphasis and frowned. "The Wood pulled you in?"

She found her pack sitting beside the door and dug through it looking for her clean shirt. "I don't know what happened for sure, but that was my guess." Her sports bra was still in one piece and mostly clean, so she stripped her shirt off and pulled the new one on. "I was trying to come up with a way to get to Torix, and I realized I don't know enough about his resources to be able to do it safely. Hence the offer to team up."

She shoved the ruined shirt into the pack and shouldered it. Aiden hadn't moved. He watched her with his arms folded across his chest, but she couldn't read his face.

"I'll take you back through the trods."

She wanted to tell him she could handle it herself, but she didn't know how far he lived from Mulligan. The trods didn't ascribe to normal geographical rules. They were really more like wormholes, folding time and space to allow for travel between magical areas. For all she knew, the cabin could be back in Wales somewhere.

Maddie's fingernails bit into her palms. He wasn't interested in sharing, but no matter how frustrating, her days of bending people to her will were over. Even if they deserved it. She relaxed her hands and remembered her mother's lessons about grace in acceptance.

"Thank you."

He gestured for her to go out the door first and closed it solidly behind them. A circle of white stones marked the edge of the property in a wide curve. Inside the circle, lush plants sprang up tall and green. The temperature hovered around perfectly comfortable, and the yard looked like it should be the middle of summer. Not a Texas summer though, those could be brutal. Summer in a place that wasn't Texas. Aiden led her past the stones, then stopped.

Outside, the trees had lost their leaves, and a brisk January wind raised goosebumps on her bare arms. A weather spell? Was that possible? How did he maintain it? She crouched to look at the circle and realized it was basically gravel, the super white kind rich people put in their driveways. Maddie grabbed one of the tiny stones and held it up to the light. It shimmered faintly, and she changed her mind. Not gravel.

Aiden traced a symbol in the air then repeated it in the dirt. A wave of prickling magic brushed against her where she touched the rocks. Before straightening, he picked up a pebble from the not-gravel and stuck it in the pocket of his sweats. Maddie stood and slipped the stone she held into her own pocket. She didn't think he'd noticed, but it was hard to tell.

"What's this all about?"

He wiped his palm on his thigh. "I know it seems weird, but the cabin is still there."

Maddie looked over at the house, then back at him. "I know, as I haven't suddenly gone blind."

He stopped scanning the trees and focused all that intensity on her. "You can still see it?"

She nodded. "The same as before, and I can sense the magic you used. I don't know what it's supposed to do though."

"Hmm." He went through the sigils again, and after the second time, Maddie was pretty sure she could replicate them. "Look now."

She looked. Trees. Rocks. Cabin. "Same as before."

He frowned. "My wards *always* work."

Understanding dawned. She'd read about wards. Very few people could cast them, but they netted powerful results. Each sigil represented something the caster intended it to do. Aiden's assumption that she couldn't see the cabin made her think this ward was meant to hide something. Not a bad idea with Torix running around free.

Maddie made a note of it and reached out a hand. She felt the charge of the magic before she actually came in contact with the ward. Her hand slid to the side as if encouraging her to go elsewhere. Interesting.

Aiden watched her with narrowed eyes. "The ward is there, but it doesn't seem to work on you."

She shook the tingles out of her fingers. "I'd say it's working. That's a strong suggestion to go away."

"That's a different thing. The ward is supposed to shield the cabin and the area around it from everyone."

She tilted her head. "Can you see it?"

"Yes. It's my magic."

"Why can I see it?"

He studied her for a moment. "I have an idea about that. Can I try something?"

She raised a brow. "Depends on what it is."

A smile crossed his face then was gone. If she'd blinked, she'd have missed it. "It doesn't involve removing any clothes, if that's what you're concerned about."

"That's not what concerns me."

He stepped closer and raised both hands to the sides of her face, but he didn't touch her yet. "I need to check the way you react to my magic."

Maddie wasn't worried about his intentions. He'd had plenty of opportunity to hurt her while she'd been unconscious. She was worried about the reaction she'd have to his touch. He waited until she nodded.

"Relax. This won't hurt." His hands pushed into her hair, and his thumbs came to rest against her temples.

She felt the slide of his rough palms all the way to her toes. Her skin felt hyper-sensitive. He tilted her head up a bit, and she saw the same heat she was battling reflected in his gaze. The threat of missing clothes suddenly felt a lot more likely.

Maddie's muscles quivered as she fought the urge to lean into him. To answer the promise in his eyes. A warm, languid sensation eased through her, and it took her a second to figure out it was his magic spreading down her body. Her nipples tightened, and she bit the inside of her cheek. If this was a sample of what his magic could do, she was in more trouble than she'd thought.

His eyes held hers, so she saw him wince when he touched the shields in her mind. His magic recoiled, then surged forward. Maddie tensed up as panic hit her. She gasped and pushed him away with her hands and her power. An involuntary reaction, but an effective one. He slid back well out of reach, and his magic retreated with him.

Maddie shuddered, as the adrenaline faded. "Sorry. I don't like it when people touch my shields."

"I noticed, but it's fine. I got what I needed."

"And what was that?"

He called a trod and stepped into the sprite-filled path as if she hadn't just blasted him back several feet. "The answer to why my wards don't seem to work on you. Somehow, you're partially immune to my magic."

3

AIDEN

AIDEN PULSE RACED from touching Maddie. He'd had his hands on her face, completely innocent, and he'd reacted as if she were naked underneath him. They'd had more contact than that during the night, but his body seemed to have decided that she was fair game since her injury had healed.

She didn't follow him into the trod right away, but it didn't take long for her to catch up. "What do you mean *immune*? Magic immunity is *not* a thing."

He sent her a look over his shoulder. "And you know everything about magic?"

She grabbed his arm and pulled him to a stop. "Where was my immunity when Torix was inserting more and more of himself into my mind?"

He stared at her hand until she dropped it to her side. Her touch made it hard to think rationally. "Did you have any inkling you had magic before Torix?"

"No. He offered his magic, and I accepted without

reading the fine print. Then he took it back when he was free."

Anger blazed in her eyes, but also fear and vulnerability. She held herself stiff, and he wanted to let his magic sink into her again. For her to relax against him like she'd done before. He hadn't felt that urge in a long, long time, and the complication made him want to curse.

"You have magic now. Where did it come from?"

She shook her head. "It's not my magic."

He waited, but she didn't say any more. Humans sometimes developed power after adolescence, but her unique situation made him suspect something else. She didn't want to share her secrets, and he accepted that. But he'd needed to know what Torix wanted from her, and now he thought he might have figured it out.

Her newfound magic.

Almost more interesting, Maddie had no trouble using the magic she'd developed. He wondered if she was at all happy that she'd gotten the power she'd wanted in the end.

This time, the trod spit them out after a short journey. They'd barely walked five minutes when the path curved and opened up to a suburban street lined with old houses. Morning at his cabin on the other side of the Wood had jumped ahead to late afternoon in Mulligan. Kids played down the street as the sun sank behind the trees. The time shift always made him uncomfortable, but he'd yet to figure out how to control it. Chaos was more his forte.

Maddie grumbled behind him. "I was trying to stay away from them."

Aiden looked over at the familiar house, dark now, and pointed to the one next to it. "The grandmother's house is empty. You can stay there for the night while you figure out what you're going to do."

After a moment, Maddie nodded. "Thanks for walking me home." She brushed past him and strode across the street without looking back.

We should team up.

He shook his head. His plan needed some refinement before he was ready to share it with her. She'd be able to take care of herself for one night. Tomorrow, if he got the answers he expected, he'd come back for her. Using her as bait would go much more smoothly if she willingly participated.

MADDIE

SEVERAL HOURS LATER, Maddie huddled in the dark kitchen, watching Jake and Sera's house through the window. Weren't new parents supposed to be exhausted? Especially new parents to a magically-inclined baby? Either they never went to sleep, or they never turned the lights off.

She'd had no trouble picking the lock on the back door, but Evie's house had been emptied of furniture and comforts. At least it was clean and kept her out of the rapidly dropping temperatures outside. A storm was blowing in, and the wind had turned from a tad chilly to downright frigid. Thanks to her time with Torix, she had a lot of trouble getting warm. Her body would be comfortable enough, but a shard of ice in her chest made her feel like she needed to shiver all the time.

Except for when she'd woken up in Aiden's bed. She'd been gloriously warm all the way through. It had stayed with her up until they'd reached the street. With every step she'd taken away from him, the ice had thickened.

Movement behind the kitchen curtains raised her hopes, but the damn light stayed on. She wanted to start a fire in the wood-burning fireplace. The logs and matches were ready, but she didn't dare until Jake and Sera went to bed. They'd definitely know there shouldn't be smoke coming out of the chimney.

At long last, the light winked out next door. A soft, flickering glow appeared in the window of their living room, like they'd left candles burning, but the lazy, floating movement belied that. Jake and Sera had sprites living in their house.

Maddie shook her head and waited a few more minutes to be sure. The master bedroom faced away from Evie's place, so even if they were still awake, they wouldn't be able to see anything.

The fire lit easily, and Maddie scooted as close as she could to the warmth. She laid down in front of the hearth with her pack under her head and wished for the millionth time that she'd kept her smart phone. Her parents had offered to pay the bill for her so they could keep in touch, but she couldn't justify the expense. Maddie could move from small town to small town in Europe on surprisingly little money, as long as she picked the right small town. Selling her phone and doing a few odd jobs had kept her going for months, and she could text or call just as well from a basic phone. Despite regular emails from her family, the lifestyle had left her feeling disconnected from the world.

At the moment though, Maddie didn't want to connect with the world. She had a more specific contact in mind. Aiden's phone had been on the kitchen counter, and it hadn't taken much time to find his number. She shivered as she stared into the fire. If she texted him in the middle of the night, would he respond? Judging by his actions thus far, he'd ignore it unless she was calling for help. That's where she hesitated. He'd helped before, but then he'd left her to find her own way to Torix.

Maddie closed her eyes and pictured him as he'd looked in the garden when he'd seen her. Even in her imagination, his eyes drew her. Magic touched her, and her body recognized it as Aiden's. She relaxed and let it sink in.

The scene morphed from a sunny garden to his dark bedroom. Moonlight filtered in through the gaps in the curtain. Aiden lay in his bed staring at her in the doorway. The blanket pooled around his hips revealing an impressive bare chest, and all that smooth muscle sent a thrill through her. Without saying a word, he scooted back and lifted the blanket in invitation.

Maddie hesitated out of habit, but what harm could come from a dream? She slid into the bed facing him, and he covered them both with the blanket. Aiden's warmth immediately surrounded her. He'd left plenty of space between them, but she eased closer anyway. The ice inside her melted away to nothing as she stopped just short of touching him.

"What are you doing here?" His voice sounded rusty, like she'd woken him up, but his eyes burned.

"I was cold."

He raised a brow. "It's a dangerous thing to enter a man's bed because you're cold."

"That wasn't the only reason."

"Is that so?" His gaze dropped to the pulse point in her neck, the lowest part of her he could actually see. Her heart began to beat wildly, and she realized she wore very little under the covers. A tank top and boy short panties. She hadn't been wearing that outfit in front of the fire, but the change didn't matter much.

Maddie didn't answer his question, raking her eyes over his expanse of skin. A delicious tension built slowly inside her, and she wasn't in a hurry to assuage it. Instead, she asked the first question that came to mind.

"How old are you?"

Aiden smiled. "Much older than you think. My kind don't age easily."

His kind, huh. "Incubus?"

He laughed. "No, but you'd make a tempting succubus."

She raised a haughty eyebrow. "Did you just call me a demon?"

"You started it."

A comfortable quiet settled inside her. Maddie wanted to snuggle closer, to confirm if the heat she felt came from him. She wondered if the reality of a lover would live up to her hazy memories. Doubt kept her still for a moment, but it had never stopped her for long.

He watched as she crossed the gap between them in slow increments. She wanted him, and the old Maddie had never been one to deny herself something she wanted. The more prudent Maddie considered the consequences before taking action.

Would he push her away? She shook her head. There were probably worse consequences than being rebuffed again.

Aiden waited for her to choose, fire in his golden eyes. Her breath mingled with his, and Maddie couldn't come up with a single reason for not touching Aiden in a dream. Her gaze dropped to his full lips, and she gave in with a slow smile. His ragged exhale ruffled her hair.

"Touch me?" The question came out as a plea, but Maddie refused to be embarrassed.

Aiden lifted his hand, and Maddie held her breath, then she had her answer.

The light touch of his fingers left a scorching trail up her neck until he cupped her cheek. She leaned into his hand, but something felt off. The warmth was there, but not the sensation. His hand created no pressure or skin to skin contact. She moved closer, sliding her bare leg against his, but the same barrier got in the way.

Aiden frowned. "Your shields are unlike anything I've ever seen."

She blinked. "My shields?"

"That's why I can't touch you. Even asleep, your shields are impenetrable. You block your mind from anyone trying to enter."

She *wanted* him to enter. Her body begged. It had been years since the last time she'd been touched by a lover. Even then, it hadn't been like this. She slid all the way against him and sighed. His arm slipped underneath her to hold her there, but she couldn't feel it.

Maddie flattened her palm against his chest and nearly whimpered in frustration. She tried to shove her shields aside, but they refused to budge. Her head dropped, and he tilted her chin up until she met his gaze again.

"You can let me in. I won't hurt you."

"I believe you."

He leaned forward and brushed his lips against hers. "Let me in."

An electric current raced through her body, singeing her nerve endings. She closed her eyes and focused on Aiden. On his clean, warm scent and the strength in his arm around her and the sincerity in his eyes. She'd reinforced her shield over and over again, multiple layers interlocking to protect her, but they were *her* shields, and *she* controlled them. One of the layers dropped off.

His stubble pricked her cheek as he whispered in her ear. "Let me in."

Maddie pulled the layers of her shield down one by one. The last barrier disappeared like reaching the surface after swimming underwater for a long time. Her eyes snapped open, and she sucked in a breath. She could feel all of him. The coarse hair against her legs, the heated skin under her hand, and the pressure of him hard against her hip.

Aiden didn't hesitate. He took her mouth, and Maddie let him in. The kiss was rough, but his hands were gentle. Their tongues danced, and Maddie arched against him. She wanted more. He shifted her under him, and she moaned at the weight of him pressing her down into the mattress. His hand skimmed down her throat and teased the curve of her breast. She nipped his lip, and he smiled against her mouth. None of her experience had prepared her for the desperation she felt for Aiden.

He kissed his way to her neck, and she felt the quick sting of a bite that he soothed with his tongue. She tangled her fingers in his hair and dragged his mouth back to hers. Before they could make contact, the room shifted again and her arms were empty.

She was standing in darkness. The area immediately around her was lit with sprites, but there was no other light. Maddie sucked in a breath to cool her ardor and fight the disorientation.

"What do we have here?" The crisp voice caused a familiar cold wave against her overheated skin.

The ice inside her rushed back, worse than ever. "You're not welcome here."

A light like a match flare illuminated Torix and his smirk. "I don't see why not? You were certainly very welcoming to our young wolf."

Maddie's heart pounded as she fought off panic. She couldn't get her shields up fast enough. The layers took time. "I have nothing to say to you."

He circled her, his eyes roving over the skimpy pajamas she still wore. "A pity, but I don't need you to speak. Why not show me where you are?"

Maddie clutched the darkness around her and pulled it tight, shivering in the cold. She couldn't let him know where she slept. Fear made her breathing shallow, but with each layer of shield she rebuilt, his image faded a little.

His eyes narrowed. "I see why I haven't been able to find you. That's an annoying little trick you've learned. Would you like to see one of mine?"

One second, he was circling; the next, he stood directly in front of her. He grabbed her wrist tightly, and black magic, shiny like oil, oozed out of him and onto her. The tendrils of magic burned as they swirled up her forearm.

He met her eyes and smiled. "Ah, there you are. Welcome home."

Anger flashed through her, chasing away the fear. Maddie planted her feet and brought her other hand up to break his hold, then she hammered silver magic at his chest with eight years' worth of pent up aggression, shoving him back a few steps like she'd done to Aiden earlier.

He raised a brow and flexed the fingers of the wrist she'd tried her best to detach. In a quick flick, he sent more magic flying at her, but she deflected with an arm wrapped in shimmery silver. "I'm not your slave anymore."

She slammed the last layer of her shield in place, and Torix disappeared. Her arm throbbed, and she hissed when she looked at it. Dark welts swirled up from her wrist where the tendrils had been, like a tattoo of stylized fire. She ran her finger over one of the welts and pain shot up her arm. That was going to be a bitch to cover up.

———————

MADDIE JERKED upright in the cold living room of Evie's house. The fire had gone out, but she was sweating and shivering at the same time. She ached in a few places, but at least her clothes had returned to normal. The tiny twinge at her neck barely registered against the pain in her forearm. She'd slept in her long-sleeve shirt, so she eased the material up and winced at the same marks she'd seen in her dream.

Predawn light began to chase away the darkness in Evie's house, where a few sprites floated around being useless. Maddie gathered her belongings and made sure she extinguished the fire completely. The last thing she needed was to burn the place down. She pulled on her coat and went out the back door, locking it securely behind her.

Frost made the grass crunch under her feet. The sun hadn't risen yet, but people backed out of their driveways leaving for work. Jake and Sera would be awake soon too, which meant Maddie couldn't stay any longer. She considered giving them another warning, maybe trying to convince them to take a trip to Europe with her parents, but she knew better than most that Sera would be able to defend everyone more easily with a base of power. The Wood, and the Fae that lived there with Evie, would help protect Sera and her family.

Maddie knew staying away from the people she loved was only a temporary solution, but there wasn't anything else she could do to negate the danger. Torix wanted her first, so she'd do her best to keep one step ahead of him. She didn't know how much he'd gotten out of her with his ooze, but he'd looked way too pleased with himself.

Her stomach rumbled, and she sighed. She'd given her last granola bar to Aiden. There were places to eat in town, but her funds were severely limited after paying for an emergency international flight. She eyed Jake's house again. He and Sera had plenty of food, and she was pretty sure they were taking her parents to the airport that morning. Unless the trod had messed with time more than she'd thought.

Maddie shook her head. She wasn't stealing from her brother and his family. It was one thing if she stopped in and said hi, but avoiding them then taking their food was wrong. Torix had enjoyed making her pop into Jake's house at the most inconvenient times for him. She'd always been forced to do whatever would be most annoying to Jake, but Jake welcomed her anyway. Love for her brother welled up and made her throat tight. She would *not* fall back on habits ingrained into her by Torix.

A pull in the center of her chest urged her to the forest. The last time she'd gone, the Wood had helped her. Her brow furrowed. Or had it? Yeah, it had opened a trod which led her to Aiden, but then they'd been attacked by that salamander. Evie had taught her about the Wood's neutrality, but Evie hadn't known everything. Maddie licked her dry lips. Trying the trods again was a risk, but she was only risking herself.

Maddie ignored her stomach and trekked back into the trees.

She'd only walked fifteen minutes or so when she noticed the sprites drifting along next to her. The Wood had opened another trod for her. Maddie wondered what would happen if she never reached the end of the path. Would she wander in the in-between forever? The prospect didn't bother her as much as it should. Torix would have a hell of a time finding her, but she'd miss the opportunity to see if Aiden's kiss lived up to her dream.

BY THE TIME Maddie reached Aiden's house, the sun had finally come up, but the temperature hadn't. The marks on her arm had faded a little, and she could touch them without having to catch her breath. She'd discovered the mark on her neck when she'd stopped for water at a creek. Aiden had bitten her. A delicate shiver ran up her spine, and Maddie blamed it on the cold. After She'd purposely tried not to think about the first half of her dream. If she hadn't lowered her shields for Aiden, Torix wouldn't have found a way in, but she was finding it hard to regret the decision.

Maddie left the trod only a few steps from the warding circle. The cabin sat clearly visible in the middle of the clearing. Sunlight reflected off the windows, and the trees cast long shadows across Aiden's garden. Smoke puffed from the chimney, promising a fire inside, but Maddie hesitated before crossing the stones.

The ward hadn't stopped her from seeing the cabin before, but her hand had slid off of it. She didn't want to walk face-first into a solid wall, invisible or not.

Maddie pulled the white pebble out of her pocket and rubbed her thumb over the smooth surface. Time to see if her theory worked.

She reached forward with the hand holding the stone and only encountered a token resistance, like pushing through a bubble, which wasn't surprising when she thought about it. The ward essentially operated as a magic bubble that rebuffed sight and people. She stepped across the threshold, and the chill left the air. The stone crumbled to dust in her palm. A light breeze, warm when it shouldn't be, picked up the fine powder and scattered it across the yard.

One-time use. Interesting.

She bent to pick up a new stone, but Aiden's deep voice stopped her. "It doesn't work from this side."

Maddie spun around. Aiden stood in the doorway with his arms crossed. Her eyes narrowed. She was disappointed to find him fully dressed, then annoyed at herself for being disappointed. "I guess I need to study up on my wards."

"How'd you find the cabin?"

She shrugged. "What, like it's hard?"

"Answer me."

"You're grumpy this morning." She sent him a sweet smile as she walked closer. "Have trouble sleeping?"

He grunted, then moved aside so she could enter. "You could say that. How'd you find the cabin?"

Maddie dropped her pack next to the door where it had been before and curled up in the corner of the couch. "The Wood sent me."

"For someone who can't call trods, you're getting a lot of use out of them."

"I can't explain that one. More interestingly, both times it sent me to you."

He closed the door after her and walked into the kitchen where plants were spread in various states of dehydration. A pot boiled on the stove, and the strong scent of lemons filled the house. Her stomach rumbled again, and she willed it to be quiet.

"You may find this hard to believe, but I wasn't planning to come here."

He watched her for a moment, then nodded. "Okay. Why don't you tell me what happened last night?"

She reached up to touch her neck, and his eyes followed the movement. "That was an accident."

He raised a brow. "And now you're here by accident. That's edging past coincidental."

Warmth crept into her cheeks. "Maybe, but I didn't mean to invade your dream last night."

"You didn't."

"What do you mean?"

"I wasn't asleep."

She held up a hand. "You had to be. It's the only way we could have interacted with each other."

He shook his head. "Still so sure you know everything. Have you ever dreamwalked before?"

"No." Maddie took her coat off and flinched as the sleeve came off her arm. She'd thought Aiden was distracted by the mess in the kitchen, but he approached her side in an instant.

"What's wrong with your arm?"

Maddie hesitated with her first instinct to hide her injury and make him back off, but he'd already seen her unconscious and weak. There was no reason to be petty. She carefully peeled the sleeve back, but she couldn't hold back another grimace when the fabric rubbed against the upper swirls of the mark.

It looked better than it had before, but Aiden frowned. She missed his smile. The errant thought slid in sideways, surprising her with its tenacity even when she tried to push it away. He gingerly picked up her arm by the fingers and elbow to check the underside. The mark went all the way around; she'd checked. His jaw ticked, and he slid the sleeve back down over the marks.

"What happened?"

Maddie met his frown with one of her own. "You first. How did I dreamwalk with you if you weren't sleeping?"

"It wasn't a dreamwalk. Neither of us is Fae, and even if we were, the wards should have kept you out. You were here in spirit."

"You're talking about astral projection. That's not a thing."

"It's definitely a thing. Even the humans are aware of it. Lucid dreaming. Spirit travel." He shrugged. "They're all basically the same idea. You go into a trance, and your spirit goes elsewhere."

She noticed he excluded her from the humans as a group, but that required a whole other discussion. Snippets of the night before sped through her mind, and the blush returned with a fury. "You couldn't touch me because it was only my mind. That's why you needed me to lower my shields."

A wicked smile curved his lips. "I warned you about the consequences of entering a man's bed."

"I *thought* I was dreaming."

His gaze skimmed over the bite on her neck. "I assume the mark on your arm happened after you left."

"Yeah. Torix found me." She expected some kind of reaction to that, but Aiden had a great poker face. "He monologued for a while, oozed all over my arm, and left when I finally got my shields back up."

Aiden's brows drew together. "Your shields aren't instant?"

"No. That's why it took me so long to lower them last night. I had to keep Torix talking and away from me while I rebuilt them." Maddie held up her now-covered injury. "Clearly, I need to work on that last one."

"Why does he want you?"

She hesitated, but keeping the secret hadn't helped her. Maybe sharing it would. "The magic inside me isn't mine. It's his."

4

AIDEN

"THAT'S NOT POSSIBLE," said Aiden. He'd suspected as much, but he'd also seen Torix suck the magic out of her.

She snorted. "That's what I keep saying, but you keep proving me wrong."

He crossed his arms. "What happened after Torix took his magic back?"

"Jake got me away from the clearing. I woke up hidden in a shallow divot under a downed tree. I felt like myself again, and I couldn't stop crying. It wasn't until a few days later that I realized I still had power. I got angry and broke a mirror across the room by throwing a shard of silver magic at it." She took a shuddering breath. "I was alone in the house, and I didn't tell any of them. I went to visit my parents in Europe because it would be easier to hide there. Then I tried to learn and practice anything I could get my hands on."

"You don't know why?"

"No. I knew it was Torix's right away. It makes me cold." She rubbed her sternum. "In here."

Aiden wanted to wrap his arms around her and warm her up, but he couldn't afford that kind of distraction. Already, his mind kept trying to wander to memories of last night during a conversation he should really be paying attention to. "It's not the same magic."

"I know. I can't explain that either. Right before Sera intervened, Torix had started pushing himself into me. Not just his mind, his essence. Sera interrupted him. It felt like a splinter broke off when—" She stopped, and Aiden's hands clenched into fists. He understood. They'd both done things against their wills, and though he'd been bound longer, she'd had it worse than him. Under Torix's influence, he'd always been himself.

She was stronger than he'd given her credit for.

"He took back the magic coating me, the parts in my mind, but he left the bit inside me. The splinter healed over, and the magic changed."

"Are you cold now?" The question slipped out, and he willed himself to stay behind the couch no matter her answer.

She tilted her head, looking inside. "I am, but it's distant." Her stomach gurgled, and she groaned. "Sorry."

"That's the second time your stomach has rumbled." He shook his head as he headed to the fridge. "Why does it feel like I'm always feeding you?"

"I may have forgotten to eat after I left here yesterday."

Aiden pulled out sandwich ingredients and considered his options. If she really possessed the last vestige of Torix's magic, and he had no reason to doubt her, she really *was* the perfect bait. It explained Torix's eagerness to reclaim his lost slave, and why he'd sent a salamander instead of a more deadly enemy. Unfortunately, Torix knew she'd returned to Mulligan.

The mark on her arm was at least partially his fault. He'd lost his mind the second she'd appeared in his bedroom in those tiny pajamas. Unlike her, he'd known it wasn't a dream, but he'd pushed her to put herself at risk because he'd wanted to touch her. That dangerous choice offered a powerful reason to track her from afar until he'd finished preparing to take on Torix.

But he needed her safe up to that point.

He put the sandwich on a plate and brought it to her. "You were right. We should team up."

Maddie did a sexy little shimmy, either for the food or the words, he couldn't tell. "Can you say that first part again?"

The words then. She inhaled the sandwich, and he wondered how often she forgot to eat. She'd have to stay with him. The wards protected her even if they didn't affect her. He glanced over his shoulder at the mess in the kitchen. Nothing time-sensitive there, but it wasn't safe to leave some of the herbs lying around. He concentrated and drew a sigil in the air. The herbs shimmered and disappeared. Maddie gasped behind him.

"What'd you do?"

She'd shared her information with him. It went against his nature, but he should probably reciprocate. "They're phased. When I'm ready for them, I'll pull them out of the in-between."

"The in-between? Like the trods? You have a pocket trod?"

The phrase was interesting, but it wasn't wrong. "Sure. A pocket trod."

"Teach me. I need a pocket trod. It would be useful in so many ways."

Aiden shook his head. "I can't. You have to be able to call trods to do it."

Her face fell, but she remained undeterred. "Teach me anyway. It might come in handy one day."

"I'll consider it, but we have other concerns to deal with first. You'll stay with me."

She raised a brow. "Excuse me?"

"If we're going to be a team, you need to stay where you're safe. With me. I don't have time to be constantly healing you." He hadn't shared all of the truth, but she looked satisfied. Her face smoothed, and mirth danced in her eyes.

"If we're going to be a team, we need a team name."

"No."

She nudged him. "C'mon. It'll be fun."

"I already regret my decision." That got him a full-blown smile, and he almost took a step back from the force of it. He'd always found her beautiful, even limp and covered in blood, but the happiness in her smile made her impossible to resist. Blood rushed south, and it took everything in him to keep from leaning over and taking her mouth to see if he could taste the joy.

Even holding back, he couldn't seem to stop taunting her. "You're welcome to join me in the bed, but I'm not sleeping on the couch."

Maddie didn't back down. Her eyes wandered over his chest before meeting his gaze. "I guess we'll see tonight how much your warning has sunk in."

His hands clenched to keep from reaching for her. "Get ready to go. We have places to be."

He pushed away from the couch and went into the

bedroom to change and gather his own pack. The full truth was that he wanted her there. In his bed. He'd wanted it since he'd first changed from the wolf in the clearing. It would be smarter to stay away, insist she sleep on the couch or the floor, but he knew his limits. She'd bared herself for him once, and he wanted another taste. It was her choice.

If she chose his bed, chose him, he planned to claim what she offered.

He'd have to be careful not to get too attached. The body could indulge, but the emotions had to remain separate. They couldn't afford to be distracted from their goal to finish Torix.

Aiden dressed in his leather pants and tunic. They may not have been fashionable, but magic inscribed into the hide protected them. He'd had them a long time, and they hadn't failed him. It was too bad he hadn't been wearing them when Torix had taken control.

He shoved a few filled vials into his pack with his other necessities. They had to travel far, and he wasn't sure of the reception they were going to get. He left the room, and Maddie stood waiting by the door.

"Are you going to tell me the plan or just issue cryptic commands?"

He liked her smart mouth. "I thought I'd start with the commands and see how it went."

She speared him with a look as she preceded him out the door. "It's not going well. What's the plan?"

"The Fae are notoriously hard to kill, even without power, and I think we can both agree that Torix isn't without power. He's borrowing it from somewhere, and we need to know where. We also need protection from future enslavement."

Maddie followed him as he exited the circle of wards

and reset them. He tossed her a stone this time. "For when we return."

"I assume you have some way to gather the information you think we need?"

"I've been asking around. I think I found the trail of one of my kin from the old days. He might know something."

She eyed him as he called a trod and gestured her into the Wood. "Where are we going?"

"Egypt."

Her eyes went wide. "There's an elemental forest in Egypt?"

He grunted and brushed past her to take the lead. "You need better teachers. The trods will take us anywhere there's a nexus. It doesn't have to be a forest."

The sprites drifted in tiny golden circles as they walked. Maddie was silent for once, so Aiden listened for the rustle of anything off the path. Usually, the presence of sprites meant they were safe, but he didn't want to let his guard down.

They walked for hours, but Maddie never complained. After a while, she asked questions and pestered him with guesses about his origin. Aiden answered her to the best of his knowledge. Her attempts to learn meant she'd be better protected. Plus, the more she knew, the less danger she'd put him in. He didn't acknowledge her guesses about his origin with anything other than a *no*. She'd never guess, but he enjoyed the pattern of her thoughts.

The sun stayed behind the trees, but the shadows shifted to the other direction at some point. Aiden verged on suggesting they break for a while when the path abruptly ended at a sandstone arch. Through the timeworn structure, a huge pyramid rose in the distance. He stepped out of the trod, but Maddie didn't follow him.

She stood surrounded by sprites and stared in awe at the sight ahead of them. Aiden remembered the first time he'd seen the pyramids, so he gave her a moment.

"I can't believe that worked," she breathed.

"Welcome to Cairo."

MADDIE

CAIRO WASN'T AS hot as she'd expected. The trod left them on an open platform at the top of a crumbling spire, surrounded by dirt and debris. More stone spires speared into the air all around them, and the pyramid she'd seen first shimmered in the distance. A balmy January breeze lifted the hair at the nape of Maddie's neck as her eyes tracked the point where metropolis met ancient desert.

Her gaze dropped as the sounds of voices drifted up to her on the wind. Several stories below them people haggled for goods in a bustling market. The wonder quickly faded as Maddie tried to brush whitish dust off of her black pants, but only succeeded in spreading it around.

"I'm surprised the trod took us here. Isn't it really open?"

Aiden sent her a dry look. "You mean like a stretch of forest in east Texas?" He tested the metal of the spiral staircase that would take them out of the tower.

"Where are we specifically?"

He glanced around, then started down the stairs. "In an abandoned mosque in Old Cairo. There was a major earthquake here a couple of decades ago that damaged most of these buildings. Before that, this trod wasn't used much.

There's one closer to Giza, but my cousin is supposed to be somewhere in the market."

"When you said kin, I didn't realize it would be direct family." She followed him down the stairs, ready to move if the steps suddenly became unstable.

He slanted a look at her. "I sometimes wish I could claim we're only loosely related, but he's the only link I have left to my father."

Maddie burned to ask more questions, but Aiden's shoulders had stiffened as he'd focused back on the stairs. He didn't want to talk about his family. She wouldn't push, and one day, maybe he'd *want* to share himself with her. That tiny flare of hope kept her mouth shut.

They went down several flights of stairs before they reached the ground. The space at the bottom barely qualified as a room; it was more of a large landing. Rubble covered the floor, and a chunk of what used to be wall almost blocked a set of large wooden double doors.

Aiden stopped her when she would have gone through the doors. "This is the biggest market in Egypt, and we're going to stand out a bit."

Her eyes narrowed. "How often have you been here?"

"Recently? Twice before. My cousin can be tricky to find."

"What makes you think we'll find him this time?"

He moved her aside and drew a sigil on the handle. "This time I've got you."

The doors opened to chaos. People and stalls and goods all crushed together. Sellers yelled over the din of a thousand people shoved into an alley. The smell of sweaty, unwashed masses hit her, and she reminded herself to breathe through her mouth. Aiden shut the doors behind them and redrew the sigil. Nothing obvious happened, but when she leaned back against the wood, the door stayed firmly closed.

Three wrinkled men sitting on stools next to the stairs raised their hookahs at her when she made eye contact. Aiden took her hand, and she smiled at the men before he dragged her into the throng.

"Do we need to worry about pickpockets?"

Aiden glanced down at her. "Do you have anything to steal?"

She clutched her pack tighter and squeezed closer to him as they wound their way down the row. "What does your cousin look like?"

"I don't know." He scanned the area around them. "I haven't seen him for a long time."

"How long?"

"About a hundred and twenty-five years, give or take."

Maddie's mouth dropped open. "You weren't kidding when you said you were older than I thought you were." She did some quick math and frowned. "That was before Torix was trapped."

He didn't respond, but his hand tightened on hers. She'd assumed he'd been caught at the same time as her, but now she wondered how long he'd been a slave. Maddie wanted to know more, but she understood his reticence. She didn't want to talk about that time either.

A sharp whistle drew their attention to a man in an alcove to their right. "I'll give you two thousand camels for that one." He crooked his finger at Maddie, and Aiden jerked her away.

"I wonder how much it is per camel," she mused.

"What?" Aiden glowered at her over his shoulder.

"Just trying to figure out what I'm worth."

Before he could answer, an orange cat dashed between

his legs and ran down a side alley. Aiden nearly pulled her off her feet when he sped after it. The alley was darker and emptier than the main thoroughfare. Tall intricate buildings rose on either side of them, blocking the sun. It looked like they'd turned onto a residential street. The road didn't provide enough room for stalls, and the doorways were all draped with thick carpets.

The cat easily outpaced them, but it kept turning around and waiting until they caught up before taking off again. After a few minutes of following it through a maze of side streets, Maddie was hopelessly lost. She stopped trying to memorize where they'd been and instead focused on holding onto Aiden's hand. He wouldn't leave her behind, but it would be embarrassing if he was forced to drag her down the backstreets of Cairo.

They stopped at a squat building surrounded by larger structures. Maddie struggled to calm her breathing, but Aiden's chest rose and fell in an even rhythm. The cat sat on the stoop, licking one extended leg.

"Is this the place?" Aiden asked.

How should she know? She opened her mouth to give him a sarcastic answer, then realized he was staring at the cat. Her mouth snapped shut.

The cat paused and looked up at him, then turned and walked past the door rug with its tail high. Maddie tugged on Aiden's hand when he would have followed it.

"Shouldn't we knock or something? It might be hard to explain that a cat told us it was okay to invade someone's home."

"The cat lives here."

"That doesn't mean it can give permission to enter."

He chuckled. "In this case it does."

She let him pull her through the entrance. The musty

rug fell into place behind her, shutting out the natural light. The clean interior consisted of a single room lit by an oil lamp with a bed, a small table, and a wooden chair. There were no other doorways or windows, and the air was stale with the scent of candle wax. The cat sat on the bed with its tail wrapped neatly around its legs.

"It's been a long time," Aiden said.

I hear you've freed yourself from your troubles, cousin.

The quiet voice had a teasing tone in her mind, and she didn't think it was referring to her. Maddie peeked at Aiden. Could he hear it too?

"For now."

That's good to know. I see you've found someone new. Why come to my part of the world with her?

Maddie looked around the room, but there wasn't anywhere for someone to hide. The cat stared at them with unblinking eyes. No, not them, her.

"We need information."

Information comes at a price.

"Even for kin?"

The cat's eyes narrowed, and Maddie accepted that it was the cat talking to them. In her mind. Through her shields. Or maybe around them. She couldn't be sure.

Especially for kin. Clan practices no longer apply to me.

Aiden sighed. "What's your price?"

I want the girl.

Maddie straightened her shoulders. Two offers in one day. Three if you counted Torix in the middle of the night. She was certainly popular.

"She's not for trade."

If you didn't bring her to trade, why is she here?

"She's under my protection."

The cat's mouth twitched and a laugh filled her mind. *Then you've brought her to the wrong place.*

A chill went down her back as her mind filled with all the terrible stories she'd heard of creatures out in the magical world. She trusted Aiden not to hurt her, but just because *he* was gentle didn't make all of his kind gentle.

Another laugh. *Calm down, human. I'm no threat to you at the moment.*

Aiden squeezed the hand he was still holding, and she looked up to meet his eyes. "He won't hurt you."

You always ruin all my fun. Fine, I ask for an unnamed favor to be determined in the future.

Even Maddie knew what a bad deal that was. If Aiden agreed, he'd be bound to whatever the cat wanted. She opened her mouth to tell the cat to go to hell, but Aiden shook his head.

"Anything except the girl."

Yes.

"I agree."

The air whooshed out of her. What was he doing? The cat inclined his head, and she felt the bonds of a spell settle over Aiden, a dusting on his skin.

It is done. His tail twitched, and she sensed a disturbing amount of triumph coming from him. *Pardon me for being rude. I'm Seth, Cat-God of Cairo. Welcome to my home.*

Aiden nudged her, and she realized the cat was talking to her. "I'm Maddie. Cat-God?"

An epithet that amuses me since I'm neither a cat nor a god. Tell me, Maddie. What's that interesting power I sense inside you?

She raised a brow. "None of your business."

He inclined his head again. *You're right. I was just curious.*

The cat turned his eyes on Aiden. *What information do you want?*

"Do you remember Torix?"

Yes, he's hard to forget.

"Do you know where he's getting his power now?"

No.

Watching his face, Maddie had the distinct feeling that Aiden wanted to roll his eyes. "Do you have a guess where he's getting his power."

That's a better question. I have a guess. There were once clans that had no power of their own, but had the ability to use the magic around them to their own benefit.

"Torix is Fae."

I'm aware of that. You asked for ideas not logical explanations.

Aiden took a step toward Seth. "And you're being purposefully cryptic."

Maddie intervened. "He did a blood ritual to bind someone to him. Is that familiar?"

A blood ritual, eh? He could be using more than one source. Or one very powerful source. Either way, it'll be hard to find out without confronting him. The cat considered her. *You intrigue me. A human with no power, but you reek of Fae magic. And you have such interesting shields.*

Maddie raised her chin. She'd talked enough about the magic, and she only trusted Aiden. It seemed like a bad idea to volunteer extra information to a false cat-god. "How is he using other sources?"

My bargain isn't with you, but I'll answer your question out of kindness. Aiden snorted, but Seth continued. *It's possible to give another creature a portion of your power. Convince enough magic-users to part with a little bit and you could end up with a lot. I see you're familiar with the idea.*

She ignored the last part. "I thought without magic you couldn't use magic?"

In most cases, that's true. For the clan I mentioned earlier, less true. There are other ways to get around that pesky rule, but they're dangerous and hard to achieve. Rare artifacts that carry strong enchantments come to mind first.

Maddie nodded absently and tried to remember the details of the scene at the bar. She'd been distracted, so she wasn't sure if Torix had been carrying a magical talisman. Maybe the knife. She shook her head and eyed Seth, then turned to Aiden.

"How accurate is this information?"

Amusement washed over her from the cat, but Aiden only spared her a glance. "He doesn't lie, and it sounds right. He knows more than anyone else I've ever met about the intricacies of magic. That's why I was looking for him, but I've never known him to help out of kindness."

I'm hurt. I've given you an abundance of information for a single measly favor. In honor of friendship and kin, I'll give you one more tidbit. There's an artifact that should interest you. A medallion forged by Lugh himself. It protects the wearer from falling under the spell of another. Seth met her eyes, and she felt like he was trying to tell her more than his words. *An immunity, of sorts.*

"Where is it?"

That's where my knowledge ends. Last I heard, it was stolen from the neck of a selkie by a soon-to-be cursed pirate who bedded her and left her behind. His ear twitched and he leaned down to lick the fur at his shoulder.

"Are there still pirates?" Maddie whispered to Aiden.

"Yes, but I'm pretty sure he's not referring to a modern pirate."

Maddie searched her mind for references to selkies, but

all she remembered was that they lived near water and they were sometimes seals. She felt like she should be surprised by the number of shifters she was encountering, but Evie had once said that the most-used aspect of magic was in changing something's form.

You'll want to seek out Cassie at the Tavern by the Sea. Maybe she'll tell you more than she told me. He hopped gracefully off the bed and walked between them to the door, but he paused before going through the curtain. *Might be best not to mention me at all, now that I think of it. She's an expert at holding a grudge. There's a nexus not too far from here. Aiden should be able to find it with no trouble. I'll be in touch about my favor.*

Seth walked into the dim alley, but when Maddie pulled the curtain aside, he was gone. She didn't sense any magic, so he probably used the cat form to his advantage. It was a hell of an exit either way.

Aiden sighed, and his grip relaxed around her hand. She hadn't realized how tense he'd gotten during the exchange.

"How did you know he'd be interested in me?"

He looked down at her and linked their fingers together. "I've never encountered someone with powers like yours before, and Seth loves a puzzle."

She wanted to ask what Seth's real form was, but it felt rude. "Well, I'm glad I could be of service, but next time, I can handle my own negotiations."

"I refuse to use people to barter."

"He was baiting you to get the best deal, or he wouldn't have given in so easily."

"Seth doesn't bluff. He wanted you. I'm just not sure what he planned to do with you."

Maddie frowned, but let Aiden lead her out of the room. Locals lingered on the side street, unlike when they'd rushed down it earlier chasing the cat. Seth was still nowhere to be seen.

"Where are we going now?"

"To the nexus. I have no idea where the Tavern at the Sea is, but I know someone who might."

"Another cousin?"

He laughed. "No, and she would be insulted to hear you say that. She's not fond of my kind."

"Your kind...pixie?"

He let loose a belly laugh. Maddie smiled, secretly glad he wasn't a pixie. They had an unnatural affection for spreadsheets. Great accountants though.

Aiden stopped abruptly and spun around. He crowded her against the wall and slid his arms around her, trapping their entwined hands behind her back. Maddie's breath hitched and then his lips were on hers.

Between the wall behind her and his broad shoulders, she was completely hidden from the rest of the alley. She'd hoped the dream had been a heightened reaction to him, but this kiss rushed through her like wildfire. Her eyes closed as she sank into it. Aiden slid his tongue against hers in a welcome invasion, and a moan escaped her.

She kissed him back, fire for fire, but he pulled back too soon for her liking. Maddie sucked in a ragged breath, and slowly eased her eyes open. When she focused, his golden eyes blazed with intention only inches away.

"What—"

"Shh." His low whisper dragged roughly along her nerve endings. "Will just walked past us."

5

MADDIE

MADDIE LOWERED HER HEAD. If Will looked their way, her light blonde hair would give them away. A loud screeching yowl echoed off the stone walls of the alley, followed by wings flapping, loud chirping, and a man angrily cursing in English. The other people on the street stopped glaring at them to turn and look toward the noise. Maddie peeked around Aiden's shoulder and saw an orange tail shoot around the corner.

Aiden grabbed her hand again and pulled her away from the commotion and through two more alleys. He stopped and drew the familiar sigil against another wooden double door. It could have been the first one for all she knew except that they hadn't circled back to the market. For a moment during the chaos, she'd considered breaking away from Aiden's hold and following Will. Was he in Egypt because of them, or did Torix have another plan? If it was the first, how did he know they'd be there? *She* hadn't even known until they'd left.

Aiden ushered her inside and closed the door behind them. It wasn't a room, as she'd been expecting. It was a tunnel.

Stone surrounded them on all sides, and a thick layer of soft sand covered the floor. Torches were affixed to the walls at regular intervals, allowing enough light to see, and sprites floated around like tiny flames.

Maddie glanced behind her. The double doors marked the entrance, but they'd clearly accessed another trod. Aiden had to stoop under the short ceiling, and Maddie swallowed hard, suddenly glad she'd never been claustrophobic.

Aiden led her deeper inside, and Maddie tried to catch her breath. Her heart still raced from his kiss, but he'd dropped the façade as soon as Seth had distracted Will. Now that they were hidden again, her anger began to rise.

Maddie glared at his back. Who did he think he was? If he wanted to kiss her, she was all for it, but using it as an excuse pissed her off. Especially because once she'd surfaced, she'd seen the dirty looks the locals had been giving them. She'd have been better off ducking back into Seth's room.

She reached out and poked his shoulder. "Are we going to talk about that show back there?"

"I wasn't planning on it."

"Let me rephrase. We're *going* to talk about it. I'll start." She smacked him lightly on the arm. "What the hell?"

He stopped walking to face her, and she realized she'd been wrong about his lack of reaction. Fire still burned in his eyes, and Maddie felt the answering heat rush through her body. "It was the first thing I thought of and we didn't have a lot of time. I could hide you since Will has never seen my human form."

"And what was your answer if the locals had done more than stare angrily? I get the feeling public displays of affection are super not okay in the streets of Cairo."

Aiden looked down the seemingly unending tunnel as the torches sputtered, and Maddie wanted to smack him again. "I admit it wasn't my best idea."

"That's all?" She waited but he didn't say more or meet her eyes. "Okay, how about the fact that Will managed to get to Egypt right behind us and happened to be on the same street. I know Seth drew him away, but could he have somehow summoned Will in the first place?"

That got Aiden's attention back on her. "It wasn't Seth, but I think he knew Will was coming. That's why he hurried us out."

"Then why didn't he just tell us?"

"And risk giving away extra information when he could sow chaos instead? I'm surprised he wasn't cackling the whole time." A muscle in his jaw twitched. "It's not Will's knowledge and presence we need to be worried about. It's Torix's. Will is a puppet. Torix either knew where we'd be or he had a way to track us."

Maddie blew out a breath as her anger subsided. "Which is it?"

"I don't know. I'm not omniscient. The only way he'd know about Seth is if someone in my clan is helping him. That's highly unlikely, but not impossible. As a precaution, I'll be more careful when consulting them."

"You think Torix is tracking us somehow?"

Aiden nodded. "I think he's tracking you."

"Me?" she squeaked.

"You contain a chunk of his power, even if it's changed."

"Yeah, but I don't use it unless it's an emergency."

"I'm not sure that's true."

Her mouth dropped open. "Are you calling me a liar?"

Aiden closed his eyes for a second and rubbed the bridge of his nose. "No. I'm saying you may be using it without realizing."

Maddie shook her head and turned her back on him. She needed to think hard about the last couple of days, and his large presence distracted her.

"Maddie?"

She held up a hand. "Give me a minute."

He shuffled around behind her and his pack hit the ground with a thunk. "Take your time. I could use a break anyway."

Maddie got the feeling he meant from her rather than from the trek through the trods. Fine with her. She paced a few steps away and dropped her own pack. She'd been living in Europe for the last year. Mostly Wales, but she'd spent some time with her parents in Norway when she'd first arrived. Despite her need to learn to protect herself, she hadn't had any contact with Torix. He'd disappeared, and she'd hoped he'd crawled into a hole somewhere to writhe in pain, pecked at by birds and powerless, for the rest of his days.

It was a pretty specific fantasy, all things considered.

Maddie tilted her head and let her hair swing around her face, blocking her view of most of the tunnel. Maybe *too* specific. What if that was exactly what Torix had done? She'd never felt good about the image that came to her sometimes. Even as a fantasy, the depiction was darker than she wanted to be. She'd fought for the last year to reclaim herself, and she wanted that self to be a good person.

The idea that Torix could still have some influence over her, even passively through his magic, sparked a chill of fear in her.

The first real contact she'd had with him had been the dream with Will, and she'd immediately booked a flight home. The threat against Jake had been a blatant manipulation, but an effective one. As he'd predicted, she'd come to him. Before that though, he'd been able to access her dream when she'd thought herself hidden. He'd implied that her shields had kept him at bay until she'd dropped them for Aiden. *Had she let her shields slip in Wales?* It was possible she'd gotten lax after maintaining vigilance for so long.

What had changed that had allowed Torix to find her everywhere except Aiden's cabin? She peeked at him around her hair. He sat with his back against the stone wall, drinking water and diligently looking away from her. She needed to learn more about his wards. In the meantime, if Torix could track her, and she wasn't fully convinced yet, they needed to keep moving.

Maddie pulled her hair back into a ponytail and shook off the fear. It didn't do any good to cower from things that she couldn't control. Better to find a way to control them.

"Ready to go?"

Aiden capped his water and stowed it before standing. "Come to any conclusions?"

"I need to know more about your wards."

He nodded and started down the path again. "I thought that might come up."

"How are they keeping Torix out?"

"I assume you're talking about the ones at my cabin. Those are actually several wards woven together. One of them is specifically for Torix. I'm not taking any chances."

"Why did it let *me* in then?" She sounded small, even to herself, and she hated it.

"You are not Torix. You have some of his power inside

you, but it seems to be changing. His centered on manipulation and fear, yours isn't that subtle."

Maddie wasn't sure if she should be offended. "What does that mean?"

"It means when you use the magic it takes the form of blades and brute force."

She stared at her feet, silent for a second. "I don't trust it."

"I can't help you with that. In my vast opinion, the magic is becoming yours, if it hasn't already."

"Vast, huh?"

"I know a lot more than you."

She couldn't argue with that. Aiden slowed as the tunnel started a gentle curve upward. "We got off topic. Can you teach me how to ward out Torix?"

Sunlight spilled across the walls of the tunnel as they came around another bend, and Aiden stopped. "I might be able to, but wards are hard to master." She opened her mouth to argue, but he stopped her by holding up a hand. "I'm not saying you can't do it. I have absolute faith you'd nail them, but I don't think the time would be worth it. Do you want to be practicing while Torix collects more power every second?"

Maddie narrowed her eyes, strongly tempted to argue anyway, but he was right. They needed to weaken Torix before he got bored chasing her across the world and went after Jake and his family. "Okay, but I still want a lesson in wards when this is over."

He watched her for a moment, but she couldn't read his face. "When this is over."

The trod ended around the next corner as they climbed a few steps up to a sunny beach with palm trees swaying in a warm breeze. Maddie inhaled the salty sea air and wished again that she could call trods on her own. If she'd spent the last year on a tropical paradise instead of a soggy village in Wales, she'd at least be way less pale.

Aiden squinted toward the clear turquoise water and started walking down the beach. Maddie stripped off her long-sleeve overshirt and tied it around her waist. She walked carefully, but the sand destroyed her balance until she finally stooped and pulled off her boots too, tying them to the outside of her pack. Each time she stopped, he got a little further ahead of her.

"Aiden, wait."

He turned and frowned. His long legs ate up the sand as he walked back to her. "I have an idea."

Maddie squealed as his hands slipped behind her back and knees and he picked her up, pack and all. "I can walk, you big oaf."

He shrugged with one shoulder. "This will be faster."

She snorted. "Yeah, until you drop me."

"Have some faith, *marenkya*."

He didn't appear tired in the slightest from carrying her, so she relaxed and hooked a hand around his neck. "What does *marenkya* mean?"

"Little fox."

She'd had worse nicknames. "Why?"

"Because you fight to survive with everything in you, strength and brains. Also, you look vaguely fox-like."

Her nose scrunched. "Great. I look like a wild animal."

His fingers dug into her side. "It's a compliment. They're beautiful creatures."

Aiden scanned the water as he walked, and Maddie tried not to pet his chest where her hand rested. If she had any doubts about his stamina, they were laid to rest. He wasn't even breathing hard. She had to concentrate to make her own breath even as his closeness sent shivers of awareness through her.

Maddie shifted her focus from the hard muscles in front of her face to the mangrove swamps in the distance. A flash of pink caught her attention.

"Oh my god, flamingos! There are actual flamingos here. Where are we?"

"The island of Andros, in the Bahamas."

"Are flamingos dangerous in the wild? Can we get closer?" She smiled up at him. "I want to see if they actually stand on one leg when they're sleeping."

Aiden laughed. "I'm not chasing a bunch of flamingos through a swamp."

"Some Uber you are."

That got him to laugh hard enough that he had to stop walking. Maddie was never afraid he'd drop her, though. He met her eyes, and his grip tightened as the laughter died down. Maddie leaned closer, but a loud splash in the distance had Aiden looking away. She let her forehead drop down to his shoulder.

What was she thinking? This was no time for distractions. They were out in the open. Torix, or more likely Will, could be following them at that very second. She didn't even know what they were doing there. That glaring oversight was a much better place to focus her attention.

"Aiden, who are we looking for?"

"An old friend of mine. Daria."

"Does she live out here?"

"Sort of. She lives out there." He pointed his chin at the expanse of glistening water. "She's a mermaid."

Up until that moment, Maddie had believed mermaids to be a myth, like the Loch Ness monster and unicorns. The fascination she'd felt at seeing the flamingos paled in comparison to her excitement at meeting a real mermaid.

She eagerly searched the water for any sign of a woman with a tail. Aiden walked closer to the waves and laughed as she used his shoulder to lift herself higher. The beach ended in a rocky promontory that jutted into the surf. Another splash from in front of them made Maddie shade her eyes so she could squint at the rocks.

They looked empty at first, but as Aiden moved closer, she could make out a figure lounging half out of the water. With her elbows resting on the rocks, a woman with short, spiky black hair had her face upturned to the sun. She wore a short-sleeve rash guard with a familiar surfing logo on it, and Maddie couldn't see anything below her waist, despite the clear water.

Nervousness made Maddie hiss at Aiden under her breath. "Is there anything I need to know in advance?"

"Don't make direct eye contact, don't mention her tail, and they like humans to stand on one foot when addressing them."

Maddie frowned up at his straight face. "You're mocking me, aren't you?"

"Yes. Mermaids are people too. They don't have any cultural peculiarities you need to worry about."

"Is that Daria?"

"Yes."

"How did you know she'd be here instead of the other direction?"

"Lucky guess."

Everything he'd told her so far had been the truth, when he wasn't teasing her, but that last answer felt false. He hadn't hesitated since they'd stepped out of the trod onto the beach, and his tone told her he wasn't going to give her more information. Aiden had known where to find Daria, and he didn't want Maddie to know how. Hurt blossomed inside her. She'd thought he trusted her more than that.

Daria didn't move as they approached the rock, but the muscles in her arms tensed as if ready to push off at any second. They stopped close enough that Maddie could make out a gleam in the water where she'd expected a tail to be. She pushed against Aiden's chest until he set her down. The sand burned her sensitive feet, so she wiggled under it until she hit a cooler layer. Maddie wanted her feet firmly on the ground for her first time meeting a mermaid.

"Daria, we need to talk," Aiden said.

Her eyes popped open, and Maddie almost gasped at the deep indigo color. "I hate when you say that." She gave Aiden a slow, appreciative once-over that sparked a surprising amount of jealousy in Maddie. They clearly had a past, and she wondered if this was why he was keeping things from her.

The vibrant purple gaze moved from Aiden to Maddie, and Daria smiled slowly, revealing sharp, pointed teeth. "You brought me a human."

Aiden took a not so subtle step in front of her, and the jealousy subsided. "She's mine."

The mermaid pouted and relaxed on the rocks again. "Why are you wearing so many clothes?"

"Why are you?" Aiden retorted.

Maddie narrowed her eyes at him. Their interaction bordered on useless, but curiosity begged her to ask one question. She stepped out from behind Aiden and addressed Daria herself. "Where'd you get a surfing shirt?"

"From a surfer. Humans are freaked out by boobs." She smiled again, more friendly, less predatory this time. "You understand."

She did. Flash a smidgen of boob and society ground to a halt. Maddie nodded knowingly, and Daria gave her a little eyebrow wiggle. Her tail emerged from the water and crashed back down, making the loud splash they'd heard earlier. Out of the water, the scales glimmered in the sun, iridescent blue deepening into dark purple at the tip.

Maddie only got a glimpse, but her eyes widened at the beauty. Did all mermaids have tails that matched their eyes? She wanted to get closer, see if the scales were as smooth as they looked. The urge built quickly in her until she had to lock her legs to stay put.

Aiden growled, and the impulse abruptly dissipated. For a second, she'd forgotten all about him. "Stop it, Daria."

She sighed and rolled her eyes. "Fine. You ruin all my fun."

Maddie blinked and dug her toes into the sand. Seth had said the same thing to him. "What just happened to me?"

Aiden didn't take his eyes off Daria, but he dropped a hand on Maddie's shoulder. "Mermaids can mesmerize with their tails. It's how they capture prey."

Maddie gaped up at him. "And you didn't think that was important information? Like when I asked if there was anything I needed to know in advance and you mocked me instead of helping?"

He shrugged. "I didn't think it would work on you."

Maddie wanted to smack him again. Of all the times to demonstrate that he didn't know everything, he chose the one where she could have gotten eaten by a beautiful mermaid. A thought hit her, and she eyed him again. "What do they do with their prey?"

He looked down and met her eyes. "They eat it or mate with it, depending on their mood."

Daria scoffed. "As if I'd eat someone that skinny. She's got practically no meat on her."

Maddie's brows lifted into her hair, and she decided to take it as a compliment. She'd just been hit on by a mermaid. A sexy mermaid. Warmth rose from her chest up her neck and into her face. That tail was potent. She shook her head, and decided to keep her eyes away from the water just in case.

Aiden didn't seem to be having any of the same trouble. "What do you know about a Fae named Torix?"

"Torix?" She yawned and stretched her arms above her head. "Never heard of him, but I don't pay much attention to Fae politics. They're always so serious and uppity. Who wants to live like that all the time?"

"What about a place called the Tavern on the Sea run by a selkie named Cassie?"

"Now *that* I've heard of. Excellent mussels. It's in a rough neighborhood though."

"What does that mean?"

She waved a hand vaguely. "Off the northwest coast of Scotland."

Maddie piped in. "Does off the coast mean land or sea?"

Daria giggled, revealing her disturbing teeth again. "Land, darling. The sea there is terrible. Have you *been* to the Atlantic Ocean? It's freezing and the fish taste like metal. So do the fishermen."

Aiden sighed, and Maddie wondered if Daria was being purposely dramatic. "Can you be more specific?"

"Callanish. Ask around. The locals know where to find it, even if they don't frequent it." She cocked her head to the side. "Why the interest?"

"Seth said Cassie might have some information for us."

Daria's face closed down, and she raised a dark, haughty

brow. "I should have known Seth was involved when you showed up here."

"He didn't know I was coming here."

She sneered. "Yes, he did. He's not happy unless he's fondling someone's puppet strings. You tell him if I see him again it won't be with mating on my mind." Her attention shifted to Maddie. "A word of advice, pretty human? Don't trust Seth. His first priority is always himself."

Aiden saved her from having to answer. "Thanks, Daria. I'll be sure to pass your message along."

Daria sniffed, then leaned back against the rocks again and closed her eyes. They'd been dismissed. Before Maddie could argue, Aiden picked her up again and carted her back the way they'd come.

She stayed silent until she thought Daria was out of earshot. "So...her and Seth?"

Aiden shook his head in incredulity. "Don't let her fool you. She has a pretty short attention span for most things. Seth tends to make sure people remember him, especially the ladies."

Maddie curled her fingers into the hair at his nape. "What about you?"

"Me and Daria?" He gave a quick, short laugh. "No. Hell no. Even if I were interested in mermaids, she's a trouble-maker. Her and Seth are perfect for each other, actually."

The question that had been pestering her all along popped out. "How did you really know how to find her?"

His lips tipped up in a slow smile. "Jealous?"

"I don't know, but that's not an answer."

He sobered. "She was watching us when we came out of the trod. Like with Seth, I knew she'd be intrigued enough about you to make herself known. We only had to wait until she was ready."

"So that pose on the rocks was staged?"

"Yes, but I expected it. I didn't want to explain in case she was close enough to hear. She'd get offended and swim off."

Relief was sweet, if short-lived. "Did you know she'd try to mesmerize me?"

His arms tightened a smidge. "No. *That* was a surprise."

They made it back to the trod quicker than the trek to the rock, and Maddie suspected he'd been slowing down on the way out to give Daria a chance to get a good look. The steps to the tunnel were gone, but a shimmering path appeared in the sand. Sprites floated over it, but they were almost invisible in the bright sunlight.

Maddie shaded her eyes and looked up at the stretch of clear blue sky. "It's been daylight in every place we've been, but the sun doesn't seem to be moving much. How much time has really passed out here since leaving your cabin?"

Aiden glanced up, then back at her. "About two days. Put your boots and overshirt on. You'll need them in Scotland."

Time moved differently in the trods. She knew that, but it couldn't have been more than a few hours since she'd woken up that morning. Sand clung stubbornly to her feet as she slid her socks on, and she sighed. The grit would chafe if she didn't find somewhere to take a shower and wash her meager clothes. Maybe paradise wasn't all it was cracked up to be.

6

AIDEN

AIDEN NEARLY OFFERED to hold her while she fought with the sand, but he'd spent enough time keeping her pressed against him. Speed had been an excuse on the beach. Daria would have shown herself on her own schedule no matter how fast or slow they walked. He'd wanted to touch her again, to see if it would appease the need spawned by the kiss in the alley. Instead, he'd had trouble keeping his hands platonic and his attention on the water.

Daria had taken advantage of his distraction. He was lucky she hadn't put more effort into mesmerizing Maddie. They didn't have time to hole up while she worked through the spell and the subsequent physical reactions. A brief image of Maddie asking for his touch flitted through his mind. It made him painfully hard, but he would never have taken advantage of her magically enhanced sensuality.

At least Cassie wouldn't be a threat.

Aiden adjusted his pants as Maddie finally stood and

donned her overshirt. The trod waited for them. She'd probably still be cold when they got there, but her layers would protect her well enough in the temperate magic of the trod. Golden sand rose around them as they walked, blocking off all sight except the path directly in front of them. Maddie stuck her hand through the wall, and a handful of glittering dust gathered in her palm. She let it fall to the ground, but a breeze picked up the particles and swept them back into the whole. Sprites floated through the walls as if they weren't there.

Unlike the other journeys, the trip to Scotland only required a short stay in the trod, for which Aiden was glad. The essential blindness in the trod made him nervous, and he couldn't stop peering into the sand looking for enemies. He hadn't forgotten that Torix's last attack had come in the nexus of the Wood. This time, he'd be armed with more than an overzealous protector.

Before they'd left, Aiden had chosen to conceal his weapons in a pocket trod in case they spent a great deal of time wandering the market in Cairo, as he'd done the previous days on his own. Egyptian authorities didn't react well to a foreigner openly carrying a sword.

The shimmering walls ended at two giant, grey standing stones bracketing the path. Beyond them, a green field dotted with more stones and tufts of grass stretched into the distance. The sun dropped behind low rolling hills, but the rest of the sky churned with thick clouds.

Cold wind slapped his cheeks as he stepped between the stones and left the path. Aiden had traveled to Scotland before, but he'd never been this far northeast. The smell of rain drifted in the air. Maddie gasped softly behind him, and he turned to see her staring in awe at the size of the stones two and three times her height. The setting sun painted her golden, and Aiden clenched his hands to keep them at his side.

The sparse fields were deserted except for the two of them. So much for asking the locals for directions.

"This is amazing." Maddie shivered and smiled at him. "Can you feel the power in them?"

"It's a nexus that's stood for thousands of years. Even the humans claim to feel it. That's why they come to places like this."

She laid her hand on the rock in front of her, and he felt her call to the stones. To his surprise, the stones answered. A wave of energy pulsed out from the center of the circle, and magic surged through him. Aiden tamped it down, but Maddie had curled forward so her forehead touched the rough surface. The magic from the stones died down, but Maddie had absorbed a large amount of it.

Aiden shook his head at the follies of youth and pulled her away from the nexus. She swung around limply, and he had to catch her before she collapsed on the ground. "Maddie? *Marenkya*? You need to let some of that magic go."

Her eyes closed, and her legs wobbled underneath her. She could stand on her own, but she couldn't find her balance. His arms kept her upright while she rode the wave of energy. She pressed her face to his chest and let out a ragged breath.

Holding her was like stepping into a whirlwind of elemental power. The core of what she had resembled Fae magic, and mixing magics was generally a bad idea. She didn't seem negatively impacted though. On the contrary, she pressed against him and shuddered. Aiden tried to shift his lower half away from her, but she moved with him.

A smaller wave of magic emanated from her and rolled over him. He grunted as pleasure spread through his body. "Maddie..." He wasn't sure what he was pleading for, but Maddie seemed to understand.

"I'm sorry. I didn't know that was going to happen."

She breathed shallowly, and her hips undulated in tiny movements with her breath. He ached as she brushed against him, and fought not to take what she was unwittingly offering. Maddie must have been thinking of them together when she released the elemental magic. The rush had stimulated both of them, and the aftereffects lingered.

Aiden shifted his hands to her waist, and tried to set her away, but she refused to move very far. The small difference took them out of direct contact, which Aiden immediately regretted. Her eyes fluttered open and the raw need there almost made him change his mind again.

Her hands slid up his chest to clasp behind his neck.

"Maddie, what are you doing?"

"What I keep wanting to do." She raised up on her tiptoes and pulled his head down to her, but hesitated.

His hands clenched at her waist, and he waited. He didn't have it in him to deny her, but this had to be her choice. Her lips brushed his, once, twice, then settled against him with an electric charge. Aiden held himself back and let her explore. She kissed him slow and deep, and he felt his urgency melt away. The moor around them was damp and bitter, but he could stand there all day with her.

Her tongue darted out, easing along his lower lip until he parted his mouth and allowed her to taste him. She made a purring noise and inched closer. A gust pushed her the rest of the way against him, but the cold touch brought him to his senses. Her legs held her without trouble, and her magic had returned to normal. He pulled away, breaking the kiss.

Maddie touched her lips with her fingertips. "What's wrong?"

"When you kiss me, I want it to be because it's *me* you need, not any random warm body."

"I'll keep that in mind the next time I'm being kissed senseless on a street corner because you're not inventive in your hiding spots."

Aiden winced. He didn't regret his decision, but she'd make sure it came back to bite him in the ass. "This is different. The effects of that elemental magic were potent, and we both responded."

Her eyes narrowed. "Are you implying I'd jump anyone who happened to be here?"

Aiden chose his words with care. "I don't know, but every time you touch me it gets harder to maintain my distance."

Kissing her proved addictive and problematic. He didn't want to hurt her, but he had no intention of getting his emotions involved again. After Lexi, life became easier without emotional attachments. At the same time, he couldn't seem to stay away from her.

She wrapped her arms around herself, and he conceded that he may have hurt her already. "I'll keep your distance in mind the next time."

Aiden accepted the warning in her voice and searched the surrounding area for some kind of tourist center. In the distance, he spotted a white building surrounded by a low stone wall. "C'mon, this way."

As they got closer, the white building turned out to be an old barn that had been refurbished into a café. A wooden section elongated the original structure and added an outdoor seating area. A second building that looked newer stretched around the first and ended in a round hut covered with the same grey rocks used to make the stone walls.

Maddie sidled closer to him when he stepped up to the door. She shivered again as a light rain began to fall. The roof of the building provided some protection, but the wind pushed the rain sideways at them. Aiden checked inside the glass and saw a desk with a rack of pamphlets next to it. If Cassie's tavern was nearby, they'd probably have an advertisement for it here. A quick spell took care of the lock. The door swung open, and a rush of warm air greeted them.

"Thank god," she muttered.

Aiden inhaled deeply before entering the building. The cold, wet air invigorated him, and he much preferred it over the lazy heat in the Bahamas. "Don't move anything. We don't want the humans to get suspicious."

Maddie arched a brow. "You know I'm human, right?"

He knew, but his senses kept telling him she was something else, something more. "I apologize if I've offended you."

She blew out a breath and rubbed her arms. "It takes more than that to offend me. What are we looking for in here besides warmth?"

He nodded at the pamphlets. "Directions."

There weren't any pamphlets for the Tavern by the Sea, but a local map pinned to the wall listed it among their pubs. The walk wouldn't take long, but rain had started to fall in earnest and darkness was approaching fast. He took stock of Maddie's leggings and boots. She wore several layers, but none of them appeared to be waterproof.

The gift shop carried a small selection of rain jackets, but Maddie refused to take one unless they paid for it. Aiden refused to let Maddie spend the last of her money on an overpriced tourist souvenir. He finally got her to agree to let him leave some cash for it with the stipulation that she'd pay him back at a later date.

Aiden suspected that she was still salty from their earlier conversation and less willing to bend. So be it. He wasn't thrilled with the way it had gone either. The smallest size jacket they had dwarfed Maddie's small frame. Her lips pressed together in obvious displeasure, but he was glad it would cover most of her clothes and her pack.

They left the money under a tumbled rock on the counter and made sure nothing else was amiss. Aiden had waterproofed his clothes some time ago. The rain fell in sheets, and large puddles formed along the gravel walkways between buildings.

Aiden relocked the door behind them, but Maddie hesitated before stepping out into the downpour. "Maybe it'll clear up if we stay here a while longer."

He sent her a reassuring smile. "It's not far to the tavern, and I'm sure Cassie will have plenty of warm food for us when we get there."

She glared at him, probably unhappy he assumed she was food-motivated, but it got her moving. The map had indicated that it would be about a thirty-minute walk, but the dirt and gravel road quickly turned into a mud track. The rolling hills they'd seen from the stones weren't very steep, but they were deceptively slick. He had to save Maddie twice from ending up on her butt, and she yanked him upright once when his foot slid out from under him.

Thirty minutes came and went, but the tavern remained stubbornly absent. Aiden's hair dripped water down his back, and though Maddie tried to keep the hood of the jacket up, the wind continually pushed it off her head. Slogging through the mud seemed to be getting them nowhere.

Before he could suggest that they head back to the tourist center to wait until morning, the rain suddenly let up. The downpour slowed to a drizzle then stopped completely before they'd crested the next hill.

Moonlight began to peek through the rapidly dissipating clouds, and Aiden strained to see any signs of another building ahead of them. Maddie looked out at the stones in the distance behind them and gasped for the second time.

"Aiden, look," she breathed.

The sky glowed in streaks of pink and green over a splash of bright stars. Maddie radiated under the bright light, and joy lit up her face. The Northern Lights blanketed the moors with spectacular color, but the sight didn't compete with the appeal of a bedraggled Maddie wearing an innocent smile. His chest ached, and he tore his eyes away.

Her rare display of happiness made him want to show her all the hidden wonders available to them, to fill her life with the delight Torix had stolen from her. Maybe one day, when they were truly free, but tonight, they had an artifact to find.

The rain stopped completely, but a chilly wind continued to blow. Aiden wanted to get inside before another storm showed up. "Maddie, let's go."

She blinked, and her smile slipped away. He felt its loss like a physical ache, so much that he almost gave in. *Never-mind. They'd find the tavern later. They could stay as long as she wanted.* Instead, he clenched his jaw tight as she straightened her shoulders and walked past him on the muddy path.

MADDIE

M ADDIE MUST HAVE VISITED WORSE places than that muddy hilltop, but she couldn't bring any to mind. On the other hand, the unbeatable show over the stones made the trek worth it. The prospect of food and warmth kept her moving forward, but she couldn't stop glancing behind them, even as more and more clouds obscured the view. She'd seen the lights in Norway, muted and quiet, but these colors stretched loud and wild. Maddie felt the prickle of their energy painted across the sky.

Hidden in a hollow only a few more minutes down the road, they found the Tavern by the Sea. Large windows filled both levels on the long, two-story building under a thatched roof. A sign with the name and a stylized seal underneath it hung over the arched front door. Maddie couldn't see the water, but the surf crashed surprisingly close-by. Cheerful torches lit the entrance, highlighting the lack of cars parked outside.

They got as far as the unlocked door before a curvy young woman with beautiful brown hair and striking green eyes blocked the way. Aiden tucked Maddie behind him, and she resisted the urge to kick him in the shin. The woman looked him up and down, then sniffed.

"Kin to Seth, are you?"

Aiden grimaced. "Yes. We need your help."

The woman, who Maddie assumed had to be Cassie, crossed her arms over her ample bosom. "Be off with you, then. We don't want your kind here."

Maddie sensed an opportunity. She popped out from

behind Aiden and looked back and forth between them. "What *is* his kind?"

Cassie's face softened as she turned to Maddie, but Aiden cut her off. "I need information about an artifact that was stolen from you."

It was exactly the wrong thing to say. Cassie's eyes narrowed at him. "I'll not give information to the likes of you. The poor frozen girl can come inside to warm herself for the night. *You're* welcome to the stable."

They looked up the coast where she pointed, and sure enough, a small building was barely visible against the darkness. If she squinted, Maddie could make out a gravel path that led in that direction.

Cassie stood back and held the door open, but Maddie hesitated. She didn't know what problem Cassie had with Aiden, but it didn't seem fair to blame him for her issues with Seth.

Maddie smiled at her. "That sounds lovely, but I need a minute with Aiden."

Cassie gave her a knowing look. "Scoundrels. The lot of them. You'd be best to remember that. The invitation stands." She turned and shut them out in the night.

Aiden glanced at the stable again and sighed. "It's not so bad. The wolf will keep me warm."

"This is ridiculous. She's never met you. How can she hate you?"

"Seth comes to mind. He tends to inspire strong emotions in women."

Maddie tried to stop a shiver, but it didn't work. Aiden noticed. He tucked a limp section of wet hair behind her ear and smiled. "Go inside, *marenkya*. There's nothing you can change out here."

She wanted to argue with him, or tell Cassie where she

could shove her conditional hospitality. Neither of those would be particularly helpful though. Aiden's smile didn't falter. "You know where to find me if you need anything."

Maddie finally gave in and rolled her eyes. "Fine, but I'm going to bring you some food at least."

He inclined his head and walked up the path to his room for the night. The whole situation was screwed up. Maddie didn't know much about selkies or Scotland or taverns, but she knew how to gather information. Too bad Aiden couldn't enjoy the warmth along with her.

Maddie squared her shoulders and opened the door to a charming great room with a bar along one wall and a large fireplace on the other. Tables with chairs were scattered around the room, and a series of large, overstuffed recliners sat in front of the fire.

Cassie stood behind the bar drying pint glasses with a white cloth. She gestured at the recliners, and Maddie was sorely tempted. Despite beginning the day in Egypt and the Bahamas, she felt like she hadn't been warm since her dream with Aiden. But they both needed food.

The only other person in the tavern, an old man hunched over his beer, sat at the far side of the bar. Cassie didn't look surprised when Maddie approached her instead of the fire. She put the glass away and grabbed a new one from a rack behind her. A young girl who looked like she couldn't be older than fifteen came through an inconspicuous door in the corner and set a plate in front of the old man. The smell of roasted meat hit Maddie, and her stomach clenched up. She really needed to remember to eat more often.

"May I order some food please?"

Cassie finished wiping her glass, then set it down carefully and leaned forward on the bar. "What are you doing running around with that ruffian?"

Maddie tilted her head. "What makes you think *he's* the ruffian?"

She snorted. "It's always them."

"He's helping me. He saved my life, and he's the best shot I have of keeping it saved."

"That's not all he's doing though, is it, girl?"

Maddie's cheeks warmed, but she refused to be embarrassed by what she'd done with Aiden. Her body, her choice. She lifted her chin. "I'd prefer he was doing more."

Cassie cackled and slapped the gleaming counter. "Isn't that always the way with the pretty ones." Her hands slid into her apron pockets as she leaned back and took a better look. "You judge his help to be useful?"

"Yes. We've worked together for years, and the first thing he's always done is protect me." The truth of Maddie's statement lodged in her chest. He'd been a wolf for most of that time, but even under Torix's power, he'd ensured her safety. "I trust him with my life, and I feel better when he's with me." She felt his absence in the bright warmth of the tavern and resolved that she'd take food to him, then stay out there.

Cassie shook her head slowly. "It's food you're after, is it?" She bellowed something in the direction of the small door. The teenager peeked her head out.

"Two more orders of the special," Cassie told her.

"To-go, please," said Maddie quickly.

The teenager waited until Cassie nodded then scurried off.

"I'll speak to you about the thing you're wanting, and when we're through and I've closed up, you can bring your man inside. It's none of mine how you spend your time. I have one spare room, and I want him gone by morning."

Maddie barely controlled her giddy wiggle. "Thank you, Cassie."

"I'm sure regret is on the horizon, but I feel a need to help." She pulled a stool up on her side of the counter and settled in. "Now, some years ago, I was gifted a necklace by a suitor. He claimed himself to be Lugh, but I can see a trickster when one presents himself. The man was utterly ordinary, but the necklace, particularly the medallion, was not. It was imbued with power I didn't recognize, and who was I to doubt the mighty Lugh made trinkets in his spare time."

The rhythm of Cassie's voice entranced Maddie. The rise and fall, the lilt, of the story pulled Maddie in so much that she didn't notice right away that Cassie had gotten up and poured two glasses of water.

"I wore that bit of magic around my neck for a time and found myself free from the machinations of those around me. I'm not without power myself, but there are many who would see me as weak. Especially once I left my people to seek my future on my own terms."

Cassie's eyes sparkled with the memory, and she sent Maddie a secret smile. "You understand that I think."

Maddie took a sip of the water and remembered how she'd felt when she'd first met Torix. Weak and scrambling for anything to make her feel strong again. She'd craved power, and Torix had offered it to her. In her stupidity, she'd accepted. Maddie grimaced, and Cassie placed a hand over hers on the bar.

"I'm sorry for that, girl. I didn't mean to awaken old ghosts."

Maddie shook her head and extracted her hand. "I'm fine. Please continue."

Cassie leaned back and took a swig of her own water. "The medallion protected me from the magic of those who would force me to their will. I left my home, and I met a dashing man." She raised a cheeky brow. "One of the pretty ones."

Maddie smiled, but she knew where this was going.

"After much convincing, I shared my secrets and my bed, and in the morning, the necklace was gone." Her eyes went far away, and she stroked her neck. "I'd done enough to build my life by then that I didn't need the magical protection, but the loss hurt. Of the medallion and the man." Her hand dropped, and she returned to the present. "He was *very* convincing."

"Do you know what happened to them?"

Cassie shook her head. "I never heard from him again, but the sea knows. She tells me that his ship was bound for Norway." She stopped talking abruptly when the teenager emerged with two plates covered in foil and two packets of silverware wrapped in napkins. The girl set everything in front of Maddie, curtseyed at Cassie, then went back into the kitchen. Maddie's mouth watered at the delicious scent of roast and vegetables.

"How much do I owe you?"

"Free for a fellow traveler. This time."

"Thank you. Truly. This smells like the best meal I've had in years."

Cassie nodded as if it were her due. "The medallion is not something to trifle with. It will only protect the one wearing it and only until it seeks a new path. Many would kill to have that ability. Some say it was lost to the waves, but the sea knows. I'd ask the trolls in Stabbursdalen what they have hidden away." She turned away and picked up her rag again.

Maddie couldn't think of anything else to ask, and she seriously doubted Seth had gotten that much information.

She wanted to tear the foil off the plate and eat right there, but she'd told Aiden she'd bring him food.

"Thank you again, Cassie."

"You mind my warning, girl. The pretty ones always look out for themselves."

7

MADDIE

MADDIE NODDED at Cassie's warning because her mom had taught her to be polite. She believed to her very core that Aiden would never toss her aside to save himself. The heavy, cumbersome plates challenged her balance, but she managed to get the door open on her own. Cold, wet air smacked her in the face, and she instantly missed the comfort of the tavern. Clouds had blocked out the magnificent sight of the Northern Lights, but once her eyes adjusted, the torches provided enough light for her to see the path to the stable.

The door squeaked as she wrangled it open, and more darkness greeted her inside. The scent of horses and leather competed with dinner, but she didn't hear any animals moving around.

"Aiden?"

One side of a giant double door at the far end of the stable stood open to the night. She picked her way down the

aisle. The barn door faced away from the tavern, but the
moon peeked out from behind the clouds enough to guide
her. The closer she got to the end, the more she could see.

In the last stall, Maddie found the wolf curled up with
his tail wrapped over his nose. "There you are. I brought
dinner." She held up the two plates, and in an instant, Aiden
was a man again.

He took the plate she handed him and peeled back the
foil to take a sniff. "Thanks. I'm surprised you were able to
convince Cassie to make a meal for me."

"I didn't. I asked to order dinner, and she had the girl
working in the back bring out two servings." The straw in
the stall looked clean, so Maddie took a chance and sat
down next to Aiden. She balanced the plate in her lap and
dropped her pack behind her. A chilly breeze drifted
through the room, but it wasn't as bad as outside. Her hair
had mostly dried while she talked to Cassie, and the rain
jacket did its job in keeping the rest of her out of the water.

Aiden had finished half his food by the time Maddie
joined him. She'd have been happy with anything edible,
but Cassie's roast reminded her of her dad's brisket. A pang
of homesickness made her pause. As long as Torix remained
free, she *couldn't* go home. Maddie refused to risk them.

Once both plates were clear, Aiden sat back with a satisfied groan. "I haven't had a good roast in a while."

"Remind me to bring you to family dinner some time."
Maddie stacked the dishes and set them aside. "Cassie told
me about the artifact."

He raised a brow. "Good work. It crossed my mind that
Seth may have sent us on a wild-goose chase, but I should've
known you'd find a way. What'd she say?"

"It's a necklace, a medallion specifically, and it's probably under the protection of some trolls in Norway."

He leaned back against the stable wall and crossed his arms. "That's going to make it tough for us to get it."

Maddie shrugged. "I don't know much about trolls. She said the medallion protects against other magic, and something weird about it choosing a new path, but that might have been embellishment. The story was compelling." Maddie frowned at the straw floor. "I felt bad for her, but I don't think she felt bad for herself. It was like she cherished the memory of the man who stole the necklace from her."

Aiden tapped her thigh with the toes of his boot. "Don't get lost in the storytelling. It's one of the ways Selkies use their magic to influence emotion."

She turned her frown on him. "I thought I was immune to magic?"

"Clearly not totally immune. The standing stones affected you."

"Daria's tail did too," she mused. "But I could shake those off easily. I felt a little loopy while Cassie was telling her story, but everything went back to normal when she stopped."

"It's a peculiar power in a strange situation. I don't know of anyone else who has even a partial immunity to magic."

The cold began to seep in again as they sat there, and Maddie shivered. The puffer coat she wore under the rain jacket kept her torso warm enough, but her leggings did very little to stop the bite from the wind when it hit her.

"It's warmer over here against the wall."

Maddie conceded that he was probably right, but she stubbornly stayed in her spot. "Cassie offered us a room once she closed down for the night, as long as you're gone by morning."

"Did she now?"

"That's what she said."

"What changed her mind?"

"My loveable personality?" Maddie tucked her knees up to her chest and wrapped her arms around them.

He smiled. "You might as well go inside if you're too afraid to sit next to me where you won't turn into an icicle."

She straightened. "I'm not afraid. And your reverse psychology won't work on me."

"Okay." He waited in the dark, the smile never wavering, and a gust of wind made Maddie hunch further into her coat.

"Fine. Scoot over." He shifted further into the corner, and Maddie sat next to him. "It wasn't because of what you said. I was cold."

He wrapped an arm around her shoulders and pulled her into his side. "I only wanted you to be warm, *marenkya*."

She *was* warm. Aiden's body gave off heat like a furnace. She hadn't noticed in the dream, but she hadn't been freezing in the dream either. Maddie tucked her legs and hands between them and curled up with her head on his shoulder. His arm snaked under her coat, but she couldn't blame him for trying to get some protection from the wind. Or for using the convenient weather excuse to bring her close. Whatever his motivation, his body heat added some warmth along her lower back.

His fingers traced lazy circles on her rib cage, and she relaxed into the repetition. Maddie sat on the floor of a stable, muddy and gross, but weirdly content. She'd eaten a good meal, Aiden kept her warm, and she felt safe.

She felt safe, but she wasn't.

Will would show up at some point. They hadn't figured out how Torix tracked her, so she couldn't get complacent. Aiden must have felt her tense up because his fingers stopped moving. They sat huddled together, sharing warmth, for a minute more, but the comfort had passed.

"We can't stay here," she said into the quiet.

"I know, but we can rest for a bit. It's been a long day."

She smiled into his shoulder. "Don't you mean it's been a long two days?"

"Yes, that's clearly what I meant. Do we have more specific directions than 'somewhere in Norway'?"

"The trolls in Stabbursdalen." She looked up at him. "You know where that is?"

"Surprisingly, yes. I've spent some time in that area. I wasn't aware they had a troll encampment there."

"Ready to be more surprised? I know one of the trolls."

He laughed. "Of course you do."

"I helped him out while I was visiting my parents after... well, after everything last year."

"I think there's a nexus in the national park there, but I don't know how far from the trolls it will be."

"That's great, but I have Oskar's cell number."

Aiden slumped down a little further, taking her with him. "Of course you do." His eyes closed. "How did you help him?"

His voice rumbled under her cheek, and she let herself relax into him again. They *did* need to rest, and Torix probably wouldn't find them that quickly when the Tavern wasn't exactly well-advertised.

"He was having trouble sleeping. My parents were camping in the national forest, so I met up with them. One night after a nightmare, I decided to take a walk. I found a rocky outcropping over a stream, and a troll skipping stones where the water pooled. He said he was waiting for me and politely asked me if I could use my magic to help him rest through the night." Maddie paused, and Aiden's even breathing clued her in that he'd fallen asleep too. Maybe that was her superpower, helping other people sleep. She'd take that any day over manipulation and death magic.

Maddie closed her eyes and shored up her shields. The rhythm of Aiden's heartbeat lulled her to sleep as well.

A CRASH and a yowl dragged Maddie slowly into waking. If she'd dreamed, she didn't remember it. Her eyes popped open when Aiden's arm around her tensed. He met her gaze and held a finger to his lips for silence.

"I don't know who you're talking about, now get on with you and your strange bird." Cassie's loud voice echoed through the stable. Maddie nodded and carefully eased off of him. Now that she knew to look for it, she could feel the weight of the magic in Cassie's words, right outside the building.

"It's poor form to lie to me." Will's voice sounded off, his normally arrogant tone overshadowed by a deeper one. She didn't need to guess to know Torix had already taken control of him.

"Sure and I'm not scared of you. This poor human may be under your thrall, but you'll not touch me and mine."

Go, Cassie. Maddie doubted Torix had gone to the trouble of traveling all the way to Scotland himself, especially since he likely couldn't call the trods on his own if she couldn't. Will still posed a threat considering the unknown nature of his bond with Torix, but with the magic Maddie sensed, Cassie could hold her own.

Just in case, they needed to get moving. Maddie stood

and dusted herself off, and Aiden followed her up. She glanced out the open door to judge how long they'd slept, but the dark sky didn't give her much information. A dizzying array of stars twinkled from one horizon to the other, signaling the clouds had passed. The Northern Lights had passed as well, but the sun had yet to make an appearance.

"As you wish, selkie. I'll find them on my own, but your obstinance won't be forgotten." Will's strange double voice tracked further away, toward the tavern.

Maddie breathed a sigh of relief that he obviously couldn't pinpoint her precise location. Movement at the end of the aisle drew her attention. A broom lay haphazardly on the floor, but she couldn't make out anything else that could have moved.

"Aiden," she whispered. "Is there something else in here with us?"

He shook his head and pulled on his pack. She did the same and realized that they were trapped in the stable as long as Will was out there. The moors around them were hilly but without any cover. They needed to get back to the stones to call a trod. Steps crunched over gravel away from the stable, but she couldn't be sure if it was Cassie or Will or both.

Aiden moved closer and lowered his mouth to her ear. "You're going to have to ride me."

Maddie reared back and raised a brow. "I don't think we have time for that at the moment."

"Trust me. Hold on tight and don't let go for anything."

"What are you babbling about?" Before the question left her mouth, Aiden changed from a man to a sleek, dappled grey horse. His coloring resembled the wolf, and his eyes remained golden. Maddie reached out to pet his soft nose, and he snorted on her hand.

Cassie taunted Will again, louder, but Maddie wasn't sure if it was because they were moving closer to the stable or if Cassie was trying harder to warn them. Either way, they needed to leave. She spotted a stool in the corner of the stall across the aisle and dragged it next to Aiden. His unexpectedly slick back reached past her shoulder.

She'd grown up in Texas, but she'd never spent any time around horses before. Even with the stool, she couldn't figure out where to put her hands to boost herself up. In the end, he knelt down while she tried not to slide all the way across his back and onto the stable floor. He stood, and she clenched her hands in his mane to keep from falling off.

Maddie leaned low over his back and whispered, "Mush."

Aiden turned gingerly toward the open door, then with a burst of speed they flew over the grass. The cold wind pushed her hood back and tossed her hair behind her. Maddie wanted to squeeze her eyes shut in fear, but she trusted Aiden. He wouldn't do anything to knock her off. She stayed low on his back, and in the distance behind them, she heard another yowl. The cry sounded like a cat in pain, but she didn't dare shift her weight to look back.

They eschewed the path in favor of following the coast, keeping the peak of the hills between them and the Tavern. The trip back the way they'd come passed in a fraction of the time even though they took a longer route, and Maddie wondered why they hadn't ridden in the first place.

The silhouettes of the stones appeared over the next hill, and Aiden slowed to a walk. He stopped in the darkness next to two of the stones, sweaty and panting, and Maddie finally looked back. A shadowy hillside marked the stillness behind them. She slid off and wobbled on the ground, but didn't fall. Aiden shifted back into a man and swayed unsteadily. He reached out for the rock, and Maddie pulled his arm over her shoulder.

"Let's get out of here."

He nodded, and the familiar tingle of magic washed over her. The space between the stones shimmered, and sprites floated into view. Aiden didn't say anything as Maddie took some of his weight. Her feet dragged a bit, sad to leave the respite and Cassie's unexpected protection behind. Maddie planned to come back some day and ask her why she'd helped.

Aiden regained strength as time passed. At some point, he reclaimed his weight, but he didn't move his arm. Maddie kept pace next to him, concentrating on breathing evenly, though her pulse raced both from the close escape and his nearness.

"Thank you," he said.

She waved his thanks away. "Why were you weak all of a sudden?"

"The wolf comes easily, but the horse is trickier."

Maddie nodded as if that made sense. "Sure. I'll bet the polar bear really takes it out of you."

He grinned. "I've never tried a polar bear."

"Not a yeti then, huh?"

"Nope."

They walked for a long while on a gravel path in the pre-dawn twilight, but the trek came to an abrupt end at a copse of trees. The trail disappeared, and they found themselves standing in a forest of pines at sunrise, but distinctly different from the forests back home. The woods in Texas brimmed with heat and bugs and underbrush. This forest in Norway boasted sparse beauty. Bright green moss covered the ground, and a trail of loose stones led between the trees.

The sky faded to light blue, though the sun hadn't crested over their particular area yet. Snow lingered in the shadows under the trees, sparkling in errant shafts of sun as the branches shifted in the breeze. Maddie's breath fogged in front of her, and she groaned.

"Why didn't I put on more layers? Every place we visit is colder than the last."

Aiden hugged her against his side for a second, then let her go to take a few steps up the path. "At least it'll be daytime here. Almost no time has passed since we left Scotland."

Maddie's face scrunched. "How do you know? I always have to check my phone."

He looked over his shoulder at her. "I don't think you'll have much luck of that here."

"Yeah, I know. Cell reception is spotty, but Oskar has a satellite phone. If I can find service, he'll answer my call." Maddie pulled her phone out of the special pocket in her backpack and checked. No service at all. Not really a surprise. "We're going to need to walk for a bit. At least it'll warm us up."

They settled into silence as Aiden created a path of his own between the trees and rocks. The air smelled crisp, and the spicy scent of pine needles wafted up to Maddie as she walked. Her muscles warmed as they moved, and she let her mind wander. She was pretty sure Aiden didn't know where exactly they were, and she was absolutely sure he had no idea where they were heading. Her phone would vibrate if it connected, so she stuffed it in the thigh pocket of her leggings where the warning would be impossible to miss.

Aiden hadn't answered her question. He'd sidestepped it

handily, which made Maddie think he'd had some practice at deflecting. Any other information she requested about magic he provided without hesitation. When she asked him something personal though, he found a way to not answer.

Maddie got that. The shard of ice and the guilt inside her never went away. She understood the sentiment of not wanting to reveal the terrible things she'd done. Maddie didn't blame Torix for all of them. In the beginning, she'd had more control. She'd reveled in the power, indifferent to who she hurt.

Sera and Jake knew about the actions, but they didn't know that she'd secretly liked the sense of power it gave her. The rules that had caused so much pain no longer applied to her.

Before Sera came to visit and Torix took control, Maddie's life had been focused in a different direction. She flexed her left arm and tried to straighten it out in front of her. A twinge of pain at her shoulder made her wince, and she dropped her arm back to her side. Ten years later, and the nerve still ached when she used those muscles.

She'd been an archer, a good one. Good enough to be in training for the Olympics. An accident on the way to dinner one night had stolen that dream from her. Her car had been side-swiped by a giant truck that ignored the stop sign at an intersection. The impact shattered her bow shoulder, and when it healed, the scar tissue caused reduced movement. She couldn't hold her bow in the proper position, so no more archery, no more Olympics. No more future.

Maddie had shrugged off the loss to Jake and her parents. She'd told them it was no big deal, that she'd been getting bored with it anyway, but a part of her died when she'd packed away her bow. She'd spent the following months making consecutively worse choices, then she'd found Torix in the Wood.

He'd promised her power, which intrigued her, then he'd tapped into her greatest wish and promised healing. Or at least, that's what she'd heard. Maddie couldn't remember his actual words anymore, but he'd never had any intention of fixing her shoulder.

After being jerked around by fate, she'd craved the ability to protect the future she wanted. It turned out she couldn't even protect herself.

"Maddie." Aiden's sharp voice snapped her out of her reverie. Her steps had slowed, causing Aiden to pull ahead of her. He stalked back, a frown marring his pretty face. "What's wrong?"

Maddie hesitated with 'nothing' on the tip of her tongue, but pushing aside her pain had started this whole mess, hadn't it? Maybe the time had come to stop hiding behind a façade of apathy.

She stared at Aiden's feet as he approached. "I make bad decisions."

Aiden stopped within arm's reach of her, and her eyes flicked up to his face. "No, you don't, *marenkya*. At least not always. I'm particularly fond of your decision to try to save me from the salamander." He rubbed his chin like he was thinking. "And the one where you crawled into my bed. I felt like that was solidly in the good decision category."

She smiled, but shook her head. "See, that's what I mean. I decided to lower my shields, and Torix found me. Bad decision."

"Only if you look at it that way. Without that decision, you wouldn't have come back for my help. Without you, I wouldn't be this close to the artifact."

Maddie sighed and gazed out into the forest next to

them. "And you wouldn't have drawn Torix's attention without me."

He reached out and picked up her hand, cradling it between his. "That was going to happen no matter what. I don't regret any of the time I've spent with you, and I'm glad I got to know the real you."

She blushed. All the years they'd spent together sowing disaster for Torix didn't provide a great foundation for a relationship. "You don't know the real me."

"Then tell me."

"And ruin all the good feelings you have going. I don't think so."

"Try me."

He stood there, holding her hand, and patiently waiting for Maddie to choose to expose herself. No more hiding. She couldn't meet his eyes, but she could stare past his shoulder and talk.

"I'm not a good person. My whole family has this image of me that *isn't* me. Torix gave me a choice, and I chose power. He didn't even have to coerce me to do most of the early stuff."

"You forget, I was there. Your early stuff was pretty pathetic for an evil genius."

She stiffened. "I never said I was an evil genius."

His thumb traced a line down her palm, and she looked up at him without meaning to. "You enjoyed the freedom of it."

Maddie's shoulders relaxed. He understood. "Yeah. Suddenly, I was the one making the rules, and my rules were all about me. Torix nudged me along toward making bad decisions, but I was already on that road."

A fleeting smile crossed his face. "I don't think your bad decisions were all that bad."

"I took advantage of Evie and tried my best to make Jake's life hell."

"Yes, it was a dastardly plan of befriending a lonely old lady and annoying your brother."

She yanked her hand away. "It's not the actions that upset me. It was the intention to cause harm."

He cocked his head. "But were you intending to cause harm? Evie taught you useful magic skills, and it made her feel useful herself. Nothing you did was actually harmful to Jake. Could it have been more that you didn't *care* if your actions harmed someone?"

Tears gathered in her eyes and trailed down her cheeks. "I tried to sacrifice him to free Torix."

Aiden wiped away the wetness. "That wasn't you anymore. We're talking about teenage Maddie. How long did that phase last? A couple of months? By that point, Torix was already leaning more heavily on you, and you weren't even out of high school yet. I know. He had me watch you before he had us work together."

Maddie opened her mouth, then shut it again. Her selfishness in the beginning had bothered her, but she'd never examined how long exactly she'd reveled in the joy of having power. Knowing that Aiden had watched her, had seen all the things she'd done, surprisingly made her less nervous about her admission. If he'd seen, then he already knew all her worst parts. Her eyes widened as an event near the end of her senior year surfaced in her memory.

"How often were you watching me?"

He looked away for a second, and when he met her gaze again, there was way too much secret knowledge in his eyes for her liking. "Probably more than you'd be comfortable with. If it makes you feel better, Torix never let me shift away from the wolf, so it was hard getting into buildings."

It *did* make her feel better. "I'm going to need you to swear to secrecy about anything you saw during that time."

His eyes glittered with mirth. "I'll keep your secrets."

Maddie sighed. This conversation had gotten off track in a big way, but some of the wounds she'd been punishing herself with had stopped hurting so bad. Her past would never be a source of joy, but maybe Torix deserved a larger portion of the blame than she'd assigned him.

She'd have to spend some time alone sorting through painful memories.

Aiden wasn't done though. "Did you ever consider that your family accepts you and loves you anyway, mistakes and all?"

"No, that would make it hard to wallow in self-pity." A small weight lifted off her chest. She'd never doubted that her family loved her, even Sera made it clear. What she'd doubted was their ability to accept the bad things she'd done. But without talking to them about it, how would she know?

Aiden smiled, and she detected a hint of smugness there. Calm acceptance was *not* the reaction she'd expected. He knew a lot more about her than she'd thought, and it made her wonder what he'd done under Torix's bidding… and what Torix had promised to him in the first place. She remembered his deflection when she'd mentioned the long time between his visits with Seth. What had Torix possessed that Aiden wanted?

A craggy new voice with a heavy Scandinavian accent broke the moment. "Are you two done sharing yet?"

Maddie's gaze shot to the pile of rocks next to them. One of the rocks blinked slowly at her, then began to stand. It rose up and up until it reached almost twice Maddie's height. Once it stopped moving, she recognized the square stature of a troll. Patches of moss covered his mottled grey skin, and a tattered piece of cloth that might have once been white hung around his waist. A black satellite phone clipped to the fabric at his hip pulled the material dangerously low. She blinked, then grinned at him.

They'd found Oskar.

8

MADDIE

"HEY OSKAR, HOW'S IT GOING?" Maddie remembered that trolls liked their personal space and kept her distance.

Aiden craned his neck up at Oskar, then stared at the much smaller pile of rocks where he'd been hiding. "How'd you do that? I didn't sense any magic until you announced yourself."

Maddie smirked, excited to finally know something he didn't. "He was in his natural state. It requires magic for them to take humanoid form." She nodded in Oskar's direction. "He has to use magic to maintain it. Once he's done talking to us, he'll go back to being a rock."

Aiden nodded and murmured, "Interesting."

Oskar chuckled, and it sounded like the crunch of gravel rubbing together. "I don't remember you being so forthcoming, Maddie."

She shrugged. "I'm getting verbose in my old age." Oskar bent over laughing, and Aiden gave her a questioning look. "It's an inside joke because Oskar thought I was a child when he first met me. I hadn't recovered my sense of humor yet. It made for an awkward conversation."

"I'll bet. How did he find us?"

"When I asked him last time, he said he followed the melody. He couldn't explain it better than that because we didn't have the right words in English. I think that's how he experiences magic, by sound."

"Okay." Aiden didn't ask any more questions, and he seemed content to stay back and observe.

Maddie's shoulders relaxed, grateful that he let her take the lead in this situation. Oskar was kind, but he didn't much like being challenged. She didn't want to find out what would happen if he started to view Aiden as competition.

She waited until Oskar had straightened up again before continuing their conversation. "I need your help."

He spread his hands out. "I can't change your past, *mitt barn.*"

She shook her head. "Not with that. We're looking for an old magical necklace. Some pirate a long time ago stole it from a selkie and brought it to this area."

"That is a very vague description."

Maddie put her hands on her hips. "You've had more than one pirate show up with a necklace stolen from a selkie?"

He mimicked her pose, but it was a lot more threatening coming from a ten-foot-tall troll. "We don't ask for histories of the treasures we keep."

She grinned. "So you *do* have treasures."

His eyebrows came together. "I forgot you are clever." He stared at her, and Maddie felt like he was searching for something. She held her breath, then sighed in relief when Oskar smiled. "Yes. You *are* clever, and a treasure of your own. Come. We'll join the others, and you can attempt the test."

"Test?" Maddie sputtered.

"All treasures must pass the test. Come, *mitt barn*." He turned and lumbered through the trees.

Maddie threw a panicked glance at Aiden, but he only shrugged and followed the path Oskar had made for them.

The troll encampment hid at the edge of a river winding through the national forest, far enough back from the shore that any wayward humans wouldn't notice giant moving rocks. Maddie used the word 'encampment' generously. A large fire marked the central space, and the trolls mostly lounged around wherever they could find room.

Maddie warmed her hands by the fire while Oskar consulted with two other trolls away from the rest of the camp. Aiden took his time joining her.

"Are you sure you trust them?" he asked quietly.

Maddie stared at the fire. "I trust Oskar. I've never met the rest of them. I'm also not okay with being tested."

"If it gets us the necklace..."

"Then *you* take the test."

"So far, none of them have acknowledged me other than when we first saw Oskar. I'd like to keep it that way."

"Great, and what happens if I fail the test?"

Aiden's silence unnerved her. At least he wasn't offering her trite reassurances. Neither of them knew what the test involved or the repercussions of failure. Maddie glanced over at Oskar. Come to think of it, he hadn't explicitly said she'd get the necklace if she passed either.

The three trolls nodded at each other, then headed back toward the fire and Maddie. Her head began to swim from holding her breath. Oskar, flanked by the unknown trolls, stopped in front of her as she sucked in air.

"You have provided us a service once before, *mitt barn*, and we again see that you are worthy."

Maddie raised her eyebrows in surprise. "That's a new one."

He kept talking as if she hadn't said anything. "Ahead of you is the test. Fail, and we part ways here." Sadness swam in his eyes for a moment, and Maddie marveled at the impression she'd left on him last year. At the time, she'd been awestruck that trolls were real and hadn't even considered saying no. Oskar's terrible sense of humor had endeared him to her. He laughed at all her snarky comments and told the worst dad-jokes she'd ever heard.

"Pass, and you may have the necklace which you seek."

She felt Aiden tense up next to her, though they weren't strictly touching. The air around him sharpened. As much as she liked Oskar and believed Aiden that they needed this necklace, Maddie wanted some clarification first.

"I have questions. What is the test? What does 'part ways' mean specifically? No offense, but how do I know you actually have the necklace we're looking for? You said before that my description was vague and never confirmed you had it or that it was the same necklace we want."

Oskar squinted over his shoulder at one troll, then the other. They didn't speak aloud, but they seemed to come to some agreement. His hand came up between them, and when he opened his fist, a golden necklace sat in his palm. The light from the fire caught the Celtic knot design etched onto a simple oval medallion. The necklace appeared normal, but she could feel the weight of the magic emanating from it.

The power in the standing stones was trivial compared to what this necklace appeared to hold.

"We have this artifact that once belonged to a selkie and

came to us on a pirate ship. It is very powerful with ancient magic that we do not like to meddle with." Oskar let her look for a moment, then closed his hand and returned it to his side. Maddie would bet a week's worth of steak dinners that he wasn't holding the necklace anymore. The heaviness of it dissipated from the air.

"When we say 'part ways', we mean you will be asked politely to leave." He shrugged with a rumbling of stone. "We don't like violence, so we try to save it as a last resort."

Maddie relaxed and smiled. "I fully support that philosophy, and we'll be glad to politely leave if that's what happens." Her smile slipped away at Oskar's next words.

"The test is in the fire. Impurities burn away. What remains is precious."

Her hands were toasty warm from holding them up a couple of feet from the flames. How hot would the middle be? The fire danced and swirled higher than her head, and the longer she stared at it the harder it got to breathe. She took an involuntary step back and bumped into Aiden. His hands dropped onto her shoulders, and his hair brushed her cheek as he leaned down to whisper to her.

"We should leave. There has to be another way to get the necklace."

She shook her head. "You saw the necklace appear and disappear. It's probably like your pocket trod. Do you have an idea of how to convince them to let it go without passing the test?"

"It's not worth death, Maddie."

She closed her eyes. The heat from the fire had chased away the chill, and the silent forest around her seemed to hold its breath. Maddie nudged the icy shard of magic she carried, and it bloomed and spread, coating her inside and out. With heightened senses, she recognized tendrils of power moving sinuously in front of her where the fire should be.

The magic inside her reached for the power, but her shields stopped it. Slowly, she pulled down several layers until the power of the fire curled toward her. She knew that power. Knew what to do with it.

"Trust me," she whispered, and Aiden squeezed her shoulders.

His hands slipped off of her as she moved forward. Maddie didn't dare open her eyes for fear she'd lose her concentration. Three steps should have brought her close enough to be seared, but she asked the fire for space. The tendrils of power bowed away from her and allowed a path through. She didn't waste any time, but she didn't rush either. One steady step after another until the fire warmed her back. She released the tendrils to their own devices, and settled her shields around her once more.

Maddie opened her eyes to see Oskar standing in front of her. He smiled and patted her on the back, nearly toppling her over. She looked over her shoulder and saw Aiden on the other side of the bonfire, his face impassive, but Oskar drew her attention forward again.

"I told them you were clever," he said.

"I passed the test?"

"Well done, *mitt barn*. The necklace is yours. Take care with it." Oskar revealed the necklace in his palm again, and this time he held it there until Maddie picked it up.

A thrill went through her when she touched it. The power pulsed and called to her, but she wasn't about to lower her shields for a second time in five minutes. She shivered as the warmth from the flames faded. As scary as it had been, when she'd been in the fire, answering the call of magic to magic, she'd felt whole. The magic had felt like hers, and the icy remnant had dissolved.

Her head drooped as the cold lodged inside her again.

She carefully tucked the necklace away in the inner waist pocket of her leggings. The slot was meant for keys, but it was the perfect size for an ancient magical artifact with unknown power. The other trolls nodded at her and wandered away. Oskar stayed by her side as she took the long way around the fire to rejoin Aiden.

"You will stay now, yes?" Oskar asked, still ignoring Aiden.

Maddie patted the back of his hand. "I'd love to, but we have important business to take care of."

Oskar furrowed his brow. "You don't understand. The fire has decided. You're a treasure given to us to protect, and we *will* protect you."

"Uhh...thanks?" Maddie realized she hadn't gotten assurances that they'd be allowed to leave if she *passed* the test. "Oskar, I'm honored to be one of your treasures, but I can't stay here. I have promises to keep elsewhere."

"It *is* tricky when treasures have minds of their own."

His face smoothed, as much as it could with deep furrows etched by time. "You'll come back. If you need us, you only have to call..." He unclipped his satellite phone and waggled it at her with a smile. "And we'll come rolling."

Maddie groaned for his benefit and had the surprising urge to hug him. It would have been like hugging a concrete pillar, and the action didn't have the same comforting connotations for trolls, so she refrained. "Thanks, Oskar."

"I'll walk you back to the trod, give me a moment to let the sentries know."

Oskar plodded away, and Maddie watched him go.

"I wonder if treasure is a bad translation of a different word," she mused.

Aiden shifted closer to her so he could lower his voice. "It seems likely given the way he was using it."

He searched her face, and Maddie counted to eleven before she lost her patience. "What? What's wrong?"

"You used elemental magic."

"So?"

"I've seen you use Fae magic, and I've seen you manipulate my wards. Now elemental magic." He shook his head. "It's supposed to be impossible to effectively use different schools."

She cocked her head. "But Torix is using magic that isn't Fae. I can tell. It feels different."

"Sort of. I think he's using items as repositories for spells. All he has to do is turn it on or off. Unless it's Fae magic, like what he did to Will. That's why I classified it as an effective use of magic. You shouldn't have been able to access the magic of the flames, let alone move them out of the way."

Maddie grunted in frustration. "What do you want me to tell you? We needed the necklace, so I opened myself to see what I could do. Turns out, that's what I could do. It surprised me as much as you."

He laughed dryly. "I doubt that."

"Are you seriously upset because I did the thing without getting myself killed and now we have the artifact that will help us get rid of Torix for good?"

His shoulders relaxed. "No. I'm a big fan of all of that. It was terrifying to watch you walk into the fire, but you asked me to trust you. I hope you'll trust me in the days that come. Your abilities keep surprising me though."

Her hackles settled. "Good. Monotony is boring."

He smiled, and it traveled from the slow, wicked curve of his lips to his eyes. In a second, she was on fire again, but with a different kind of flames. "I'd never call you boring, *marenkya*, and I can't wait to see how else you surprise me."

Maddie swallowed hard, but she couldn't convince her overheated brain to come up with an answer that didn't involve them naked in bed together. The knowledge in his eyes made it clear she didn't have to say anything. She felt her face heating as Oscar joined them, and it gave her the impetus to break eye contact with Aiden.

"Do you have everything you came for, *mitt barn*?"

She pulled the necklace out of her pocket and held it out. The subtle glow in her palm could have been from the sunlight, but she didn't think so. "Yeah, let's get out of here."

Oskar trudged into the trees, once again making his own path. Maddie shoved the necklace into her pants again and noticed that Aiden waited until she started moving to follow. He kept pace a step behind her, but close enough to touch.

"What are you doing?" she muttered over her shoulder.

His hand grazed her back as she stumbled on a root then righted herself. "You heard the troll. We have to protect the treasure."

"So you're walking behind me like a creeper?"

"You protect the necklace. I'll protect you."

Maddie tripped on another root and cursed her inability to talk to someone behind her while watching the ground in front of her. The problem was that his presence distracted her in a distinctly non-creepy way. She *wanted* him to touch her, and it made the rest of her clumsy.

Since her magic fire trick, the cold air hadn't bothered her. Too bad, the frigid temperature might have cooled down her raging hormones.

Oskar paused in front of a small creek to let them catch

up. As she got closer, Maddie realized the creek had only looked small next to the massive troll. She didn't remember passing over any water on the way to the encampment, but to be fair, she hadn't been paying much attention at the time.

"We're not far now. Do you need a break?"

The water looked clear and fresh, and Maddie's bottle could use a refill. "Maybe a quick one." She eyed the speckled green and grey rocks on the embankment. They glistened in the sun, and she'd bet they were slick. The current whipped leaves and sticks away from them faster than she was comfortable with.

Oskar crouched near the water, and Maddie watched him curiously. All he did was dig his fingers into the mud at the bank and close his eyes. His strange meditation offered another example of the many things she didn't understand about trolls.

She waited a moment, but Oskar looked like he might be there for a while, so Maddie slipped off her pack and dropped it on a dry-looking patch of brown grass. She stretched her arms over her head, arching her sore back, and caught Aiden staring. The hunger on his face sparked an answering heat in her. She took her time holding the stretch, letting him look his fill. Their eyes clashed and held.

Maddie knew she had a decision to make when they returned to his cabin. The tension between them had only increased during their travels, and she badly wanted to release it. She'd been reticent to get involved with him in the beginning, but that had been before she'd gotten to know him. Before she'd trusted him. While she still had no intention of letting her feelings get out of hand, Maddie could see no harm in enjoying themselves together if it was what they both wanted.

And Aiden's heated gaze assured her he wanted it as much as she did.

Her arms dropped to her sides. Aiden took a slow step toward her, and prickles washed over her. For a second, her reaction to Aiden seemed weird, but then her brain caught up. She knew that feeling.

The prickles were a warning.

Realization dawned on Aiden's face at about the same time that she figured it out, but they were too late. Oskar shouted in surprise and fell forward into the pool. He made a mighty splash, and his head surfaced as he sputtered incoherently. Something dragged him downstream before he braced himself and plunged his arm into the now-frothing current. Maddie flung her pack over her shoulder and tried to run to him, but Aiden grabbed her around the waist.

"No, wait," he said quietly, watching the water.

Oskar bellowed, and Maddie struggled against Aiden's hold. "Let me go. He needs help."

"If you rush in, he'll have to stop fighting or risk hurting you too. Give him space to defend himself."

Maddie connected with a heel to Aiden's shin. He grunted in pain, but didn't let go. "Dammit, Aiden."

"Maddie, use that clever mind of yours."

Oskar heaved something grey and slimy deep into the trees. The water calmed. His hip cloth dripped into the stream, which had leveled out somewhere above his knees. Maddie's fear began to recede, and she noted that the water went deeper than she'd first thought. Aiden kept his arms around her, but less restraint, more embrace.

She leaned back against him and sighed in relief when Oskar snarled in the direction of the grey thing and climbed onto the bank.

"What was that?" Maddie asked.

"*Bäckahäst*." He spit the word out as he continued to watch the forest around them, but it didn't mean anything to her.

"Was that a kelpie?" Aiden directly addressed him for the first time. She thought for a second Oskar would ignore the question, but he eventually turned back to them.

"Yes. They're also known as kelpies. That one must have been desperate to attack me in such a manner."

Maddie patted Aiden's arm around her midsection, and he belatedly released her. "What was it trying to do?"

"Pull me deeper into the water." He tsked. "It was a foolish plan. This water can't hold me, even with the kelpie's power." Oskar shook himself and sent droplets flying.

Maddie wiped water off her arms and tried not to think about how close she'd come to being between the kelpie and Oskar. "I thought kelpies were native to Scotland...or maybe Britain? I can't remember exactly, but further south than here."

Oskar sent her an amused glance. "There are no laws that keep them there. We should leave."

"Okay, but I have to pee first."

Both men turned to look at her. "What? I've been holding it forever. I can be quick; it'll only take a second." Before they could protest, she walked a few steps away from them and slipped behind a couple of close-growing trees. She heard them grumbling behind her and smiled as she took care of business. "See, I can still hear you complaining. Everything is fine."

Maddie adjusted her leggings back up and felt the pocket to make sure she still had the necklace. A rustle in front of her made her roll her eyes. "You don't have to follow me everywhere, Aiden. I promise I can pee by myself and not—" Her words cut off abruptly as she made eye contact across several trees.

It wasn't Aiden looking back at her.

The grey creature appeared wet, but it might have been a trick of the light. Its body resembled a seal but with four slender legs holding it up. Weird fins wrapped around each of the legs. They must extend out when it's in the water.

The kelpie had seemed much smaller when Oskar had tossed it into the forest. On four legs, she only came up to its shoulder. It tilted its head at her and sniffed the air with a long horse-like snout. Unlike a regular horse, this thing had slitted eyes on the front of its face, and it was watching her.

Maddie stood as still as she could.

It hadn't attacked yet, and she didn't know what was holding it back. The thin lips parted to reveal rows of jagged teeth as it made a clicking growl. Her chest tightened at the sight of those teeth, and she focused on getting air into her lungs without drawing more attention to herself.

A hand wrapped around her sore wrist, and a second later, she jerked backward. Maddie yelped, but by some miracle, she kept her feet and darted past Aiden, away from the kelpie.

"Run!" she barked, but the breath was wasted. They were already speeding back the way she'd come. He'd lost his grip on her arm as she twisted, but he stayed a step behind her the whole time. Her arm ached where he'd grabbed it, right over Torix's mark.

Where was Oskar? She tried to listen for sounds of pursuit as she slalomed around trees, but she couldn't hear anything over her panting. They reached the stream and veered away from the water. She'd seen it pull Oskar down and didn't want to mess with it on its home turf.

Where was Oskar?

Maddie had no idea where her panicked sprinting led her. She abruptly stopped, and Aiden crashed into her. As she'd suspected, silence permeated the forest behind them. Either the kelpie was part ninja, or it had stopped chasing them…or it hadn't started at all.

"Where's Oskar?" She gasped the words at Aiden as she bent at the waist and tried to breathe.

He scanned the trees they'd run through, not even winded. "He was on the other side of the kelpie. I came in behind you, and he went around."

"How…" Maddie held up a hand and gulped in air for a second, then stood. "How? I could hear you arguing?"

Aiden uncapped his water and handed it to her. She took several grateful swigs, then returned it to him. "We wanted the kelpie to think that."

Her eyebrows shot up. "You knew it was there?"

"Approximately, yes."

"And you still let me go off to pee alone?"

His eyes found hers. "I believe your exact words were 'you don't have to follow me everywhere, Aiden.'"

Maddie threw her hands up. "That would have been a great time to *actually* follow me. What was the plan?"

Aiden shrugged. "I'd get you away from the kelpie, and Oskar would try to snap it in half."

Maddie winced at the image that conjured up, but the memory of those jagged teeth made her glad Oskar had thick, stone-like skin. "How far to the nexus?"

He glanced behind them again and pointed in the direction they'd been running. "Like Oskar said, we're almost there. Only a minute or two more."

Maddie started walking, but her heart pounded in her throat from the fear followed by the surprise sprinting.

Cardio. Need to work on the cardio. "Can your spidey-sense tell us where the kelpie is now?"

"Strangely, no."

She picked up her pace. "Isn't that bad?"

"Absolutely."

The fear crept up again, and Maddie ruthlessly pushed it away. Aiden had told her to use her clever mind, and she fully planned to do that. Just as soon as they found the damn nexus in the middle of the damn forest. She felt the tingle of power ahead of them and breathed a sigh of relief.

They'd reached the nexus, but a twinge of conscience made her pause. Oskar could be injured, were they really going to leave him to fight that thing on his own?

A wave of magic from the necklace at her hip enveloped her. Time seemed to slow down, and she suddenly knew where the kelpie was hiding. She turned to warn Aiden, too late again.

He must have sensed something as well because he whipped them around to position himself between her and the kelpie. It appeared beside them on four silent legs, and its jaw snapped closed with a wet crunch. *Fucking ninja kelpies.*

Aiden grunted in pain, but she felt a rush of magic slam into the slimy body, sending it skidding a couple of feet back. Her arms were trapped at her sides by Aiden wrapping himself around her, and she could only steady him as he slowly collapsed. Maddie couldn't track the kelpie with Aiden in her face, and blood slicked his sides, making it hard for her to maintain her grip.

"Call the trod!" Maddie shouted.

Aiden's head lolled sideways, but the familiar shimmer appeared between the trees. His dead weight made them easy prey. A mix of adrenaline and magic gave Maddie the strength to heft him. She flipped around and wrapped an arm around him, tucking herself under his shoulder to support his weight. Before the kelpie could muster another attack, she dragged him through the sprites and onto the path.

9

MADDIE

THE TROD CLOSED BEHIND THEM, leaving Oskar and the kelpie in Norway. Maddie used the magic she'd called to half-carry, half-drag Aiden the blessedly short distance the trod required to get them back to Aiden's cabin. She'd never been so happy to see log walls before.

With a deep breath, she carefully lowered Aiden to the forest floor so she could dig out the white stone to get through his wards. Once he was face down on the ground, she couldn't get back under him. They needed to get inside, but Maddie didn't want to add to his injury. She ended up pulling him by one arm through the circle, up his gravel path, and into his cabin.

Maddie kicked the door closed and released her magic, allowing her strength to return to normal. Blood covered Aiden's back. The kelpie had torn his shirt to hell and ripped off a chunk of muscle over his shoulder blade. Somehow, the mangled mess barely oozed blood. Maddie tossed her pack by the door and went in search of clean bandages.

Maybe boiling water? She wasn't a medical professional, and Evie's advice about magical healing only said to let the body do the heavy lifting. Not entirely helpful.

Memories from a first-aid class she'd taken at least a decade ago said to apply pressure and call 911. She snorted as she grabbed a clean towel out of the bathroom. The latter certainly wasn't going to happen, but she could press on it while she called someone who might actually be able to help.

Aiden hadn't moved from where she'd left him sprawled on the floor next to his couch, but his shoulder had stopped bleeding. Shiny pink skin around the edges of the wound slowly expanded. Maddie sat down hard on the floor next to him, clutching the towel. As she watched, his shoulder closed up on its own.

They'd left a trail of blood across Aiden's yard and into the house, so she used the towel to clean it up, checking on him every few minutes. His slow, even breath helped her fight off the anxiety that his sudden healing produced. Her lizard brain insisted she do something to help him, but what?

As a last resort, Maddie checked his pulse. She held her hand to his neck for a good thirty seconds before she gave up. His pulse was...well, he had a pulse. She didn't know what a normal pulse would be for a human, let alone him. As much as she liked their guessing game, it would be a whole lot more helpful if she knew what he *was* before she tried to heal him.

With nothing left to do, Maddie flopped on the couch and closed her eyes. Exhaustion made her limbs heavy. They'd taken a nap in...Scotland? All the places they'd journeyed sort of blurred together. Will had interrupted that one. Torix had messed with her sleep the night before. If his plan was to sap her energy through lack of rest, it was working beautifully.

Maddie had expended a lot of magic to get Aiden back to his safe zone, and she questioned the relative safety after busting through his wards. He probably needed to renew them, but she didn't know how to do that. Guess those instructions would have been a good use of time after all.

Fatigue swamped her. Maddie struggled to stay awake, to come up with a plan for what to do next, but her body was simply shutting down. Her gritty eyelids refused to stay open, so she gave in and let the darkness take her.

FOR ONCE, nothing interrupted Maddie. When she woke, night had fallen again. She cleared her parched throat, then groaned at the sticky dried sweat on her skin. Her stiff muscles protested when she tried to roll off the couch, almost ending up next to Aiden on the floor. Moonlight lit the room well enough for her to see him breathing, but her expertise maxed out at making sure he wasn't dead.

Maddie stood over him, hands on her hips, and weighed the risks of showering while he was immobile. Couldn't be any worse than passing out next to him. Several hours must have gone by, at least. She pulled her phone from her leggings to confirm her suspicion, surprised the pocket had kept it in place. Not bad for the amount of movement she'd done.

Torix had scared her away from Evie's house the morning of January twenty-third, and if her phone correct, she'd survived to early morning on the twenty-eighth. They'd been traveling for five days, but maybe a day and a half had passed for her. No wonder all the magical creatures never seemed to age.

She plugged in her phone and pursed her lips. Aiden hadn't shifted an inch from where she'd dropped him. Maddie flipped on the lamp and crouched next to him to examine his shoulder.

He felt warm, but not feverish. Nothing marked the place he'd been bitten other than his torn shirt. She ran her fingers along his shoulder blade until she hit the jagged edge of fabric. Not even a scar. The smooth skin tempted Maddie to keep going, to slide her hand under his shirt and follow the line of muscle down his back.

Maddie shook her head and lifted her hand. He'd gotten hurt because he'd been shielding her. The least she could do was keep her hands to herself until they could both enjoy it. She blew out a breath and sat back on her heels. Maybe a cold shower was in order.

The cabin door only sported a simple deadbolt. Better than nothing. She locked it, and silently promised Aiden that she'd be quick in the shower. If something attacked them, she'd deal with it when the time came.

His small bathroom came well-stocked. She found plush towels folded inside the cabinet, along with separate bottles of shampoo, conditioner, and body wash, unlike her brother's all-in-one soap monstrosity. With the door open in case of catastrophe, she stripped off her dirty clothes. The cold shower wasn't a bad idea considering she'd had to talk herself out of fondling Aiden's back not five minutes ago, but Maddie couldn't resist cranking the handle as hot as it would go.

A groan escaped her when she stepped into the water, and for a second, she just stood there with her eyes closed and let it beat on her sore muscles. Steam rose around her, and she didn't waste any more time.

After the shower, Maddie stood in Aiden's bedroom, wrapped in one of his towels. The problem with living out of her pack, one of them at least, was the lack of clean clothes. Everything she had with her was either torn or covered in blood and sweat. Most of it was both. Maddie stared speculatively at Aiden's wardrobe. She *really* didn't want to put on dirty clothes now that she'd finally cleaned off the filth.

She shrugged. Better to beg forgiveness than ask permission.

Maddie didn't have to search long to find some soft, cotton shirts that would work. She chose a deep green option that came down to mid-thigh. Unfortunately, her undies were as dirty as the rest of her clothes. The shirt alone would have to do.

She peeked her head out the doorway to make sure Aiden hadn't moved, then rinsed her bras and panties in the sink. He'd have to deal with her underthings hanging on his shower rod. The rest of her clothes would have to wait, but she had an idea where she could get more.

Maddie sat cross-legged next to Aiden on the floor, making sure all her good parts were covered in case he woke up, and pulled up the contacts list on her phone. First things first, she had to check on Oskar. It took over fifteen calls before someone picked up Oskar's phone, but the person who answered wasn't Oskar. The unidentified troll spoke with deference, but he wouldn't share specifics. He told her not to worry about Oskar's recovery, that he'd been injured, but he'd survive. They'd take good care of him because he'd protected her and killed the kelpie. She thanked the troll and hung up.

One less thing to worry about, and at least Oskar would benefit from their encounter.

The next call made her hesitate. Sera had insisted on sharing Zee's number in case of emergencies. Maddie scowled at her phone while her finger hovered over the call button. The Fae had gotten her into this mess, and now she was supposed to trust them to help her get out of it?

Torix was Fae, but they'd separated themselves by branding him Dark Fae. Did the distinction really make a difference? Sera, who was half-Fae in her own right, said it did. Maddie dropped her hand, letting her phone thunk to the ground as she looked over at Aiden.

He could have died. Oskar could have died. Maddie was beginning to accept that she couldn't do this on her own. How many more people she cared about needed to get hurt before she sucked it up and asked for help?

The answer had to be none.

Maddie pressed call and counted six rings before Zee picked up, grumpy and half-asleep. A low male voice in the background had to be Ryan, and she smiled at the familiar rumble. He'd always hated being woken up in the middle of the night.

Ryan had been her brother's best friend since high school, and for a short while, Maddie's secret boyfriend. Her time with him had been a bright spot in the blur of Torix's darkness, despite the manipulation she'd been forced to employ. When Ryan cared about someone, he went all in, but she'd always known he wasn't meant for her. Probably the reason Torix had allowed the relationship as long as he did. A taste of what she couldn't have.

Her eyes wandered to the man face-down in front of her. Nostalgia aside, she'd never felt for Ryan what she did for

Aiden. He believed in her, and made her believe in herself. More importantly, being with Aiden felt right.

And your instincts have always been so trustworthy...

Maddie frowned at her inner voice and asked Zee to meet her at the cabin with a change of clothes. To her surprise, Zee agreed without asking questions. The best directions Maddie could give to the cabin involved either walking around aimlessly or hoping a trod deposited Zee in exactly the right spot. Both options sucked, and even if Zee could control the placement of the trod, the trip through could take an inordinate amount of time that Maddie didn't have.

Ryan said something in the background, and Zee told Maddie to turn on her phone's GPS for tracking. They planned for Maddie to wait fifteen minutes, then go outside the circle so Zee could find the cabin. Maddie didn't like the idea of potentially weakening the circle more by going through it again, but she needed help.

Bringing in another Fae should have made her uneasy, but relief lifted the massive weight of her responsibilities. While she waited, Maddie retrieved the necklace from her wadded-up pants in the bathroom. She examined the medallion, turning it over in her hand. The magic pushed against her, but she was able to resist it. She didn't plan to tell Zee about the necklace, but she'd have to reveal *some* secrets if she wanted information. The Fae didn't give much away for free.

Maddie snorted. Or anything at all.

Her current ensemble didn't have pockets, so she tucked the necklace into a zippered pouch inside her pack. She considered the option of wearing it, but Maddie wasn't ready to test its power just yet. Fate seemed insistent that she be the one to carry it around, but would it have protected Aiden from the kelpie's bite if she'd given it to him? The question haunted her.

Aiden needed to wake up. Maddie missed his touch and his smile and the way he actually paid attention when she talked. He seemed to know *way* more than her about most things, but when she *did* have knowledge, he didn't dismiss her. He listened, and he learned. More than anything else, she missed the way he understood her. He saw her, all of her, and he liked it.

After the requisite fifteen minutes, Maddie put on her boots and tromped across the yard. The cabin hadn't exactly warmed her with the fire out, but she'd had other things on her mind. Outside, she'd expected to be thoroughly chilled by the time she reached the white circle, but the ambient temperature wasn't too bad.

The other side of the circle, however, had to have been near the freezing mark. Her breath came out in white puffs as she checked the GPS and held up her phone. Why did it always have to be cold? Maddie wrapped her arms around herself and hopped from one foot to the other to build up warmth. Her phone chimed. Zee's text said she was almost there.

Trepidation worked its way through Maddie as she stood out in the open with no weapons and practically no clothes. Stupid horror movie heroines often died this way. The thought wasn't comforting. Maddie glanced at the white circle behind her and considered stepping back inside, but Aiden had assured her the wards kept this place hidden. Without her GPS, she'd be leaving Zee to wander the woods in the middle of the night.

When she turned back, a tall woman with bronze skin and green eyes stood a few feet from her. Zee crossed her arms, showing off impressive biceps in a tight pullover, but her face showed concern instead of the consternation Maddie had feared. A few more intricate braids had made their way into Zee's long, dark hair since the last time Maddie had seen her in a group chat.

She looked like an Amazon going to battle, and for once, Maddie valued Zee's resolute attitude toward magical problems.

"Hi, Zee." Maddie added an awkward wave and instantly regretted it. Zee made her nervous, and she hated feeling anxious.

"You said you needed magical help."

Maddie nodded. "Let's go inside. It's freezing out here." She turned, intending to go back to the cabin, but Zee grabbed her arm.

"Inside where?"

"The cabin?" Maddie gestured toward the building in front of them.

Zee shook her head. "I only see trees."

Belatedly, Maddie remembered the wards, the whole reason she'd had to come outside. She grimaced. *Not so clever now, are you?* When had her inner voice become such a bitch?

Maddie shrugged off Zee's hand. "Do you know anything about wards?"

Zee's brows shot up. "Not much, I'm afraid."

"Okay. I have no idea if this will work." She clasped Zee's wrist and tried to pull her across the circle of white stones. They met resistance at first, but Maddie added a quick burst of power around them both, and Zee stumbled through.

Zee's eyebrows climbed higher. "This is unexpected." She reached a hand out to touch a tall, fern-like plant near the edge of the property. "Temperature controlled," she mused. "Weather too, probably."

Maddie waited at the cabin door while Zee adjusted to the change. "I know it's cool, but Aiden is inside and I'd feel a lot better if you'd look at him."

Zee left the plants and joined Maddie at the door. "How did you find this place?"

"Aiden brought me here."

"Who's Aiden?"

Maddie opened the door, and Zee gasped softly. "That's Aiden. He got bit by a kelpie protecting me. He passed out pretty quickly, then his shoulder healed itself, but he hasn't woken up and it's been hours." Maddie sucked in a breath. "I need to know how to help him."

Zee's gaze hadn't left his unconscious form. "I know him..." Her eyes narrowed. "The wolf. Of course. He's a shape-shifter."

Maddie snorted. "He's a lot of things." She ushered Zee further into the room and closed the door. "Can you take a look at him?"

Zee nodded absently and crouched down next to his formerly injured shoulder. She tossed a small bag that Maddie hadn't noticed earlier onto the couch, then held her hand over the torn area of his shirt. "Clothes for you. How long did you say he's been asleep?"

Maddie ignored the bag and sat on the other side of Aiden. "I didn't check the time when we got back, but it was close to mid-day. Maybe twelve hours?"

"Mmm." Zee stacked her palms and a pale green glow emanated from them. Maddie slid her hand into Aiden's and watched Zee carefully. She didn't trust the Fae, but this one had been vetted by her family. Still, if Aiden showed one sign of distress, she'd pull on every drop of magic she had to get Zee the hell away from him.

"What does a kelpie bite do?"

"It kills, usually. Let me concentrate."

They sat there in silence, and Maddie's fear ratcheted up with every second that passed. *What was wrong? Why was it taking so long?* She squeezed Aiden's hand, and tried not to imagine the worst thing that could happen.

Finally, the glow disappeared, and Zee let her arms drop back to her sides. "He's a tricky one."

"Is he going to be okay?"

Zee met Maddie's eyes. "Yes, but he'll rest for a while longer. Probably until mid-day tomorrow." She stood and stretched.

"Did you heal him?"

"No. He'd already healed himself, but I checked him thoroughly for more injuries. He made it hard because his nature is to obscure. Every time I tried to look closely at something, my magic shifted away. Very like the wards placed outside this cabin. Tell me, how did you find him?"

Maddie stayed seated next to Aiden, even though her position meant looking way up to talk to Zee. "He found me. Then he saved me. Twice."

Her gaze sharpened. "Saved you? What were you in danger from?"

Maddie weighed her words very carefully here. Too much information and Zee would try to take over, too little and she'd get suspicious. "Mostly my own bad choices. Also, some kind of giant magical lizard. I'm fine, clearly. Does Aiden have more injuries?"

Zee studied her for a second, then relented. "No. He's simply recovering from overexerting himself. You have feelings for this creature."

Insult flared at Zee's casual dismissal of Aiden as a person. "He's not a creature. Okay, yes, I have feelings for him, but we're not bound or anything." She'd heard the stories from her brother, but considering her part in them, she'd tuned most of it out.

Zee's face softened. "There are worse things."

Maddie swallowed at the sudden lump in her throat. Zee had heard *her* story too. "I told Sera, but I'm going to tell you too. Torix is still out there causing trouble. Be careful because he's pissed."

She nodded and crossed her arms again. "You're going to go after him, but you shouldn't go alone."

"I'm not alone."

Zee let her eyes fall to their joined hands and sighed. "Very well, then I have information for you."

Maddie winced. "What will this cost me?"

"Nothing. The information and the healing, or lack thereof, are my gift to you." She held up a hand when Maddie tried to argue. "Don't test me. Accept it and say thank you."

Maddie definitely didn't trust handouts from the Fae. There was always an ulterior motive. She gritted her teeth and ground out a thank you. Zee didn't seem to care that the gratitude was forced.

"Torix wasn't always a Dark Fae. He earned that title because of his actions against humans a long time ago, but before that, he was one of us. We all have skills we excel at, but his was more unique than most. In fact, I've never heard of another Fae with his ability." Zee crouched again, so they were closer to eye-level. "He could use other forms of magic."

Maddie blinked. *Just like her. How much of him was inside her?* Suddenly, she wanted to tell Zee everything and beg for guidance. The power she held made her scared and excited at the same time. Part of her wanted to hold it tight and claim it as her own, but more of her was terrified of the price she'd pay. Would she become like Torix? That fear distanced her from the magic and gave her a damn good reason to keep it locked away.

Zee watched her with hooded eyes, and Maddie stopped her freefall of thoughts, landing on one important realization. This was a test. Zee wanted to see how much Maddie knew, always playing an angle. But Maddie wasn't in the mood for games. As strong as Zee's mental abilities were, Maddie trusted her shields absolutely.

Zee would learn nothing from her thoughts. *Her face, though, was probably saying a lot.*

Maddie stroked Aiden's hand and attempted to adopt a nonchalant expression. "What you're telling me is that even without his magic, Torix is dangerous? So, the exact thing I was just telling you? That's really helpful, thanks."

The intensity left Zee's eyes, and she scowled. "Your brother's right. You *are* a brat."

Maddie shrugged. "I'm the same person I've always been." *At least in the last year.*

Zee shook her head. "Okay, it's late, and Ryan's waiting for me. I respect that you don't want to give any more information than necessary, so for time reasons and in the interest of staying on Jake's good side, I'm going to assume you know more about Torix's abilities than I do. I don't know what he's planning, but he's always had a plan. When you confront him, and I know you will, you need to keep in mind that Fae magic will always be his strongest, so he'll reach for that first." She nodded to the bag on the couch. "I brought you another gift. It belonged to my second before she took over as leader, and I think it'll help you combat Torix's abilities. Use it to channel all the magic at once. Even he shouldn't be able to defend against that." She eyed

Aiden's prone body. "Provided you can survive long enough to use it."

Her tone dripped with doubt, but Maddie ignored it. Zee had given her a lot in the last hour without demanding payment. The time she'd spent with Ryan, or maybe Ryan himself, had mellowed her. Maddie hoped Ryan got as much out of the relationship. *Couldn't be worse than you.* She was going to strangle her inner voice.

Maddie sighed and let go of Aiden to stand. "I'll try my best. Let's get you home to your stud-muffin."

Amusement and love filled Zee's eyes at the thought of Ryan, and Maddie felt a pang of jealousy. Not for Ryan, but for the strength of Zee's feelings for him. She wanted someone to look at her the way Zee had just now at the thought of Ryan. Her eyes drifted to Aiden again, and unbidden, she remembered the look he'd given her before the kelpie had attacked. Maybe she wasn't paying enough attention.

Maddie escorted Zee back out past the wards. She had to pull Zee through them again, and the crossing wasn't any easier than the first time. Once outside, Zee looked back and shook her head. She waved and muttered about researching wards as she walked into the trees.

Aiden and her clothes waited for her inside, but Maddie lingered in the garden. Zee, with all her knowledge, didn't know what Torix planned. *Maybe if she'd shared the whole truth...* No. Besides, Zee seemed to know that Maddie wasn't powerless. She'd brought a weapon of some sort, after all.

Channel all the magic at once. Easier said than done. Maddie wasn't even sure if she could channel one type of magic. The phantom warmth of the enchanted troll flames licked her skin, and she conceded the point. She'd channeled other magic before, weaving elemental and Fae together so she could walk through fire. No reason to think she couldn't do it again.

Resolved, she left the garden to its slumber and went inside. It felt wrong to take Aiden's fantastic bed while he slept on the floor, and the exhaustion had passed anyway. She sank down next to him and picked up his hand again. The touch reassured Maddie. Something Zee had said about Aiden came back to her.

"Your nature is to obscure. I get that. It's a lot easier to hide than let people in."

Aiden squeezed her hand and spoke without opening his eyes. "Not from you."

Maddie's heart sped up. He didn't look entirely conscious. What had he meant by that?

He shifted slowly, pulling her down next to him until she lay against his side with his arm wrapped around her. Aiden grunted contentedly and seemed to fall back to sleep, but his hold didn't loosen. Maddie smiled as she tucked herself more firmly against him and closed her eyes. While the floor wasn't ideal, she wouldn't trade her current position for anything.

The wards would protect them, and Aiden rested warm and healthy next to her. Maddie relaxed and let herself fall asleep.

10

AIDEN

AIDEN CAME AWAKE with his face buried in Maddie's hair. She lay half-underneath him on the floor of his living room, and though his shoulder ached mildly, he wasn't eager to get up. The last thing he remembered was putting himself between her and the kelpie, then intense pain. He frowned. Maddie had yelled to open a trod. He must have done it, but how had she gotten him home?

She shifted, rubbing a leg against his, and he let the concern go. Her even breathing told him she slept. Maddie hadn't gotten much rest the last few days. Especially since she'd apparently taken care of him after his injury.

He took a deep breath and filled himself with Maddie's luscious scent, a combination of his soap and a unique, bright spark he associated with her. His hand pressed into her lower back, and the soft cotton he encountered there made him realize she'd changed her clothes. A careful glance down revealed bare, toned legs intertwined with his.

The hem of one of his shirts ended at the top of her thighs. *What was she wearing beneath it?*

He closed his hand gradually, gathering the fabric, and watched it inch upward. All the playing they'd done up to that point, and this slow slide might kill him. He was hard and aching, and he had to stop.

She trusted him enough to sleep in his arms, a comfort he hadn't had since Lexi, and he wouldn't take advantage of it. *At least, not more than he already had.* He forced his hand to relax and dropped his head back down next to Maddie.

"Why'd you stop?"

Aiden's gaze shot back to her face. A half-smile greeted him, and he met the heat in her eyes. "I thought you were asleep." He tried to prop up on his elbow, but his shoulder twinged with pain, and he winced.

Her sharp eyes followed him as he eased back down. "You're still hurt."

"I'll be fine in a minute." He traced her collarbone along the edge of the shirt. "This is suddenly my favorite shirt."

Maddie batted his hand away and sat up to examine his shoulder. "Mine too. Let me see."

He laid down fully on his stomach, sadly, without her underneath him. Her fingers smoothed over his skin, leaving a trail of fire behind. "You scared me. Your shoulder was torn up, and I didn't know what to do." She smacked him lightly where the bite had been. "That was stupid. I can take care of myself."

Aiden disagreed. Not about taking care of herself. Clearly, she could take care of both of them when she had to. But he didn't think his actions were stupid. That kelpie could have killed Maddie, and he'd taken the hit for her instead. He'd do it again in a heartbeat.

"I said I'd protect you." He couldn't see her, but he heard the soft indrawn breath.

She tugged at his ruined shirt. "Take this off."

He rolled over onto his back, ignoring his healing shoulder, and pulled her on top of him where he wanted her. The shirt rode up, but not high enough for his liking. "You first."

Maddie braced herself with both hands on his chest and sat up. She straddled his lap, her hair wild and her cheeks flushed. His hands slid down her sides to rest at the curve of her waist. His cock nestled tight against her, and it took everything in him not to hold her in place and thrust upward. As if she'd read his mind, she rolled her hips, and he groaned.

Her fingers dug into him through the fabric over his chest. "I want to be very clear here." Another long, slow roll, and he grit his teeth to hold himself still. "I'm thankful for what you did, but in the future, you are not allowed to sacrifice yourself for me. Got it?"

Aiden almost lost his grip on his self-control. He flipped them around, settling between her thighs, and pulled her wrists above her head in a loose grip. Her eyes blazed into his. "What I do with my life is my choice. This is yours." He released one wrist to trail his hand down the sensitive skin of her inner arm. Her breath hitched when he reached her breast, and she arched up with a moan when he brushed her hard nipple.

He let her take more of his weight and leaned down to put his mouth against her ear. "Make your choice."

She pulled her remaining wrist free and wriggled underneath him until she'd yanked the shirt over her head.

Nothing. She was wearing nothing under his shirt.

Her eyes captured his again, and her voice came out low and sure. "You. I'll always choose you."

A thrill of pleasure went through him, and he let go of the last vestiges of restraint. He'd wanted her for what felt like forever, and she lay open and eager in front of him. The fire inside him demanded he take her now, but he forced himself to gentle his touch. He slipped his hand into her hair, stroking her cheek with his thumb. Her skin was so soft, everywhere. He kissed her, light and sweet, and she sighed against his mouth.

The kiss quickly deepened. His mouth grew hungrier, his tongue demanded everything from her until she arched into him. Her hands tore at his shirt, his pants, anywhere she could reach. Their fingers tangled together to remove his ruined shirt, and Aiden backed away for a second to kick off his pants and grab a condom from his abandoned pack.

She raised a brow, naked and utterly confident on the floor. "You came prepared."

He grinned and couldn't get back to her fast enough. By the time he was finally—*finally*—naked against her, neither could catch their breath. She dragged her tongue across his chest and nipped the muscle there.

Aiden wanted more.

He gathered her hair in his fist and brought her mouth back to his. Maddie wrapped a leg around his hip and used the leverage to rub herself against him. The deliberate, slick pressure urged him on. He nudged her opening, slowing her when she would have rushed ahead.

"Aiden..." The breathy plea of his name struck something deep inside him. A sense of possession. A claim.

He lifted his head to watch her eyes as he pushed forward. Watched the satisfaction move across her face with a smile. Her nails dug into his bicep, and he welcomed the pain.

"More." Her demand sang through him. He pulled back,

then plunged in, and she gasped. Maddie moved with him, and they surged together feverishly, all heat and need.

Her muscles tightened, her eyes dark and glassy with passion, and she whimpered. Aiden drank the sounds from her mouth and splayed his hand behind her hip to change the angle. She fought release, clinging to the peak of her pleasure.

"Let go, *marenkya*."

Maddie clenched around him, and her head fell back with a moan. He buried his face in her neck, buried himself in her, and let the wave take him too.

Aiden stayed there, breathing her in, until his heart stopped pounding in his ears. He knew he was heavy, but Maddie didn't seem to be in a hurry for him to move. She trailed her hand up and down his back with a light touch. Two could play that game. He kissed her neck and teased her with his tongue, tasting the sweat on her skin. Her breath hitched, and he vowed that in the future he'd take the time to taste every inch of her.

His hand tangled in her hair, so he tilted her face toward him and took one more long, drugging kiss. He retreated far enough to lightly rest his forehead against hers, and his cock twitched inside her. If he didn't move soon, they'd never get off the floor. Not a bad idea, actually.

Aiden groaned, levering himself up and away. He stood and offered Maddie his hand. She let him pull her to her feet, then stretched like a cat, completely comfortable in her nudity. He took care of the condom, but he couldn't take his eyes off her. Red marks marred her skin, and Aiden felt a twinge of guilt for taking her against the hard wood. The wide smile on her face made him think she didn't mind too much though.

She didn't say anything when he grabbed her hand

again, only raised a brow in question. He backed toward the bathroom, drawing her with him. "Interested in a shower?"

"I already took one, but I'm happy to scrub your back."

They lingered in the shower until the hot water ran out. Maddie went back to the living room while Aiden pulled on cargo pants and a long-sleeve shirt. No point wearing armor inside the wards. He'd gear up again before they left.

Maddie had dressed in another pair of black leggings and a black long-sleeve shirt when he rejoined her. Her previous clothes were wadded-up in a pile with the green shirt she'd been sleeping in earlier. He'd never be able to wear that shirt again without thinking of her.

Hands on her hips, she frowned down at the pile. "These all need to be washed, but I didn't see a washer or dryer around here."

Aiden chuckled. "That's because I don't have one. I go to the laundromat like a normal person."

Her gaze shot to his, disbelieving. "You do not."

"I do. For the normal clothes. The magically protected ones have to be cleaned separately."

She sighed in disgust. "Well, I guess I'll try really hard not to get *these* clothes bloody."

Aiden wanted to reach for her again, and after stopping himself out of habit, he realized they'd blown past the time for restraint. He crossed the distance between them and wrapped an arm around her waist from behind. She relaxed back, and a sense of rightness came over him. *She belonged there.*

He pushed the thought aside and brushed a kiss against her ear. "I knew you were going to be a distraction."

"You started it."

"Did I? I seem to remember waking up with you underneath me."

"Semantics." She turned in his arms and linked her hands behind his neck. "Honestly, I'm all for taking a day and spending it in your big bed, which I haven't gotten to try yet, but kind of a lot has happened in the last couple of days. We should probably come up with a game plan."

Aiden deposited her on the part of the couch not covered in clothes. "Fill me in on what happened after the kelpie bite, and I'll make breakfast."

She tilted her head as he walked into the kitchen, tucking her leg under her and sitting sideways so she could watch him. "Why don't we start with what the hell happened *with* the kelpie bite?"

"Kelpies are venomous. Their bite, like the salamander's, will knock the victim unconscious. Unfortunately, the victim is usually in the water when the kelpie bites them, so they drown soon after."

Maddie shuddered. "Well, that explains why you passed out so quickly. At least you were able to call the trod first."

He frowned while pulling eggs and milk out of the refrigerator. "I don't remember doing that, but the last bit is pretty fuzzy. How'd you get me back here?"

"I carried you. Well...part of the way, I dragged you. The kelpie didn't follow us into the trod. Oskar was injured, but I think he killed it before it could come after us. He's fine, by the way."

Aiden grunted as he made French toast. He was glad Oskar would recover. The troll had come through when they'd needed him.

Maddie continued without waiting for a response. "I dropped you on the floor and freaked out for a minute while your shoulder healed all on its own. Care to tell me about that?"

She sounded curious, but not angry. Maddie surprised

him again with her ability to adapt to situations out of her control. He didn't like to talk about himself, but she'd proved she could handle hard information. More importantly, he'd come to trust her. "It's hard to damage me in a way that will be permanent."

"Are you saying you're immortal?"

He grimaced. "Not quite. I can be killed. If the kelpie had bitten me in the water, I would have drowned like everyone else."

"Not a mermaid." She sounded proud of herself.

He smiled and flipped the bread. "You're right. Not a mermaid." Aiden pulled out two plates and glanced at her. "My body will usually heal anything that injures me but doesn't cause death right away." Her brow furrowed, but he didn't want her to think about it too deeply. "How did you get me through the wards?"

"The same way I got you through the trod, I carried-slash-dragged you."

Aiden turned off the stove, plated the food, and brought it to the table. "That shouldn't have been possible, but I feel like I say that a lot about you."

She joined him at the table and shrugged. "I only know what happened, not why. I dropped you inside, you healed, I passed out for a while, I showered, I checked on Oskar, I called Zee—"

Aiden's head jerked up. "You did what?"

She straightened her shoulders and took a bite, waiting until she swallowed to answer him. "I called Zee. I needed to make sure you weren't secretly dying while I napped. She came out—"

"She found the cabin?"

"Stop interrupting, and I'll tell you. I went outside the circle, and she followed my GPS. When she got here, I pulled her through the ward." Aiden opened his mouth to interrupt again, but Maddie glared him into silence. "She was impressed by your little paradise. After she reassured me you were going to be fine, we had some girl talk, and I walked her out."

He hadn't missed that she'd glossed over part of the explanation, but the part with the wards bothered him more. "You *pulled* her through the wards? How?"

"I held her hand and walked through with her. There was a bit of resistance when she crossed the circle, but I pushed some magic at her and she popped through."

Aiden chewed thoughtfully. No one should have been able to cross the wards without a keystone, and he'd only given her one when they'd left. His was probably still in his pocket when she'd carried him over, but he hadn't known they'd let unconscious creatures through without intention.

"You showered before calling Zee?"

Pink spread across her cheeks. "You looked like you were sleeping, and your shoulder had healed."

At another time, he would have enjoyed teasing her, but he needed more information. "Did you have the keystone with you when you escorted her through the wards?"

Maddie glanced at the couch, then back at him. "No. I was wearing your shirt at that point. I'm assuming the keystone is the little white rock you gave me."

He nodded, then leaned back. "Fascinating. Without knowing anything about wards, it seems like you're extending your natural abilities to another creature. You're amazing."

She blushed again and ate her last bite. "Remember that the next time I almost get us killed while peeing."

"Where's the necklace?"

"In my pack. Your shirt didn't have pockets, and neither do the leggings Zee picked out."

That explained her anger at the dirty laundry. She'd had to ask Zee for clean clothes. "We're definitely going to experiment with you and the wards after all this is over." He didn't add *if they survived*, but Maddie grimaced and stood to take their plates to the sink.

She knew as well as he did they'd been lucky so far. Torix was playing with them. He'd intended the attacks to subdue instead of kill, but he could change his method at any time. Aiden didn't plan to wait for that to happen.

Maddie moved with efficient grace as she washed and dried the dishes. Her blond hair swung in a ponytail as she moved, and he vividly remembered the silky feel of it against his face. Her words came back to him. *I'll always choose you.*

Aiden smiled ruefully. He'd chosen her too. At some point when he hadn't been paying attention, she'd broken through the walls he'd built after Lexi. He could try to shore them up now, but it was far too late. She'd become more important to him than his plan for revenge.

Aiden accepted that he could never use her as bait, and let go of his original plan. The competing agendas inside him aligned with a new goal. Stop Torix before he got to Maddie. Creatures would keep coming until they neutralized Torix. His hands curled into fists under the table as the urge to keep her safe consumed him. He'd stand between her and Torix until his last breath. Maddie was his, and nothing would harm her.

MADDIE

MADDIE TOOK her time putting away the dishes. Aiden watched her with hooded eyes, and something about his posture told her he wasn't thinking about backing her against the counter. *She* was thinking about that, but she considered it a natural side-effect of all the naked time that morning.

When she had nothing else to keep her hands busy in the kitchen, she sighed and met Aiden's gaze. "I'm procrastinating."

"I can see that."

"Torix terrifies me," she blurted out. Her fear made her feel weak, but he needed to know. "We have the necklace, and the next logical step is to use it against him, but all I want to do is hide under the covers in your bed. Preferably with you next to me. Some warrior I am."

His face softened. "There's nothing wrong with being afraid. You have more of a reason than most to be wary."

"Not more than you," she said quietly.

Aiden inclined his head. "Maybe, but you're stronger than your fear."

Maddie pushed away from the counter and approached him. He scooted his chair away from the table to give her room to slide into his lap. His arms came around her, and Maddie's spike of fear subsided. He had so much strength in him. Her head rested on his shoulder, and she let herself relax against his heartbeat. When had he become so important?

"I won't let anything happen to you." His voice rumbled against her, and she remembered him saying something like that before, when she'd been scolding him for the kelpie bite. A fierce protectiveness rose up inside her. He wasn't the only one who could make promises.

She raised her head to meet his eyes, golden and intense. "That goes both ways. We'll keep each other safe."

A smile tipped the corner of his mouth, and he nodded. "Okay, but that means I have to come with you the next time you have to pee."

Maddie giggled, all her fear forgotten. "Perv." She smacked his chest playfully, but Aiden winced and hunched over, rubbing his temple. The smile drained from her face. "Aiden?"

He shook his head. "I'm okay." When he straightened, he leaned sideways to search out the window.

Maddie propped herself up to look, but she didn't see anything unusual. "What?" Before he could answer, an orange cat streaked across the yard, well inside the boundaries of the wards. It disappeared under a full rosebush, but Maddie had seen enough.

"Was that Seth?"

"I hope so. He punched through the wards hard enough to give me a headache, but he hasn't said anything, which is unlike Seth. He loves the sound of his own voice."

Maddie reluctantly got off Aiden's lap and backed away from the window. "Can he hear his own voice when he communicates telepathically?" She rolled her eyes at herself. "Nevermind. Not important right now. What's he doing here?"

Aiden got up and checked the other windows on the way to the bedroom. "Let's find out."

Maddie followed him to the doorway and watched him change into his full leather armor. Last time, he'd left the top— she couldn't remember the name for it—behind, and the leather definitely would have protected him from the kelpie if he'd been wearing it. In any other circumstance, she'd have thoroughly enjoyed herself. Aiden in leather was a fantasy all on his own without adding in the knowledge of what he looked like naked. *Who was she kidding...she'd enjoyed herself anyway.*

He opened the locked cabinet in his wardrobe, and Maddie got her first look inside. Vials lined up behind bunches of dried herbs, small pouches, and a lump of something she couldn't make out.

The questions nearly choked her, but it wasn't the time. He grabbed two vials, a pouch, and a flat stone she hadn't seen at first. She concentrated, and this time when he closed the cabinet, she could feel the small pulse of magic he used to lock it. How interesting. There were so many things she had yet to learn.

Aiden paused while filling his pack and tilted his head to listen. She'd assumed Seth would communicate with both of them, but it looked like she'd been wrong. Or at least, *someone* seemed to be talking to Aiden.

He nodded, and his attention came back to her. "We have to go. Is your pack ready?"

Maddie frowned. "Yeah, what's wrong?"

"Something is trying to take down the wards."

"Something besides Seth?"

"Yes." He urged her into the living room, where he grabbed the rest of his gear.

"I thought no one could find them?"

"You may have left a mark on them when you pulled Zee through. I'm not going to go check now, and I don't have time to reinforce them. We have to go."

There'd be time for more answers later, she hoped. Maddie grabbed her pack, glad she'd thought to stuff the dagger inside when she'd refilled it. She steadied herself and lifted her chin. "Okay, where to?"

He took her hand and led her outside to his garden. The forest looked peaceful around them, but Maddie knew looks could be deceiving. If she turned her head just right, she could see the shimmer of the wards like a giant bubble surrounding them. At the far end of his property, almost hidden under a lush honeysuckle bush, stood a stone arch.

They stopped in front of it, and Aiden set the flat stone into an indentation she hadn't noticed. A moment later, magic flared, and a shimmer similar to the wards appeared between the pillars of the arch. Maddie leaned closer. It wasn't a trod; there weren't any sprites or a path of any kind.

Aiden moved toward the shimmer, but Maddie hesitated, stopping him. She'd never heard of anything like this, and strange magic made her nervous. Maybe they were overreacting to a stray cat running around.

Go!

She jumped at the lashing voice in her head. Seth had finally deigned to speak to her. Aiden squeezed her hand, and she tore her gaze away from the arch to face him.

"Trust me." He implored her with those golden eyes, and the unease in Maddie calmed. Whatever it was, wherever it led, Aiden wouldn't hurt her. She believed that absolutely.

Maddie nodded and followed him through the shimmer.

11

MADDIE

THE SWEET, warm air on the other side reminded Maddie of Aiden's garden. She'd tried to keep her eyes open on the way through to see what happened, but the change was almost instantaneous. They'd appeared in a forest, but different from every forest she'd been in. She tilted almost horizontally trying to spot the tops of the ancient trees surrounding her, taller than the redwoods she'd seen once on vacation with her family. This place looked like her world, but not quite.

Maddie gaped at the flowers bigger than her head growing all around the arch. They ranged in color from soft, delicate pink to vivid purple with multiple layers of petals and long antennae-like centers. She leaned down and gently touched one of the flower antennae, and the petals snapped closed over her hand. Maddie squeaked and jerked back.

She checked to see if Aiden had noticed, but he'd been busy running his hand over the top of the arch. He stopped and fiddled with something in the very middle, then pulled a flat stone from the top. The magic dissipated, and the shimmer disappeared.

Maddie gasped. "It's a portal!"

Aiden grunted in assent.

"Where are we?"

"My home."

Maddie raised a brow. "That's not very specific."

"Remember my pocket trod?"

"Yes?"

"This place is like a bigger version of that. The human world became dangerous for my clan, so they made a new home here."

Maddie didn't think her eyes could get any bigger. "They?"

"I was born here. This was the only home I knew."

A burst of knowledge hit Maddie. "Until Torix."

He nodded and carefully stowed the stone in his pack. "Seth left for Terra—"

"Terra?"

"What we call your world. Lexi and I followed him. Torix was waiting for us." Aiden had tried to keep his face carefully blank when he'd said the name Lexi, but Maddie saw the pain flash in his eyes. She hadn't heard the name before, but then, there was a lot about Aiden's past she didn't know. Like all of it. But this name was special.

Maddie could figure out what happened next. Torix enslaved Aiden, Seth escaped to survive on his own, and she'd bet they wouldn't find Lexi in this pocket world. Most likely, Torix had killed her. Three of them had left, and none of them had returned.

Aiden scanned the area around them and inclined his head at a path through the trees that looked the same as every other direction. "The clan is that way."

Maddie wasn't ready to leave just yet. Seth hadn't come through the portal. The panic in his voice had been real, and Maddie's worry about what they'd left behind increased.

"Why didn't Seth follow us?"

Aiden's jaw ticked. "He's not allowed back. The portal is locked against him."

She propped her hands on her hips, inexplicably angry. "Why? If we were in danger, so was he. We can't just leave him behind."

Aiden's eyes stayed trained in the direction of his clan. "He knew what he was doing. Seth is proficient with wards. He told me to take you and run while he reinforced, and I quote, 'the tangled mess I should have outgrown by now.'"

Seth's irreverent attitude and Aiden's confidence that he'd be okay made Maddie feel a bit better, but that didn't explain Aiden's reluctance. She put a hand on his arm. "Who's Lexi?"

He stiffened. "My wife."

Pain sliced through her. Maddie recoiled internally, but didn't back away. *He'd been married to another woman while getting naked with her?* Her hand tightened on his arm. "You have a wife?"

"I *had* a wife. She betrayed me to Torix, and then Torix killed her."

The pain in her chest disappeared, replaced by the need to comfort. She slid her arms around his waist and pressed herself close. "I'm sorry." She *was* sorry, but relief left her lightheaded. She'd fallen too far to save herself at this point.

He curled around her, holding her tight and dropping his head next to hers. Maddie knew pain, and she'd do whatever she could to help ease his.

"How long ago?"

His breath tickled her ear. "A hundred and twenty-five years or so. I was a wolf for a long time."

She wanted to ask more questions, to find out what happened. How had Lexi betrayed him? Why? How had he stayed sane for that long? But she didn't. He had his reasons for keeping quiet, and she trusted that he'd tell her when he was ready. She thought of one relevant question though.

"Why didn't you come back when we were released?"

He raised his head and straightened, but kept her against him. "I promised myself I wouldn't come back until Torix paid for what he'd done."

Maddie winced and tried to pull away. "And you had to break that promise because of me."

He held her in place and met her eyes for the first time since they'd come through the portal. "I *chose* to break my promise for you."

The solemn intent in his voice settled inside her. Since the dream in Wales, they'd both changed. She hoped for the better. A long history stretched between them, most of it painful, so Maddie resolved to help him focus on now.

She stretched up on her toes to plant a quick, hard kiss on his mouth. When he started to deepen it, she danced away, and his hands fell to his sides. "Enough dawdling. Your clan awaits."

She kept her tone light and confident, even though the prospect of meeting his family inspired a wealth of dread. *What if they hated her?* Aiden gave her a look that said he knew what she was doing, but he led her toward his people anyway.

They walked hand in hand through the forest, and Maddie's head swiveled back and forth finding something new and amazing approximately every six seconds. A rustle from behind a leafy fern covered in berries made her tense up; things kept attacking her from bushes in the woods. Aiden ignored it, and a few seconds later, a tiny squirrel creature with a fluffy tail popped out.

It had dark brown fur with lighter rosettes like a reverse leopard, most likely to help it blend with the shadows in the trees. Long whiskers poked out of a small triangular face and quivered as it sensed the air. Maddie contained a squeal of delight, but her joy must have been written all over her face. Aiden took one look at her and slowed to a stop.

"A *caid*. They're harmless."

Maddie watched it stuff its mouth with berries while flicking its tail at them. It sniffed a bright blue vine twined around the base of a giant pine, then scampered up into the branches far above them.

She stared after it, craning her neck to see where it went. "How are there creatures here if you guys created this space?"

Aiden scratched the side of his nose. "I've wondered that myself. Most of my clan believe what the elders tell us about our history, but some of us think they may have exaggerated their roles in creation."

"You think they found a convenient pocket dimension and claimed it for their own?"

He shrugged. "That's one theory."

Maddie noticed he didn't reveal if he believed it or not. Another thought struck her. "I'm finally going to find out what you are."

He smiled and shook his head. "It's not a secret, *marenkya*. There's just not an easy way to explain it."

"Does that mean you're *still* not going to explain it?"

"Not now. Let's keep moving. We're almost there."

A few minutes further and they cleared the trees. Aiden paused for a moment as the view opened up. The path dipped down into a valley surrounded by cultivated fields and led to a cluster of small houses. At first glance, the village appeared primitive, but Maddie saw glass globes lit up outside each house and a softly burbling fountain in the middle of the space. The simple design, three large basins stacked on top of each other, indicated an understanding of plumbing she hadn't even considered until that second. People milled about in the fountain area, talking and trading goods.

She squeezed Aiden's hand, and he looked down at her. "Ready?" she asked.

He pulled her closer and brushed his lips across hers. "I'm glad I could bring you here."

Maddie wanted more of his teasing mouth, but he started walking again. A hush fell over the crowd as one by one they looked up and noticed Aiden. Shortly after entering the village, Aiden caught sight of a woman across the way and abruptly stopped.

The woman laughed with her head thrown back, the action somehow reflected in her whole body. A swath of red fabric draped over one shoulder, tucked in at the waist, then flowed down into a short skirt in the front and a train in the back. She only appeared about ten years older than them, but Maddie had learned a long time ago to not trust appearances.

Her gaze landed on them at the edge of the square, and her eyes widened. Familiar golden eyes. "Aiden!"

Maddie leaned closer to whisper to him. "Everyone speaks English?"

He chuckled as he led her forward. The closer they got, the more relaxed he seemed. "It's a spell that lets everyone understand each other. The elders maintain it."

She nodded at the woman approaching them while

ignoring the other people in toga-like outfits that tried to flag her down. "Who is that?" Maddie had an idea, but it would be nice to have it confirmed before she had to interact.

"That's my mother." Aiden stopped at the edge of the village, and Maddie took a deep breath to prepare herself. She could see where he got his good looks and his confidence.

Maddie pulled her hand free at the last second, a smart move because his mother didn't stop when she reached them. She threw herself into Aiden's arms with a wild laugh. "Aiden, I've missed you."

He gathered her close, and Maddie tried to back away. Before she could take more than a step, his mother's arm snaked out and latched onto Maddie's sore wrist. Maddie hissed, and the other woman gentled her grip. She patted Aiden's cheek, then turned those golden eyes on the arm she'd captured.

"What have we here?" Cool fingers traced the red mark that had faded but still ached. She tsked. "This is nasty business. It could use the touch of a healer."

"Mother." Aiden's warning tone surprised Maddie.

"A healing. That's all. I promise not to meddle." Her gaze lifted to Maddie's face, and magic seeped into her until it hit her shield. His mother raised her brows with a smile. "Better than I expected."

A soothing sensation encircled her wrist and moved slowly up her arm. When Maddie peeked at it, the mark had disappeared along with the ache. Faint ripples continued across her chest and spread through her body. Maddie felt refreshed, as if she'd been cleansed. *What had just happened?*

"That's enough." Aiden stepped between them, and his mother took a step back with her hands in the air.

"I was simply trying to help." Her smile hinted at a deeper motive, but Maddie couldn't read more than that. "Aren't you going to introduce me?"

Aiden let out a long-suffering sigh. "Why, when you enjoy so much doing it yourself?"

She snickered at him. "You've been away too long." Her attention shifted back to Maddie, and she sobered. Power suddenly gathered around her like a cloud, and Maddie took a step back. "I am Keris Morgan, also known as Eris, Goddess of Chaos."

"Only the humans call you that," Aiden muttered. The goddess glared at him, and he stood a little taller.

Maddie eyed him in disbelief. "You're a *demi-god*?"

He flinched. "It's not like that. The humans were easily impressed and vastly more imaginative than my ancestors gave them credit for."

His mom waved his protest away. "Oh, don't be so modest." She took both of Maddie's hands in hers. "They worshipped us, then they blamed us for their ailments, then they turned on us." Her strange golden eyes twinkled. "But I think we don't need to fear that from you."

"No, ma'am." Maddie's hands shook, and she hoped no one noticed. Her mind refused to focus on the impact of Aiden's heritage. *How did one address a goddess?*

"Call me Keris. Those humans never could get my name right." Keris tucked Maddie's arm through hers and strolled into the village. "And who are you?"

Maddie narrowed her eyes. Her shields protected her mind from intrusion, but she'd never tested them against a deity before. Aiden took up a position behind them, and Maddie wished she could see him.

"I'm Maddie Thomas. Goddess of nothing."

Aiden snorted behind her, but his mom laughed. Keris

was almost as tall as Aiden, but she slowed her stride so Maddie didn't have to run to keep up. The other people stared at her curiously as she was paraded along. Once they'd passed the bulk of the crowd, Keris leaned her head toward Maddie and spoke softly.

"I can smell him on you."

Maddie gulped. It was the weirdest thing anyone's mother had ever said to her, and she'd worked for Janet for *years*. She didn't know how to answer, but Keris didn't seem to expect one.

"You're a strange choice for him, but I can see his dedication to you. Tell me, are you worthy of my son?"

Maddie laughed dryly. "Probably not." *Definitely not.* "But I'll never abandon him." She knew Aiden could hear her, and she knew Keris understood her meaning.

The self-proclaimed goddess slowed and sent her a look that could only be described as imperial. "We shall see."

Maddie's stomach ruined the somber moment by gurgling loudly.

Keris smiled and changed direction. "Come. We'll eat, and you can tell me all about what you've been doing in Terra."

They followed the smell of roasting meat to a small round building with smoke coming out of a hole in the top. Maddie inhaled deeply and sighed in happiness. Brisket at last. Keris procured three plates covered in dripping meat and flatbread from the grizzled man inside. They sat on a stone bench nearby, and Maddie tried to take her time with her food. She caught Aiden watching her with a knowing look and blushed.

Aiden relaxed and smiled, chatting with his mother and what seemed like every person in the square. After the plates had been cleared and returned, Maddie nearly glowed with contentment. The village provided food, safety, and a break from the constant running they'd been doing, at least for the time being.

In a rare moment of quiet, Aiden captured her hand and pulled her close to rub his lips against her temple. Maddie had questions to ask, but Keris shooed Aiden away. "I want some time alone with Maddie. Go visit the challenge ring."

Aiden's brow furrowed, but Maddie sent him a reassuring smile. "I'm okay. Go ahead." She had things to discuss with Keris too.

He lifted her hand and kissed her fingers. "If you're sure. Mother can show you the challenge ring when you're ready."

Keris linked her arm through Maddie's and tugged her away. "I promise to take good care of your human."

Aiden didn't look convinced, but he strode off in the other direction.

Maddie waited until she thought he was out of earshot before digging for information. "You don't seem surprised that I'm here instead of Lexi."

Keris' stride remained steady, leading them in a wide circle around the outer buildings. "Word got to us that Lexi was lost. I never believed her to be a good match for Aiden, but I regretted her death."

Maddie guessed Seth had sent the information, but Keris hadn't mentioned him. It could mean that they didn't know—unlikely—or that there was a taboo against talking about him. Or something else entirely. Until she learned the nuances of this place, Maddie thought it best to volunteer as little information as possible.

"As for you, I was *surprised* he brought a woman with him. Time will tell if I'm *pleased* by it." Keris sounded as if she didn't care either way, which terrified Maddie. She didn't want to know what the results would be if Keris *wasn't* pleased. Either way, her love for her son seemed genuine.

The conversation made Maddie miss her own mom. She'd been blessed to be surrounded by good people who loved her, even when she'd been more Torix than Maddie.

"How much do you know about her death?"

Anger flashed in Keris' eyes. "I know she helped a Dark Fae lure my son away from his home and into danger."

Maddie chose her next words carefully. "Why was he left there?"

Keris sighed, and a gentle breeze lifted Maddie's hair. *Please let that have been a coincidence too.* "You need to understand. My people believe strongly in dealing with the consequences of your actions. Aiden chose to leave, urged on by Lexi." She shook her head in remorse and gestured at the thriving land around them. "This place is paradise for us. The elders work hard to make sure we have no reason to *want* to return to Terra. It's safer for everyone if we remain here. Aiden broke the rules and left without permission. The consequences of that became clear immediately, and the elders closed the doorway. Only Aiden or Lexi could activate it from the other side to come back."

They walked a little way into a field of knee-high grasses, and Keris stopped, staring at the horizon. The joy she'd had when they first arrived had been overtaken by grief. Maddie couldn't imagine not knowing what had happened to someone she loved for hundreds of years, and not being able to do anything about it. She wondered where Aiden's dad was, if he'd been around for that moment. Gods or not, it had to have been torture. Maddie had the strangest urge to hug the tall woman next to her, but Keris held herself stiffly.

Instead, Maddie blurted out the first thing that crossed her mind. "I have the Dark Fae's magic inside me."

She'd surprised Keris. The slow turn of her head made Maddie think it probably wasn't the best information with which to distract her. "Do you?"

Might as well keep going. "I hate it. He made my life hell for seven years, and I can't escape him even now. All the things he made me do with his magic, the people I hurt." She had to stop talking and take a deep breath to center herself. "I don't want anything of his."

Keris stared at her a moment, then burst out laughing. "Child, you *earned* that magic. I heartily approve of your disgust for him and his power, but it went to you for a reason. Use it to make him pay."

Maddie met Keris' eyes and saw the same thirst for revenge she kept hidden inside herself. She *wanted* to make him pay. She wanted to torture him and destroy all the things he loved. The darkness in her thoughts scared her, but Aiden's words came back to her. *It wasn't you.* She'd told herself that repeatedly, but only recently had she started to believe it.

"Thank you," Maddie said.

Keris nodded regally and twined their arms again to walk back to the village. Neither said anything more, but the silence gave Maddie time to compose herself. She'd dealt with a lot of revelations lately.

The sound of chattering people got louder as they took a narrow road between two large buildings. They rounded a corner, and Keris stopped them at the edge of another gathering. A rudimentary ring had been drawn on the ground, and people surrounded it, jostling each other and cheering. Maddie couldn't see who was in it at first, but she'd bet they'd reached the challenge ring.

The crowd thinned for a moment and revealed Aiden. He grappled an older man, and Maddie could tell he held back from the careful control of his movements. The man got in a lucky shot, and she gasped. Aiden absorbed it and surged forward to toss the man onto his back outside the circle.

Maddie's heart slowly descended from her throat. Somehow, she hadn't realized that Keris had meant for Aiden to be fighting in the challenge ring. He laughed and helped the older man up, clapping him on the back.

A voice jeered in the crowd. "The mighty Aiden has finally returned to defend his title."

Aiden dusted himself off casually. "I welcome all challengers."

A giant of a man with shoulder-length light brown hair and massive shoulders pushed through and stepped into the ring with a cocky tilt to his head. "You've gotten slow in Terra."

Aiden grinned. "Still faster than you, Oren. Do you offer a challenge?"

Maddie wanted the newcomer to say no. She wasn't sure she could watch Aiden get beat to a pulp while everyone cheered. Out of the corner of her eye, she saw a sly smile spread across Keris' face. The goddess of chaos appeared to be up to something.

"I do. Do you accept?" Oren's booming voice brought Maddie's attention back to the ring.

Aiden looked confident of his victory. "Of course."

"Then I name a new prize."

Aiden's smile dimmed but he played along. "You've lost interest in my title after all, eh?"

Oren searched the crowd until his gaze stopped on Maddie. A sense of foreboding shot through her. "I want the human."

Aiden's smiled dropped as he followed Oren's attention to Maddie. Their eyes met and held. "No."

Oren shrugged. "She's unclaimed. That makes her fair game. What say you, clan?"

The crowd roared, and even Keris clapped. Maddie looked at her in betrayal. "Shouldn't you stop this?"

Keris shook her head. "This is our way." She nodded at the ring. "Aiden knows that. Besides, Oren won't hurt him. They've been friends since birth."

Maddie's head swiveled back to the dirt circle, where Aiden had lost his playful demeanor. "I won't let you claim her."

"Then don't lose."

Maddie would have backed away, but Keris had a steel grip on her arm. The group parted so Keris could escort her to the front. Aiden stood on the opposite side of the circle from her, with Oren between them. The competition no longer resembled a good-natured match between friends. Oren was huge, but Aiden was...Aiden. Maddie bit her lip and tasted blood.

Aiden sent her another glance, this one asking her to trust him, and shifted his weight to the balls of his feet. In a flash, the contest began. They moved so fast Maddie could barely follow them, trading blows then backing away.

Maddie forced herself to adopt a confident face so the people sneaking glances at her wouldn't know the panic she fought. "What happens if Aiden loses?"

Keris scoffed, but kept her focus on the action. "Aiden doesn't lose. The challenge ring is usually there for arbitrary titles and bragging rights, but occasionally, it's used for a more serious trial. In this case, Oren gets the right to claim you."

Maddie sucked in a breath as Aiden took a hard kick to the stomach. "What does that mean?"

"He joins his power with yours, binding you together."

It all sounded a little too familiar, and Maddie had trouble pulling in air. "I don't get a choice in the matter?"

Keris patted her arm. "Of course, you do." The panic receded enough that Maddie could concentrate on the fight again. "Whoever wins the challenge, gets the honor of the prize, but as the prize, you get the option to deny the victor. It also means neither of you will be permitted to bind yourself to anyone else until the victor is defeated."

Aiden moved in a blur, performing a complicated throw that Maddie almost didn't catch. "What happens if Aiden wins?"

"Then you have a harder choice to make."

Minutes later, the bout ended, and relief flooded Maddie. Aiden had won, as promised.

Oren laughed from the dirt outside the ring. "It appears I chose the wrong prize."

Aiden ignored him, his eyes only for Maddie. The people around her backed away as he approached, and Maddie's heartbeat raced. He reached her and dragged a thumb across her lower lip where she'd bitten it.

His mouth followed his thumb, and she met him halfway. The world fell away in a dizzying rush as his arms surrounded her. His magic settled over her with a light touch, and she felt the choice. Accept and be bound, or deny his magic and reject him. Maddie didn't need to consider. She gladly accepted his claim, and staked her own.

He paused and smiled against her mouth as his magic met her shields and sank in. The layers remained in place and strong as ever, but he was inside them all the same. His magic fit perfectly alongside her heart, warm and welcome.

Maddie deepened the kiss, but a cheer from the crowd brought her back to reality. They were making out in front of his clan.

And his mother.

His mother, who had triumph written all over her face, clapped and smiled. Aiden pulled back enough to raise a brow at her. "I thought you weren't going to meddle?"

Keris shrugged, not at all sorry. "I was simply speeding things along." She clapped her hands to get the crowd's attention. "Enough challenges for today, I think." A few grumbled, but the people dispersed fairly quickly. Oren had regained his feet, and he inclined his head at her with a smile before sauntering away.

Safe in Aiden's embrace, Maddie didn't care what Keris' motivation had been. Not long ago, she couldn't have imagined sharing herself with another person, but times had changed. *She'd changed.* Maddie rested her forehead against Aiden's chest and waited for the next surprise coming her way.

She didn't have to wait long.

12

MADDIE

I should've known Keris would take advantage when I sent you here. Seth's voice whispered across her mind, and Maddie felt Aiden tense. He must have heard it too. She searched his face, but other than the muscle twitch, he didn't reveal that his exiled cousin was somehow talking to them.

Keris still looked smug. *She can't hear me. Or see me. Contrary to what they think, they don't know everything about magic.* Maddie coughed to cover her laugh. She didn't know how to respond to him without talking out loud, and Keris hadn't left them alone yet.

"I'll give you some time, but I suggest you don't linger here too long." Keris gave her a knowing look. "I removed the mark he was using to track you. You have a lot more power at your disposal now. Use it wisely." She reached up to kiss Aiden's cheek, then walked back toward the house where they'd found her. A second later, she casually called over her shoulder, "Tell your cousin I said hello."

Dammit. The soft curse floated out, and an orange tabby

appeared in the shade of one of the buildings away from where the people had spread. Maddie narrowed her eyes. He hadn't been there before. The cat meowed at them, and she wondered if she'd ever get to see Seth's true form. Talking to a cat wasn't all that weird, but curiosity ate at her. The appearance of the rest of the clan implied that his people were humanoid, but who knew at this point? Was Aiden's true form the human one...or something else? Maddie pushed that disturbing idea to the back of her mind.

Seth walked around the back of the building, and Aiden pulled her along with him. Once out of sight of the rest of his clan, Aiden spoke in a low voice. "How'd you get here?"

The cat's tail twitched. *No worry for my health? I'll keep that in mind the next time I save your ass.*

Aiden rolled his eyes. "I knew you'd be fine. Though if anyone here catches you, I'm going to deny everything."

That's fair. I came to tell you I've fixed your wards, and it's safe to return to your bubble.

Maddie stiffened. "It's not a bubble. It's a home."

Aiden sent her sidelong glance, but didn't add anything.

Fine. It's safe to return to your home. Torix and his puppet have left.

Maddie shivered. "Torix was actually there?"

Yes. He followed something to the cabin, then targeted your hack job on the wards. But thanks to my skillful intervention, he never penetrated them. He's unaware of the cabin, but he'll be back.

Seth stuck out a leg and started bathing himself. Maddie looked down at her now healed arm. Keris had said he'd been tracking her through the mark. The answer seemed so simple that she felt stupid for not thinking of it.

A loud clatter came from the other side of the building,

and Aiden shifted so she was pressed against him with her back to the wall. She thought the cat snorted, but the warmth of Aiden's hands at her waist distracted her. One touch and he churned her hormones into a frenzy. His hair tickled her cheek as his head came down to speak quietly in her ear.

"No one will question us finding a bit of solitude after the challenge ring, but they'll be suspicious if we're speaking to a cat."

Maddie understood his point, but it seemed a shame to waste the solitude. She ran her fingertips down the planes of his chest, over soft cloth and hard muscle, and stopped at the waistband of his pants. His grip on her hips tightened.

"Maddie..." The warning growled into her ear sent shivers racing down her back.

Should I come back at a more convenient time? Seth's sarcastic tone penetrated the haze of desire that had descended. Maddie blew out a breath and closed her hands into fists against Aiden's stomach. She'd be good. *So good.* Seth was right. He risked... something to be here, and they should pay attention. Aiden tucked his thumb under her shirt to brush her bare stomach, and Maddie almost lost it again. *Focus.*

"Why is this so hard all of a sudden?" she asked. Both man and cat snickered. She hadn't known a cat *could* snicker. "You know what I mean."

Aiden loosened his grip and put a sliver of space between them. "It's the ritual from the challenge ring. Sharing our magics is intimate, and it temporarily amplifies our other needs."

"So it'll go away?"

"Yes."

That depends.

Maddie looked down at the cat sitting nearly under their feet. "You'd better hope it's soon or you're going to get a show."

He blinked at her slowly. *Wouldn't be the first time.*

Aiden's shoulders shook with laughter. "He's teasing you. Neither Seth nor I have ever been bound by the challenge ring before."

"Not even with Lexi?"

Aiden sobered, and Maddie regretted her question. She'd spoken without thinking. He'd married Lexi, surely they'd been connected this closely.

"No. Not even with Lexi."

Heat spread through Maddie, and her heart swelled, doubly glad she'd accepted his claim. He'd offered her something he'd given to no one else, and she'd damn well cherish it.

If we're all done getting emotional, I was trying to tell you that Torix knows you were at the cabin, even if he doesn't know the cabin exists. I sensed something when he was probing. Something powerful that wasn't Fae, and it's growing. Even with my wards protecting you, I'm not sure how long it will be safe.

"We should head back." Aiden's voice strained with the words, but Maddie understood. The longer they stood there, the harder it became to maintain logical thought. He turned his head slightly to breathe in deep against her neck. Her center tightened at the sensation, and Maddie had to focus on multiplication tables to keep her grabby hands to herself.

I'll see you on the other side then. The cat scampered away toward the trees, and Maddie realized he'd never told them how he'd gotten through the portal in the first place. Aiden pressed a kiss to the sensitive spot below her ear, and the thought floated away.

Now that they were alone, he was free game. Maddie

pulled his shirt free from his pants and flattened her palms against his bare skin.

With a groan, Aiden dropped his restraint and palmed her ass so he could lift her into a better position. Maddie wrapped her legs around his waist and pressed against him, trying to relieve the ache. The intoxicating pressure wasn't nearly enough. *More.*

Maddie tipped her head to the side, searching blindly for his mouth. He pressed her more firmly into the wall to prop her up and plunged his hand into her hair. She locked her hands behind his neck for leverage, meeting his demand with her own.

The kiss burned wild and hungry, but Maddie couldn't get close enough. *More.* The slide of his tongue against hers. The pull of his hand fisted in her hair. The pent-up desire for him to touch her right *there.*

None of it was enough. Maddie needed all of him, needed to be naked against him, inside and out.

She tore at her shields, desperate to have nothing between them. One by one they came down, until there was only the core of her open to him.

His magic filled her, and hers reached for him. They intertwined in a tangle of power that left Maddie gasping. Aiden sucked in a breath and pulled back enough to touch his forehead to hers. A calm moment in the storm.

She'd been mistaken before. *This* bound them.

Aiden lifted his head and gazed at her with blazing eyes. "You're mine, *marenkya.*" *Yes.* She couldn't vocalize the words, but he knew. He leaned in, stopping just shy of her lips. "And I'm yours."

Her heart turned over, and she grinned, finding her voice. "Damn straight." Fire raged through her, but he kissed her softly. His hand gentled in her hair. Maddie lost herself in the tender moment. Her body quivered, but she wouldn't rush this.

In the quiet, a bird screeched above them, and Maddie belatedly remembered they were outside, only a few short steps from the rest of his clan. The magics inside of her urged her to finish it, to hell with who might see them, but Aiden pulled back.

"I want you in my bed, but on our terms. Not because I underestimated the strength of the binding."

Maddie let her head thunk back against the wall. "I'm not complaining, but maybe we could do both?"

Aiden kissed the hollow of her throat, then grazed his teeth along her skin. Maddie whimpered when he stopped and pressed into her. It wouldn't take much to send her over the edge.

His hand left her hair and slipped between them, delving into her leggings to stroke her slick opening. Maddie cried out, and he caught the sound in his mouth. She moved against him, helpless to stop the spiraling pleasure. His fingers pushed into her, matching her rhythm, while he circled with his thumb.

"Come for me." His rough voice sent her over the edge.

Maddie clung to him as she let go with a long, low moan. Aiden didn't release her right away. He held her tight between his body and the wall as he pulled his hand free. His golden eyes, bright with passion, met hers, and he licked his fingers. The fire that had ebbed with her climax roared back to life.

She pulled his mouth down to hers, and he traced her jawline with his knuckles.

Her taste on him fed the ravenous magic inside her. She finally realized she felt his hunger as well as hers through the connection. With him rock hard against her, Maddie was ready and willing to keep going.

Aiden brushed his lips over hers, then lowered her legs to the ground and set her away from him. "We need to get back."

Maddie sighed heavily. "Are you sure?"

His hands clenched into fists. "It's taking everything in me to keep my hands off you right now, but we can't stay here. My mother is up to her old tricks, and the longer we wait, the more likely she'll find a way to keep us here." His eyes traveled the length of her, as if memorizing the moment. "You need to put your shields back up."

Maddie's heart already pounded in her throat, and the magic inside her revolted at the prospect of locking him out again. She wasn't even sure she *could* with his magic so entangled with hers. As a test, she raised a couple of layers, and Aiden winced from several feet away. The raw overwhelming hunger muted a tiny bit.

His power swirled inside her, but her shields cut off most of the connection. Maddie took a step forward, but he moved back, keeping the distance between them.

She clenched her jaw. There had to be a way to protect herself without excluding him. The night with Zee and the wards came back to her, and she remembered Aiden saying she'd extended her abilities outside herself.

Well, if she could do it for Zee, she could do it for Aiden. Maddie felt for the magic that connected them and tried to twist her shields to fit around it. A few seconds of effort caused her to sweat and pant. The effort required too much magic to encompass both of them.

"Raise them, Maddie. I'll be fine. I want you protected."

She shook her head. "I'm not going to hurt you to protect myself. Seth said the wards would hold for a while.

We have time to come up with a plan. Besides, there's no guarantee my shields will keep Torix out if he really wants in."

He smiled. "They will. If they can keep me out, they can keep anything out."

"Fine." But instead of raising the rest of her shields, she released what few she had up. Both of them sighed in relief at the free flow of magic again, but the urge to jump him returned with a vengeance. "I'll raise them when we leave the wards around your cabin. Until then, you'll just have to resist the allure."

Aiden's smile turned wicked, and a fresh wave of need jolted through her. "I have no intention of resisting once we're somewhere safe." He gestured for her to precede him into the woods.

AIDEN

THE IMAGE of Maddie with her face flushed from his touch and her lips swollen from his kisses wouldn't leave him. He kept replaying the noise she'd made as she came around him, driving himself insane. His body wanted to join his magic inside her.

She stepped around a fallen tree, and he felt her answering longing. The truth hit him hard. The claim from the challenge ring had locked into place as a mate bond. He had a *mate*, a once in a lifetime connection that his clan revered.

No one had warned him about the intense magic from

the challenge ring, though from what he understood, it didn't *usually* result in a mate bond. Even more reason that his mother should have given him a heads up since she'd most likely set up the entire scenario. Had she recognized Maddie as his mate?

He'd been gone a long time, but he'd only heard of one other instance of a warrior claiming a mate as a prize. When a young Keris had claimed his father.

Aiden couldn't take his eyes off Maddie's lithe body ahead of him, and he shook his head. He didn't know why his mother had orchestrated the challenge ring that way, but then she'd been a mystery to him even before he'd left for Terra. She probably expected him to thank her. He scoffed quietly. Maddie glanced at him over her shoulder, and Aiden's heart stuttered. Maybe thanks were in order after all.

They reached the doorway without incident, and Aiden replaced the power stone. The shimmer returned, and he walked through it without a backward glance. Unlike the last time when he'd gone through with his ex-wife, nothing attacked them on the far side.

Maddie appeared a moment later, and Aiden removed the second power stone. The cabin and the surrounding woods looked unchanged. Before, the warding circles had given off a hint of magic, but now with Seth's tinkering, they blazed with power. Aiden walked closer and shook his head. *Subtle job, cousin.*

At least the wards provided Maddie safety while her shields remained down. He crouched and trailed his hand along the white stones, feeling the magic ripple. Seth had done as he'd promised. It would take time to get through them without a keystone, so Maddie would be able to rebuild her shields if something attacked.

He stood and started back toward the cabin. Maddie had

gone ahead of him, leaning against the open doorframe with her arms crossed. The magnetic pull of her had subsided a little as they crossed back into Terra, but he could still taste her on his tongue. Seth had given them a reprieve, time to make a plan of attack, but more, time to let the binding settle.

Tomorrow would be soon enough to start hunting Torix.

Maddie watched him with hooded eyes as he climbed the stairs, but moved into the cabin before he could reach for her. Inside, Seth the cat curled up on the couch.

It took you long enough.

Aiden sighed. "Are you ever going to tell me how you do that? You're not supposed to be able to use the doorway." His hands itched to gather Maddie close to him, but with Seth watching, he chose to keep his distance.

The cat stretched and sat up. *Not today. I've been keeping an eye out, and Torix is nowhere near here. He's been spending time skulking around that little town nearby, but mostly it's his minion doing all the work.*

Maddie perked up. "What work is Will doing in Mulligan?"

Before today, he was harassing your brother's wife. First, he tried to grab her, but she damn near broke his wrist and tossed him on his ass. After that, he kept his distance and just stared menacingly. Honestly, I'm not even sure that part is Torix's bidding. They seemed to be waiting on something, until this morning. Torix summoned his minion, and I followed them here.

Maddie had tensed when Seth mentioned Sera, and her fear had rushed through him, but she'd relaxed again by the end of the report. "Thanks for your help, Seth."

My pleasure. The smugness in his voice made Aiden nervous. Seth's ear twitched, and he tilted his head toward Aiden. *It looks like your plan is coming along well. She's all*

primed as bait. I'll take my leave so you can complete the bind-
ing. Just don't take too long, even I don't know what Torix is
hiding.

Aiden took an angry step forward, but the cat flashed past him and through the open door. A wave of turmoil came from Maddie, and he shifted his attention to her. She stared at him with narrowed, hurt eyes. *Damn his conniving cousin.*

"Complete the binding?"

He held up his hands. "I don't know. My knowledge here is limited, and Seth likes to cause trouble. This constant need for you does stem from our magics, but none of this was intentional."

She stalked toward him. He could feel the anger and hunger coursing through her in equal parts. Her eyes searched his, and she nodded. "I believe you, but we have another issue to deal with."

Aiden took a careful breath. She stood close enough that his control was already slipping. "I don't want to fight with you."

"That's too bad because we've already started. What did he mean about the plan? What plan?"

Aiden rubbed a hand down his face. Seth just couldn't leave without stirring up trouble. "It wasn't a coincidence that I found you in the Wood."

Maddie snorted. "No shit. You followed me there. I figured out that much, but the why was a little hazy."

"Torix called you back, and you came. I wanted to know what side you were on."

She leaned forward. "And…"

Aiden clenched his hands at his sides to keep from reaching for her. "Then the salamander attacked, and I was busy trying to save your life."

"For which I've thanked you, but that doesn't explain why."

Aiden paused, knowing her frosty attitude would only get worse. "I needed you for bait."

She nodded, and scorn erupted from her. "You wanted to use me to get to Torix. Or more accurately, to get Torix to come to you. Except he showed up a little too soon right? You weren't ready for him yet, but you did a great job of convincing me to stick with you. The sex was a huge bonus." She struck out with her words in an effort to push him away, but she hadn't raised her shields. The futile attempt didn't hide the pain he felt in her. Pain he'd caused.

Aiden had intended her to be a means to an end, but somewhere along the line, she'd become more important than defeating Torix. More important than everything.

The depth of his feelings for her scared him, but he couldn't let her believe he'd been using her. "It wasn't like that, *marenkya*. I never intended for you to get hurt."

"What *did* you intend then?"

She was so fierce, so sure he was playing her, that Aiden told her the truth. "I intended to watch you and keep you at arm's length until I was ready to take on Torix." He couldn't resist touching her any longer, cupping her cheek and running his thumb along her lower lip. "Then you tossed me that granola bar and stared at me with knowing eyes. I watched you for so long, and I wanted you to see me. The real me."

Her eyes closed for a second, those hazel eyes that had captured him in the first place. When they opened again, the anger was gone. He'd known she would understand. Like him, she'd been hidden away, unable to connect with other people. She craved that connection as much as he did. "You wouldn't let me keep you at arm's length."

"Distance is stupid," Maddie muttered. "Like your dumb plan. Everyone knows bait is more effective when the bait is..." She jerked her head away from his hand. "Would you stop that? I can't think of a good comeback when you're getting me all hot and bothered."

Aiden dropped his hand and took a few steps back to grip the countertop. He hoped she could sense the truth in everything he'd said. "You never stopped being hot and bothered."

"Maybe, but that's not the point." She jabbed a finger at him. "I don't appreciate secrets that have to do with me. Why not just tell me in the first place? Clearly, I'm well aware Torix wants me."

He shrugged one shoulder. "I didn't want to risk you running away."

"You literally told me you didn't want to team up when I offered. What did you expect to happen?"

"I expected you to write me off and team up with your family. They'd keep you safe while I found Seth and got what I needed. I underestimated the love you have for them."

She huffed out a breath. "I want to stay angry, but this whole no shields thing is making it hard."

Aiden almost—*almost*—made a joke about other things being hard, but he was trying to keep his mind out of his pants. Seth's announcement about completing the binding had surprised him as much as her. The more he thought about the idea though, the more sense it made. The claiming created an intimate sharing of magic, and the mate bond moreso. At the moment, the power ebbed and flowed between them, but the ritual demanded closure.

He dropped his head to his chest for a second, pushing himself back against the cabinets. His arm muscles strained, but his conclusion remained the same. Sex would lock the bond in place, and he didn't want Maddie tied to him because of his mother's machinations.

Decision made, he raised his head. "Since you're not angry anymore, we should talk about the binding."

Maddie raised a brow. "I wouldn't say I'm entirely done being angry, but sure, let's change the subject."

"You didn't know what you were getting into. Hell, *I* didn't know what we were getting into. If Seth is right, and he usually is, sex would make the binding permanent, so I'm giving you an out. If you tell me to stay away, I will."

Maddie shook her head and walked toward him. "I may disagree with your terrible plans, but I chose you, Aiden. I'm not going back on that." Fears he hadn't let himself examine too closely melted away in the face of her determination. Lexi had betrayed him for reasons he still didn't understand, but Maddie wasn't Lexi. She belonged with him in a way Lexi never had.

Maddie stopped in front of him and reached up to brush a kiss along his jawline. "I don't want you to stay away."

His fingers flexed involuntarily on the granite. She'd asked him to stop while they talked, and he'd respect that. The edge of the counter dug into his back as he held himself still.

"You're right. I'm not angry any more. I don't care about the binding, about Seth, about manipulations done by your mom or anyone else." She leaned closer, and her breasts grazed him, igniting another surge of need. "I care about you. I trust you, and I'm proud to be bound with you. It goes both ways though."

Aiden turned his head toward her. "I'm already yours."

Maddie smiled, and a wave of anticipation damn near made his knees weak. Some from him, but most from her.

That involuntary reaction convinced him better than any of her pretty words that she embraced their bond.

Before he could act on it, she patted his chest and moved away. "Good. I'm glad we have that settled. Now about Torix."

Aiden groaned and willed his mind to follow along. "You're going to be the death of me."

"Don't be dramatic. I'm thinking we rest up, and first thing tomorrow, I go hang out in the nexus until Torix shows up. You wear the necklace and use your convenient wards to keep yourself hidden. I'll distract him, and when his guard is down, you murder the fuck out of him. Okay?"

He frowned. "No. Not okay."

"It was *your* plan."

"Like I said, the plan changed." Aiden pushed away from the counter to grab the pack she'd dropped inside the door. He wanted to carry her into the bedroom and keep her busy for the next lifetime or so until she forgot all about Torix, but even that probably wouldn't shift her focus. The next best idea involved taking care of Torix first, *then* celebrating with Maddie. His jaw clenched. Either way, he wouldn't let their former master anywhere near her.

"Where do you think you're going?"

He dug through the inner pockets of her pack for the necklace. "I'm going hunting. I need more information about the source of Torix's power before I confront him. You're going to stay here where it's relatively safe."

She stalked up to him and yanked the pack out of his hands. "You're not going without me. I'm the bait remember?"

His frustration boiled over, and he slammed his hand against the wall. "Dammit, Maddie. Can't you understand that I don't want to risk you? I can't lose you to him. Not again."

She dropped back to the soles of her feet as the fight slipped out of her. Her hand cupped his cheek, and he leaned into it. "We're stronger together."

"I won't use you as bait."

"Your first plan sucked, but I understood it. I *do* make good bait. Your second plan pisses me off though. Protective instincts are all well and good, but you're not the only badass around."

He grimaced. "Believe me, I know."

"And you're not leaving without me."

Short of tying her to the bed, Aiden knew there was no convincing her to stay. She was determined to face the problem head-on, and he was determined to keep the woman he loved out of harm's way. *Loved?*

Fuck.

Aiden shook his head and paced away from Maddie. He'd promised himself he wouldn't get sucked into that trap again after Lexi, but he couldn't make himself regret his current predicament. What he'd felt for Lexi paled in comparison to his feelings for Maddie. She watched him with her arms crossed while he paced. He'd do anything to keep her safe.

Anything.

Aiden stopped and met her eyes. He didn't have time for more reconnaissance. Tomorrow, he'd go after Torix on his own, and he'd make damn sure Maddie would be safe.

Tonight...tonight, he'd take for himself.

13

MADDIE

SHE HADN'T EXPECTED to convince him. In fact, she'd been mentally preparing to follow him and save his ass again. Instead, she'd watched him come to a decision. The emotions flowing between them were too jumbled for her to figure out what it was, but his eyes met hers and a frisson of excitement went through her.

If the hunger in his eyes signified anything, he wasn't leaving any time soon.

"Aiden?" The question came out husky and rough.

His gaze trailed down her body and a smile flitted across his face as he walked purposefully toward her. "I think we've talked long enough."

"Thank goodness." She exhaled a jagged breath, and Aiden pulled her against him to capture it.

He groaned against her mouth, and Maddie let go of her restraint. She'd tried to resist touching him long enough to have the necessary discussion, but it had been torture.

Anger had been the most effective tool to distance herself, and she gladly released it.

Whatever Aiden had decided, she was on board.

His hands dragged up her stomach, taking her shirt and sport bra with them. She lifted her arms so he could pull them all the way off, and cool air caressed her heated skin. His clever hands found her breasts and teased her with soft touches. Taking his time, enjoying the moment.

Maddie pushed his shirt up, eager to feel his skin against hers. They stumbled into the bedroom, neither willing to let go. Aiden broke their kiss to shuck his shirt and pants. Maddie grinned at the sight of him full and heavy for her.

He followed her down onto the bed and feathered kissed down her neck, leaving rough patches where his stubble scratched her. Maddie didn't care. She arched up, but he seemed to be determined to go slow this time. When his mouth finally closed on one nipple, her head dropped back and currents of pleasure shot directly to her core. She buried her hands in his hair to keep him there, pulling the hair tie loose. Aiden chuckled against her chest and paid the same careful attention to the other breast.

He worked his way down her stomach, lowering her leggings as he went. She kicked off her pants as his hands traced the curve of her ass. The magic between them lashed at her, insisting they quicken the pace, but Aiden paused and looked up at her with glowing golden eyes. Maddie drew a shallow breath. The corner of his mouth tipped up, and while holding her gaze, he ran his tongue inside the line of her low-cut panties.

With excruciating care, he eased her panties down her legs until she was naked in front of him. Maddie felt the heat of his mouth a second before a long, slow lick echoed in every sensitive part of her. He used his hands and his tongue until she shivered and clenched the bedding in tight fists. Power and tension coiled within her, with release just out of reach. Aiden murmured words she didn't understand against her skin, and a zing of magic ricocheted into her setting off explosions along her nerve endings that pushed her over the edge.

Maddie lay still for a moment catching her breath, and Aiden pressed a kiss where she was still highly sensitive. He pulled back, but Maddie's hips jerked toward him. Her nipples ached, and she wanted his mouth on her again. But more, she wanted to taste him. Maddie pushed on his chest until he stood, then slid off the bed to her knees.

"It's my turn." Her hand closed around his shaft, stroking him firmly. She licked the glistening tip, then smiled at him.

He wrapped her hair around his fist, and Maddie reveled in the power to make him groan with a swipe of her tongue. It didn't take long for him to reach the edge of his control. She felt it in the clench of his fingers in her hair, the thrust of his hips as he took her mouth.

Maddie looked up at him through her lashes, and Aiden cursed, pulling her off him and dragging her to her feet. She licked her lips as he eased her back onto the mattress. Maddie watched as he grabbed a condom from the wardrobe to sheath himself. His burning eyes never left hers as he stalked forward. Aiden lifted her leg and kissed the inside of her ankle, her knee, her hip. A fleeting flick of his tongue against her clit, then he was moving over her, his hair loose and wild around them.

He worshipped her breasts as his cock nudged her entrance. *Finally.* Maddie arched up to meet his thrust. As Aiden sank into her, their magic surged like they'd completed a circuit. Maddie gasped at the feeling of utter *rightness.* He moved slowly at first, pulling out almost all the way before plunging forward again. She opened her legs wider, and he leaned forward to change the angle.

His mouth captured hers, and he kissed her slow and deep, his tongue mimicking the rest of him. Aiden slid his hands into hers, guiding her up to grip the headboard above them. They rocked together, urged on by the magic swirling inside them, until Maddie couldn't tell where she ended and he began.

She teetered at the edge of a precipice, reaching for him with her body and her magic. He reached back, and the connection locked into place. A jolt of fused power sizzled through her, and she trembled, then fell. Maddie gripped his hands until her nails dug in. Aiden pressed his face against her neck and slammed into her as he followed her over.

SOME TIME LATER, Maddie lay spread across Aiden's chest, naked and grinning as she traced paths through his sparse chest hair. Their shared magic had settled contentedly inside her. "Why are you always sniffing me?"

Aiden laughed. "My kind have advanced senses of smell compared to humans. Everyone has a unique scent, and I happen to really like yours."

"Well that's a relief. I thought it might be some kind of fetish thing." *Not that it would bother her.*

"I can also smell my mark on you after we've been together."

That explained his mom's weird comment earlier. She yawned, fighting to keep her eyes open. "What do I smell like?"

"It's hard to describe since it's not a scent so much as a series of feelings it evokes." Aiden pulled the blankets out from under her and covered them both, curling her into his side. His hand trailed lazily down her back and up again. Maddie's eyes fluttered closed as his voice rumbled beneath her cheek. "Blinding, fierce light tempered by softness and compassion. Freedom. Home. Mine."

Home. They'd gone to his home, and he'd rushed back here with her. Would he leave her once Torix was dead? *Mine.* The magic bound them, but that wasn't all. She'd given herself to him, and she refused to regret it, no matter what the future held. They'd defeat Torix, protect her family, and then she could daydream about a life with Aiden.

Maddie was drifting off, but she wanted to tell him something.

"I love your shoulders," she mumbled. *No, not that.*

He chuckled. "Good to know."

Her relaxed body refused to stay awake in his warm, squishy bed, but she gave it one final effort. "Torix..."

Aiden brushed a kiss against her temple. "Sleep, *marenkya.* I'll keep you safe."

She roused once in the night reaching for Aiden, terrified he'd been taken away from her. He held her until she calmed, then the heat built again. Maddie reached for him in an entirely different way, but something niggled in the back of her mind. Something she'd meant to tell him earlier.

MADDIE WOKE up the second time alone in Aiden's bed. She could tell because she was starfished sideways, and she couldn't feel the warmth of anyone near her. Her body ached, despite the luxury around her. *Next time, stretching.* She pulled the pillow closer and inhaled Aiden's scent. Maybe there was something to his sniffing after all.

The daylight filtering through her cracked eyelids implied she should get moving, but Maddie wasn't a morning person on the best of days. Jake had accused her of being part sloth once because it took her so long to get out of bed.

She rolled over and blew blonde frizz out of her face. The ponytail had disappeared sometime in the night, and her hair had a mind of its own when it wasn't contained. She sat up, naked. *No surprise there.* But her clothes had mysteriously disappeared. Maddie distinctly remembered the sound of her leggings hitting the floor last night.

The room wasn't well-lit, but she could see enough to know that there weren't any piles of clothes on the floor. She hadn't taken Aiden for a clean freak, but he must have moved them. Maddie threw the covers off and hit the bathroom.

She found a neat stack of several pairs of undies that she'd washed yesterday – *the day before?* – and silently thanked her mom for instilling a sense of prudence. Her pack with her toothbrush was still in the living room, but she did her best rinsing her mouth out, finger combing her hair, and washing her face. Clad in underwear and nothing else, Maddie sauntered out of the bedroom expecting to see Aiden.

The cabin was empty.

Maddie frowned. Last night had been amazing, and she'd finally felt like she belonged, completely connected to Aiden. She'd expected to wake up with him this morning, but clearly that wasn't happening. A warm breeze that did *not* belong in January wafted across her bare skin from an open window. She spotted her long-sleeve shirt, bra, and leggings neatly folded on the table. Her panties were missing, but there were plenty of clean ones in the bathroom.

Belatedly, Maddie remembered that Seth had been prowling around the house yesterday. Nothing stopped him from being there now since he could apparently come and go through the wards as he pleased. She quickly got dressed and peered out the window.

The plants in Aiden's garden swayed gently in the breeze, but the man was missing. Her boots had been lined up neatly by the door, so Maddie laced them up and went out to look around. Her frown deepened. The knee-high vegetables in his garden didn't do much to obstruct her view. She could see from one end of the empty circle to the other.

Where was Aiden?

A gust pushed through the trees, and Maddie glanced up. The sun peeked past the canopy, so it must've been almost noon. Nothing made any noise beside the wind. She shook her head at the sensation of being alone in the world.

They'd expended a lot of energy last night, so it made sense that she'd needed to rest, but even she didn't normally sleep this late. The shimmer of the wards caught her attention, and Maddie watched the sheer magic undulate above the stones. Unlike before, she could see them clear as day, and strangely, she could feel the wards as if she'd cast them herself. The magic in front of her wasn't flowing so much as floating.

When she reached out, her hand slid to the side like it had before, but the ward felt solid this time, smooth and hard to the touch. No matter how much she pushed, it didn't give at all. With a grunt, Maddie stepped back and narrowed her eyes. What had Seth done?

Aiden had said the keystone didn't work from the inside, but she might as well try. Maddie shrugged and picked up a white pebble. She encountered the same solid shell, and the stone didn't do anything to help her. There had to be some way to get through it; after all, Aiden and Seth were both gone.

Weren't they? Maddie glanced back at the cabin. She hadn't done an exhaustive search. It wasn't likely she'd missed either of them in a building that basically had three rooms. She walked the perimeter of the ward, hoping to find some portion of the yard she hadn't seen before. Her good mood from that morning slowly dissolved, replaced with churning suspicion in her stomach. The more time that passed, the angrier Maddie got. If Aiden had stepped out for coffee and donuts, she was going to maim him. In an entirely non-sexual way. No matter what her quivering thighs thought.

She discovered a small garden shed, but it wouldn't have been able to hide her, let alone someone Aiden's size. Seth would have fit inside nicely, but somehow, she didn't see the cat strolling in there and latching the door behind him.

Out of places to explore in the yard, Maddie went back inside the cabin to check one more time. Her pack hadn't moved from where she'd tossed it during their tussle the night before, so she grabbed her cell phone and checked her messages. Nothing. Aiden hadn't even left her a convenient note explaining where he'd disappeared to after promising to keep her safe. Hard to do if he wasn't there.

She eyed her phone. Would he answer? Only one way to find out. She scrolled through her contacts until she found him, but the call went directly to a terse voicemail. His grumpy voice made her smile, then sigh in frustration. At least this time no one was unconscious.

The memory of Aiden's injured shoulder and Zee's visit reminded her of the weapon in her pack. She'd been carrying it around this whole time, but she hadn't really had a chance to examine it. Her coat had been the only thing she could think of to sheath it, so she pulled out the wad of puffy material and unwound it.

The dagger had a wood handle with a slightly curved blade. Zee had made it sound all mystical, but when Maddie picked it up, it felt like any other knife. Not like the necklace. That thing pulsed with magic. Maddie's eyes returned to the bag. Magic she should have been able to feel while digging through her pack.

A horrible suspicion bloomed, and Maddie searched frantically through all the inner pockets. No magic current pulled at her. She emptied the bag onto the ground, searching for a golden necklace among her possessions.

The dagger was right where she'd left it, but the necklace was gone. *Son of a bitch.*

Maddie hurriedly restuffed her pack and ran out the door. That idiot had gone after Torix on his own. Fear and anger fought for prevalence, but Maddie needed her mind, not her emotions, running the show.

Aiden hadn't left for donuts and coffee. He'd decided to hunt down a deadly Fae that had whooped both their asses once before and had several dangerous creatures at his disposal. One of those creatures had nearly killed Aiden. Without her, the kelpie probably would have dragged his body into the water, never to be found. And now he was facing Torix and his menagerie alone. Why did men have to be so frustrating?

She reminded herself that the necklace would protect him if he remembered to put it on. He'd gone to the trouble of stealing it, surely he'd also wear the damn thing. Maddie slid to a stop at the edge of the yard and nearly bounced off the ward. She ran her hands over the smooth surface, but everywhere she pressed was the same. An impenetrable bubble. Frustration got the best of her, and she punched the translucent wall, wincing when her knuckles smarted with the impact.

The wind rushed through the trees outside, then tossed her hair in her face. If air could move through, that meant it *wasn't* impenetrable. Something blocked *her* from leaving. Urgency pushed at her. Aiden could be fighting for his life right now, but she forced herself to stop and take a deep breath. Brute force wouldn't work. She needed a better plan.

He'd said she was partially immune to his magic, and after last night, she had a hefty dose of that same magic inside her. Maddie groaned. Could it be that simple? She could use his magic. The power felt different than what she was used to, but then, most things were at this point.

Maddie nudged the dormant mix of magics, and they flared to life. Warmth bathed her as the familiar sensation of him swept out from her center. Except...this time felt tamer, less intense.

Last night, there'd been a deep connection involved, along with heightened emotions, and a whole lot of really awesome sex. This morning, the bond diminished to a pale shadow of that. Was the intensity based on proximity? Was their visceral bond destined to fade?

She closed her eyes and probed the connection. Something came between them, like a veil. The sensation reminded Maddie of gauze or gossamer. Her eyes popped open. Or a shimmering, translucent ward. She stared at the visible wall again and cursed.

All the training and knowledge she'd sought became worthless in the face of a magical bubble cast by a fake cat.

Trapped on the wrong side of the bubble, Maddie gritted her teeth. Panic tightened her chest at the missing link to Aiden. She felt like part of her had been sectioned off and placed out of her reach. If they survived this, she was going to shave Seth bald.

Maddie breathed in and out slowly and set aside her plans for revenge to focus on the problem in front of her. The awakened magic made it easier to sense the nuances of the wards, but she still didn't understand them. She flattened her palm against the surface and searched with her power, discovering several layers of protection, like in her shields. The ward let her prod and tease the layers apart, but when she tried to pass one, they all snapped back together. When she used primarily Aiden's magic though, the response slowed drastically. The layers wouldn't let *her* magic through, which was probably why Torix couldn't find her here, but it let Aiden's magic pass.

Guess it wouldn't do to have him bouncing off his own prison when running off to be a martyr.

Maddie shook her head and ruthlessly shoved that thought aside. Aiden wasn't going to die, unless she killed him herself. Her complicated feelings made concentration difficult, but she refused to give up and leave him to face Torix alone. The magical bubble wrap pissed her off, but despite her frustration, Maddie recognized her own knee-jerk protective instinct. Aiden pushed past all her defenses and truly saw her, the good and the bad. She wasn't letting that go without a fight. They'd address his glaring lack of trust later.

Her frantic thoughts had done nothing to calm her, so Maddie tried applying logic. The magic inside her waited, warm and whole. Granted, Maddie didn't know how this particular binding worked, but if Aiden died, wouldn't she be able to feel it? The ward masked his emotions, but her physical sense of him, while fainter than before, pointed strongly toward alive and well. She didn't want to think about any other option.

She took another deep breath and backed away from the wards. Time to use her clever mind. Aiden's magic would get her through, but she needed a plan for after that. Maddie held up her hand and silvery magic curled into a ball in her palm. She'd resisted using it out of fear. The fear that accepting it would bring her one step closer to the person Torix had tried to make her become, and that she'd use that power to hurt the people she loved. What Torix had given her before had been a façade, a shallow excuse for magic that she could never seem to fully embrace. *This* magic was different.

The ball lengthened into a bow with barely a thought, and Maddie smiled. At some point, the ice shard she'd always associated with it had melted. She'd been using it as a shield to separate the magic from the rest of her, a shield she'd created and blamed on Torix. After the challenge ring, there couldn't be any half-measures. She'd had to take responsibility for the power inside her or risk losing the choice altogether.

Given the option of Aiden or her fear, she'd banished the ice. With it gone, she'd gained a level of control she'd never had before. With Aiden, she'd finally felt warm.

Her other hand formed an arrow, which she nocked and tried to draw back. Sharp pain shot down her arm from her shoulder to her elbow, and she released the magic. The bow and arrow dissolved, and Maddie let her dreams from the past dissolve with them. There was no going back, not even with magic.

She was a different person, one she quite liked, and that

person had a shitload of power with which to kick a Dark Fae's ass. Maddie raised her chin and adjusted her pack with the dagger inside it. Her shields were still down. Once through the wards, Torix would find her.

He'd expect her to fight back, but he wouldn't kill her until he'd reclaimed his magic. That gave her some time to figure out a way to separate him from his magical batteries. Aiden's magic threw an unknown variable into her plan. Well, that and the source of Torix's power. Maddie suspected the connection between her and Aiden would return in full force on the other side of the barrier, and he'd come running. She decided against trying to keep him away. He was a demi-god; he'd make great backup.

Oh, and she'd have to be careful not to end up a zombie again. No big deal.

Right. Maddie focused on filling her tight lungs instead of the prospect of facing her biggest nightmare, literally. Her plan terrified her, rushed and crazy and not thought through, but she was out of time. After everything that had happened, Maddie didn't think Torix wanted another round of controlling Aiden. She was pretty sure the asshole would jump straight to death, with maybe a small foray into some light torture first.

As she approached the wards the final time, Maddie promised herself she'd make Seth teach her how he'd locked her in. She looked forward to practicing on Aiden.

The sun had finally moved beyond the trees and shone directly on the yard, including Maddie and the circle of white stones. She squinted at the brightness, checking one last time for holes in her plan. Reckless stupidity aside, it was the best she could come up with.

Aiden's magic responded smoothly when she called it. Distinct qualities she associated with Aiden enveloped her.

Strength and protection and a base that was constantly shifting, just slightly. Was this what Aiden meant when he described her smell?

An interesting thought, but not particularly useful at the moment. She urged the magic to slide over her like a skin-suit, covering every inch. It seemed particularly suited to the act of shielding her. Maddie wasn't surprised, considering Aiden's current location.

Once his magic covered everything, Maddie pushed against the ward with her hand. It passed right through with no resistance, but when she pulled back, the pressure increased until it pinched her hand painfully before she slipped free.

Maddie frowned at her red fingers. The ward had tried to close on her. Like when she'd been testing it before. Aiden's magic created an opening, but it didn't stay open for long before the ward adjusted. *Damn Seth and his ingenuity.*

There was nothing else to do. She'd have to run through and hope for the best. Head first, just in case. Maddie took a couple of quick breaths, counted to three, and sprinted as fast as she could for the circle. At the last second, she lowered her head and tucked in her shoulders. Most of her passed through without effect, but the closing ward caught her boot and tripped her.

She tumbled forward, but managed to stay upright. A moment later, emotion slammed into her. The full force of Aiden's frustration, worry, and determination hit her, followed by a shot of panic as he realized she'd moved past the wards. Maddie had to let go of his magic and center herself again to sort through it all. As a result, the nice, warm coating of power seeped back into her. They really should've practiced more with the bond thing.

Without the layer of Aiden's magic protecting her, the

much colder temperature outside the circle shocked her. If Maddie had been smart, she would have taken ten seconds to grab her jacket, but the weather had been the last thing on her mind. Her breath frosted the air in front of her, and she shivered.

The trees around her weren't really familiar, but she knew the Wood came right up to the circle there. Maddie hadn't been able to call trods before, but she hoped that had been a repercussion from locking away the magic as much as possible. She'd believed she couldn't do it, so she hadn't been able to. *My, how things had changed.*

She wrapped her arms around her middle and set off into the forest, calling a trod as soon as she could feel the elemental magic. Sprites floated past her, and her muscles unclenched as the temperature leveled off. Maddie aimed for the nexus of the Wood and tried to keep her magic as hidden as she could until she arrived. She'd prefer to do battle in a place where there wouldn't be any collateral damage.

Once there, she'd open herself and call Torix. It wouldn't take him long to find her, and she hoped he'd be in such a hurry that he'd leave his lackeys behind. If not, she was in for a lot of trouble.

14

AIDEN

AIDEN HADN'T SLEPT MUCH. He walked through the forest in the late morning light, stopping occasionally to inhale deeply. The mundane forest chilled him, but he'd forgone the trods. Torix wouldn't be able to hide in the in-between and affect Terra. That particular skill was unique to his clan.

Torix had drawn Maddie back to the Mulligan area because he needed to physically get his hands on her, which meant he'd gone to ground somewhere nearby. Aiden searched for Torix's scent as he moved. The hunt would have probably been easier as a wolf, but he didn't want to confront Torix in the form of his enslavement.

Shortly before dawn, Maddie had fallen asleep again, but he'd stayed awake. He'd tried to memorize the feel of her curled up against him to hold on to for later. Even if he managed to defeat Torix, Maddie wouldn't react well to him warding her in the cabin. The mate bond made it difficult to imagine she'd turn her back on him, but she was surprising and stubborn.

Aiden smiled. The image of Maddie asleep in his bed kept disrupting his concentration. He'd have much rather been there next to her than freezing his ass off in the woods. When he'd first left, he'd cursed the cold for making his fingers and nose numb, but that had been hours ago. The temperature had risen enough that he could feel his face again.

The wind barely stirred the pine needles, but it brought him teasing whiffs of Torix that didn't linger long enough to provide much information. The sporadic scent made pinpointing a direction difficult. Aiden tried to follow the traces that mixed Torix with his Will-zombie. They'd want to overpower Maddie when she returned.

And Torix knew she'd return. He used Will's harassment to taunt her. She'd do anything to protect her family, and the harassment would only get worse until she acted. Or until Aiden ended it.

He stopped beside a large prickly bush and took stock of his location. His cabin occupied a wooded area on the far outskirts of town, almost to the halfway point between Kilgore and Mulligan. When he'd left that morning, he'd headed toward the Mulligan part of the forest, but now he was fairly certain he'd been led toward Kilgore instead.

Aiden scanned the trees while he took a swig of his water. Something else had been following him for a little while, and he wanted to get a better look at it. Not Torix or Will. He'd recognize those trails. Something that knew how to disguise itself. He had a good guess what.

Out of the corner of his eye, he spotted a familiar orange tail.

Seth must have tired of his game. If he hadn't wanted to be spotted, he wouldn't have been. Aiden capped his water and waited. The cat ambled out of the brush, stretched, and blinked up at him.

"Why do you insist on taking that ridiculous form?"

Cats are small, agile, and pointy. What else would you want in a form?

"The ability to defend myself against a bigger opponent."

The cat stared at him. *That supposes I plan to fight my opponents. I'd much rather flee and find some other way to win than strength.*

Aiden rolled his eyes. "Sometimes you don't have a choice, cousin. Can you please change? I feel silly talking to a cat."

The humans are a bad influence on you. A second later, Seth became a man dressed in jeans and a long-sleeve shirt.

Aiden hadn't realized how much he'd missed his cousin until they stood face to face. He hadn't changed much in over a century. The same height and build Aiden had inherited from their respective fathers, but topped with shorter, dark red hair.

Seth spread his arms with a mocking smile. "Happy now?" Aiden hugged him, expressing his relief at having his cousin back through several manly thumps on the back.

"Did you finish the wards?"

Seth's smile dimmed. "Yes, but if Maddie comes after me, I'm putting all the blame on you."

"I'll gladly accept it as long as she's safe."

Seth sighed. "About that. You know she'll figure out a way through sooner rather than later. I've never met anyone with abilities like hers."

The breeze picked up, and Aiden raised his face to the wind. Hints of Torix, like every time before, but no real direction to focus on. He grunted in frustration. "How would you know?"

"I've been following you two." Seth waggled his eyebrows when Aiden glared at him. "You should thank me. I've saved your ass several times. And let's not forget I risked my beautiful hide invading Cassie's stable. She's not a big fan right now."

Aiden grunted again, this time in agreement. "I'm just assuming you deserve her ire. She wouldn't talk to me either. Maddie had to work her magic."

Seth's gaze sharpened. "Maddie used magic on Cassie?"

"No. Her personality. Everyone we met with wanted Maddie in some form or another."

Seth rubbed his jaw, seeming deep in thought. "Maddie and Daria and Cassie... all together at one time."

Aiden speared him with a look. "I'd be careful what you're implying there."

Seth laughed. "Why? Are you looking for a fight that badly? Besides, Maddie denied me, and Cassie would rather light her tavern on fire than let me step foot anywhere near her."

"Skulking around her stable must have felt great for you."

Seth shrugged. "I'll take what I can get. If you're done procrastinating, want to share your terrible plan with me?"

Aiden crossed his arms. "Can't you just pluck it from my mind and then conveniently blurt out the worst part, and only the worst part, in front of my mate?"

Seth tilted his head. "Your mate, huh? I hadn't realized."

Aiden resisted the urge to throttle him. "Which part of the bond were you unclear about? You seemed pretty fucking knowledgeable when you were getting in the way.

How did you know about completing the binding, by the way?"

"Once upon a time, I listened when the elders spoke. The challenge ring doesn't reward you with a mate, only a binding and supposedly increased power. I haven't tested it. Keris sensed something I didn't and took advantage." Seth whistled. "She *really* took advantage."

Aiden scoffed. "She was just causing trouble, as always."

"Well, yeah, of course, but she also made sure you'd have the best motivation to not do anything stupid." Seth frowned. "Except it looks like you're doing something stupid, so clearly, she can't anticipate everything. That's refreshing."

Aiden shook his head and started walking again, knowing Seth would follow. "I'm hunting Torix."

"With Maddie behind the wards instead of helping you?"

"Yes. The bond made it so she couldn't raise her shields without cutting us both off from part of our magic. She won't use her shields, and I won't deliver her to Torix defenseless."

Seth snorted, and Aiden glanced back at him. "Defenseless? You think she's defenseless? You're still not paying attention. You wouldn't be wearing that shiny bauble if it weren't for her."

The golden necklace felt heavy around his neck, and somehow sad. *No...disappointed.* He knew better than to discount ancient magical trinkets, but assigning moral judgements seemed like a step too far. Aiden didn't want to examine the fact that he was probably projecting his own emotions, so he changed the subject.

"What's done is done. I'm going after Torix alone."

Seth sighed. "Not alone, I guess."

Aiden grumbled, but there was no dissuading Seth when he decided on something. Better to keep moving. Seth walked along in silence for almost an entire minute.

"What happens to Maddie when she figures out how to get past the wards, and she will, if Torix kills both of us?"

"He'll come for her with everything he has, steal her magic, and probably regain some semblance of his former power which he'll then use to torture her for a long time." Aiden spoke casually, but the fear of that exact outcome gripped his heart. If he died, whatever magic remained within him would revert to Maddie, so he hoped the boost would give her a fighting chance. More likely, if Torix figured out the bond between them, he'd try to contain Aiden's power somehow.

Seth scowled. "That's what I remembered from last time. I just wanted to be sure."

Last time. Three of them against Torix, or so he'd thought. Seth's exile gave Lexi an excuse to travel to Terra. She'd convinced Aiden to follow Seth through the doorway. Lexi excelled at manipulation, only displaying aspects she thought they'd like and keeping the rest of her hidden.

Like the part where she obsessed over a Dark Fae, then traded her husband for power.

They'd only dated a few weeks, and while he'd enjoyed her company, they'd rushed the marriage. Aiden couldn't believe he'd ever thought himself in love with her. The strength of his feelings for Maddie threw his half-marriage with Lexi into stark contrast.

Seth cast several sidelong glances at him while they walked, but allowed Aiden to stew in silence.

Twenty minutes later, they weren't anywhere closer to Torix as far as he could tell, and Seth was equally useless. Aiden kicked a pinecone into the brush, then looked up at the sun peeking through the canopy. Almost noon, Maddie would be up soon. He'd given her a light suggestion to sleep, but it only lasted so long.

Seth peered into the brush after the pinecone and shook his head. "This isn't working."

Aiden turned on him with a growl. "No shit, cousin, but I don't have a better way to find Torix."

Seth raised a brow. "You mean besides bringing Maddie along and fighting him together? You know, at your strongest?"

"I told you. I'm not using Maddie for bait." There had to be another way to find him.

"You make it sound so sordid. There's nothing wrong with bait if you have a solid plan in place to deal with the consequences. This 'wander around until you trip over Torix' plan sucks, and unless you lock her away until Torix is dead, Maddie will always be bait." Seth braced his hands on his hips with a sneer. "How do you think she'll feel about being locked away again? How would you?"

Aiden frowned. "I'd never lock her away. She'd—"

"What do you think you did this morning?"

Aiden opened his mouth, then shut it again. The wards functioned to keep Torix out, but he'd had Seth adjust them to keep Maddie in for a while. Ideally, Aiden would have been back before she woke, so he hadn't considered Maddie's reaction to being stuck inside. Seth was right, protecting her was one thing, but he'd become her captor.

"Fuck."

Seth nodded sagely. "Yeah. I was waiting for you to realize on your own, but you're as hard-headed as your mother."

Aiden's stomach roiled as he realized in his attempt to save his mate, he may have driven her away for good. Seth clapped him on the back and turned toward where the wards stood strong.

"It's not too late to fix it. We can come up with a better plan. One where you don't run off half-cocked and get us both killed."

Aiden shrugged him off. "I should have known you were only worried about yourself. The last time I came running it was to help you, and it cost me my wife and my freedom."

Seth threw his hands up. "How is Lexi's bad decision my fault? I didn't ask you to come after me, and *I* certainly didn't trade you to some asshole for more power. Not that it did *her* any good."

Aiden remembered the look of surprise on Lexi's face when Torix had turned on her. They'd come through the doorway not long after Seth, but instead of his cousin, they found a Dark Fae waiting for them. Torix had pulled Lexi to him and sucked some of her life away. She'd whimpered. That little noise stuck with him more than anything else that happened after. Even knowing the truth, he wasn't sure she'd feigned it.

Torix offered him a deal. Servitude in exchange for Lexi. Without Seth for backup, Aiden agreed instantly. Torix tossed him a knife and told him to slice his palm, then hand it back. Jaw tight, he'd done as instructed. Moments later, Torix forced him to shift and trapped him as a wolf.

Aiden watched Torix let Lexi go as promised. But instead of running, Lexi sidled up to him and slipped her arm through his. Her fear abated, replaced with a smirk he didn't recognize. He tried to shift, to talk to her, to tell her to get away, get home. Torix's magic held him in place, and Lexi met Aiden's eyes as she congratulated Torix on a plan well-executed.

Aiden still didn't know why she'd chosen Torix over

him. If she'd been unhappy, she could have asked for a divorce, and they'd have gone separate ways. Luring him to Terra seemed like a vast overreaction. She hadn't bothered to explain.

Torix, for his part, ignored Aiden once he'd gained control. He turned his focus on Lexi. With a growl trapped in his throat, Aiden stood helpless as Torix trailed a finger down her face and leaned in for a kiss. Lexi responded, and Aiden felt part of himself die. His wife had betrayed him in every way that mattered.

Seconds later, her eyes popped open and she tried to pull away. Through his pain, he watched Lexi become pale and struggle against Torix's hold. She weakened, then Torix dropped her limp body at his feet. Aiden raged at the loss of his trust, his freedom, and even Lexi. The growl finally escaped, and Torix turned back toward him.

He flicked his fingers, and Aiden struggled to breathe. Torix leaned down so they were eye to eye and spoke softly.

"You're mine now, wolf. Better to accept your lot and make the best of it. I hate having to kill my toys before I've had a chance to play with them."

Aiden vowed to fight with everything in him, even if it resulted in his death, but before he could follow through, an orange tabby cat came racing out of the brush, spitting and hissing.

Seth hadn't been gone; he'd only been hiding. Torix smiled dangerously, and Aiden could suddenly breathe again. "Ah, Lexi had said there might be two of you." He cast a sidelong glance at Aiden and took a step toward Seth. "Tell me, wolf, what would you do to protect this one?"

Aiden managed a shake of his head to warn Seth off. He couldn't bear to lose his cousin along with everything else. Seth either saw the shake or sensed that Aiden needed him to run. He paused in his theatrics, then turned and took off in a spray of pine straw. That had been the last time he'd seen his cousin until Maddie had lured him out in Cairo.

Seth watched him now with guarded eyes. "I'm sorry for leaving you, and for what happened to Lexi. Well, not *sorry*, she got what she deserved, but I'm sorry for the effect it had on you. You protected me, and it wasn't your fault that you couldn't protect Lexi. There was nothing you could do, literally. Maddie isn't Lexi, and you need to get that straight if you plan on keeping her."

Aiden's fists clenched. He'd made the same argument with himself, and hearing someone else say it didn't make it easier to implement. "I know. I know Maddie is her own person. I know Lexi wasn't my fault. Losing Lexi was hard, but losing Maddie would destroy me."

"You love her?" Seth asked.

"I love her."

Seth nodded. "Then trust her. Let's go back and get her before Torix really does show up. You can grovel for forgiveness later."

Aiden hesitated, then nodded. His Maddie was fierce, powerful, and determined to fight her own battles. He couldn't tuck her away until the danger had passed if he wanted to have any chance of a life with her after. And he wanted a life with her. They just needed to survive first.

Seth rolled his eyes. "Finally, you're making sense. Don't take this the wrong way, but you're a lot broodier than you used to be."

"And you're a lot more devious. How long did it take you to figure out how to bypass the banishment?"

"Not as long as it would have taken you." Seth grinned.

Aiden snorted as he stepped over a fallen branch. "Not

all of us are geniuses. At least you were able to take care of Lexi, whether or not she deserved it."

Seth sobered. "What do you mean?"

Aiden stopped moving at the confusion on Seth's face. "Her body. Torix had complete control over my form in the beginning. It wasn't until the Fae stuck him in a tree and curbed his power that I could exert myself. He took me back to that part of the woods often though. I think it was a subtle torture for me as well as a way to keep an eye on the rest of the Fae. He liked to multi-task."

"What does that have to do with me?"

"I never saw Lexi's body again. I assumed you'd taken care of it somehow."

Seth shook his head slowly. "No...I'd been freshly banished. The most I could do was send a message through the doorway for Keris. I thought *you'd* taken care of her body."

They stared at each other in dawning horror.

Lexi was dead. He'd *seen* her die. Their bodies could recover from most injuries, but having the lifeforce sucked out of them circumvented the healing. Her power had vanished, eaten by Torix. He'd felt it.

Seth grasped Aiden's forearm. "Could she still be alive somewhere?"

The prospect hit him in the gut. His malicious wife could be alive. Was it possible? Humans could have found the body. Or Fae. Or dryads. Or really any of the other races that populated the planet. It would be impossible to find out if someone had discovered the body of a random woman in a desolate section of woods on another continent over a hundred years ago. The internet was a marvelous thing, but there were limits.

Seth jostled Aiden's arm. "Seriously. Would you be able to tell?"

Aiden grimaced and shook him off again. "I doubt it. We never connected that way. If she was nearby, I'd get a sense of someone from our clan, but it's never happened. If she did survive, wouldn't she return home?" The first thing he'd done upon being freed was contact his family. He'd vowed not to return without killing Torix, but he'd wanted them to know he lived.

Seth scoffed. "And risk the chance someone found out she'd sacrificed her husband, who also happened to be the son of the clan's leaders? Yeah, if I were her, I'd for sure stay in Terra where she could at least push around the humans."

"That does sound like her. And Mother would definitely have told me if Lexi had returned when we reconnected last year. Punishing Lexi would have been the highlight of her century. If Lexi's in hiding, we should find her. She's—" A breeze brought a hint of Torix's scent to him even though they'd turned back.

Seth lifted his face to the wind and inhaled, then frowned. "Is that what you've been following this whole time?"

"Yeah, I know Torix is somewhere local. I was hoping to surprise him, but the direction keeps changing."

"That's not a real scent. It's really subtle magic layered to seem like a scent."

"Are you sure?"

Seth sniffed once more, this time in the direction of Aiden. "Yeah. You and Maddie are strong and clear, but that one is like a bad photoshop job. Why would Torix want you running around the woods chasing a false trail that leads consistently away from the cabin?"

Aiden didn't need Seth's sarcasm to figure out Maddie

was in more danger than he'd realized. He cursed, then took off running. The cabin wasn't far. Most of the time he'd spent wandering had been in large circles. Seth crunched through the leaves behind him, no longer cloaking himself in silence like he usually did.

The bond assured him of Maddie's health, but Torix's scent trick had easily fooled him, so Aiden hesitated to take anything for granted. Once he got to her, nothing would make him leave her side again.

When they were still too far away from the cabin, Aiden felt the wards shudder. He picked up speed and considered changing into a faster animal, but he couldn't with his focus split. If Torix had found the cabin, the wards had lost their biggest defense, hiding in plain sight. Maddie believed herself safe inside them, and she'd be unprepared.

A second shudder, bigger this time with a familiar hint of magic woven through, made Aiden stumble. Torix wasn't trying to break into the wards; Maddie was pushing her way out.

She cleared the circle, and a wave of anger and worry nearly knocked him over. The return of the full force of his magic, mixed with hers, unmasked the fake scent he'd been following. Without realizing it, he'd handicapped himself when he'd separated them.

"Dammit. Seth, can you get there faster?"

Seth panted, but kept his pace. "Not with whatever she just did to my beautiful wards. It feels like someone just rubbed my fur the wrong way."

The fake-Torix scent disappeared about the same time Aiden's sense of Maddie distorted. She'd figured out how to call a trod. He'd bet she planned to lead them to the nexus. The clever girl knew Torix would track her, and Maddie could wield the elemental power that filled the nexus to the brim. Hopefully, Torix didn't have a way to use that magic against them.

Aiden took a sharp right and pounded through a new set of brush. They'd been travelling parallel to the boundaries of the Wood, so they crossed over almost immediately. He called a trod and hoped the sprites helped him catch up to Maddie. His fear for her squeezed the breath out of him, but fear lied. He and Maddie *were* stronger together, just like she'd said.

It was time he stopped letting fear run the show. Like she'd said before, he wasn't the only badass around. Maddie could handle herself, and he'd be whatever she needed him to be in the fight. If he could only get to the nexus in time. Aiden had made a lot of mistakes today, and he refused to let Maddie be the one paying for them.

15

MADDIE

THE TROD only made Maddie walk a short distance before reaching into the nexus. Sprites followed her into the clearing, and the path disappeared. Maddie had no need for the flat stone in the middle of the circle, barely visible under the pine straw, but she took note of it anyway. Muted daylight lit the trees around the clearing, and shadows darkened further into the woods. She suspected that anyone attempting to penetrate the shadows would end up back in the clearing, but she'd never tested it.

She nudged her power to search the area and discovered another obstruction between her and Aiden, probably because of the nexus. His power intertwined with hers, but something obscured her sense of him.

In the short amount of time between leaving the wards and entering the trod, Maddie had checked on Aiden. He hadn't found Torix yet. She knew what Aiden felt like in battle, and though he'd been annoyed, he hadn't been fighting. A part of her hoped that whatever was annoying him kept at it because he deserved a little discomfort after what he'd done to her.

She didn't sense anyone else. *Unless they could cloak themselves...*Maddie told her pessimistic inner voice to shut up and dropped her pack near the edge of the trees. Her hand closed over the dagger Zee had given her, and a strange prickle of anticipation met her. She frowned and drew back.

The magical, aggressive dagger seemed to pout when she didn't pick it up. She eyed the pack and decided having a weapon outweighed the risk of its potential sentience. Unfortunately, Maddie didn't have anywhere to stash it that wouldn't immediately be obvious. Her leggings weren't meant to double as a sheath.

She tapped the outside of the pack as an idea dawned. Maddie knew how to make herself stronger using magic, but she'd never tried making something else light. She shrugged and retrieved the dagger, ignoring the glee emanating from it. Might as well try now. Light and unobtrusive.

Silver magic curled around the hilt and engulfed the blade. A second later, the dagger weighed next to nothing, and she had trouble looking directly at it. Excellent. She carefully tucked it into the waistband of her leggings, thankful they were tight enough to hold it in place.

The plan seemed great until she tried to actually walk. When she took anything more than a tiny shuffling step, the long, awkward blade pressed painfully into her leg. Torix had to touch her to steal her power, so she needed to be agile. Maddie shook her head in frustration and pulled the dagger out to leave it next to the pack, much to its chagrin. She tilted her head and stared at the area around it for a moment, then concentrated and changed the spell.

Weightlessness was great, but she needed it to come when she called. Wrapping a razor thin tendril of magic around the hilt made it so she could pull it to her at any point. The magic would stretch, and she tried to make the look-away spell extend to the tendril as well. Maddie couldn't tell if it had worked because she could feel the location of her magic. Without trying, she could see it with her eyes closed. Aiden probably could too, but Torix shouldn't be able to sense it.

Maddie rubbed her sweaty palms on her thighs and took a deep breath. The pulse of elemental magic in the Earth below her should have been comforting, but thanks to Zee, she knew Torix might be able to use it just as well as she could. That didn't mean she wouldn't pull on it in an emergency, but there was no point in juicing herself up ahead of time. Without more information, she'd done everything she could to protect herself.

Reaching out to Torix proved to be harder than she'd expected. A great big ball of fear tried to lodge itself in her throat, making it hard to focus. Eventually, she had to close her eyes and picture a man with pointed features and a sinister smile. She shuddered, but pushed through the cold terror to essentially toss a magical rock at him.

One moment she was alone in her mind, the next, Torix's amusement washed over her. *Finally come to your senses, dear?*

If you want me, come and get me. Maddie slammed a shield between them to sever the connection. A single thin shield wouldn't keep him out if he pushed, but as she'd thought, he was more concerned with getting to her physical location. If he did succeed in breaking through, she'd throw up another one, and she'd keep doing it as long as she needed to.

Every time a leaf rustled in the quiet stillness of the nexus, she tensed up. It didn't take long before a path opened, thankfully on the other side of the clearing from where Maddie waited by her pack. The sprites appeared first, and she fought a sensation of betrayal. Sprites protected, and Torix was the last person who deserved protection.

A lanky man wearing jeans and a green sweater with the sleeves pushed up to his elbows strode out of the trod. He resembled any other human she'd encountered except for the bolt of terror that she experienced when she looked at his face. Brown hair swept back from sharp features and otherworldly green eyes, and Maddie forced herself to confront his smirk with her chin high.

The path closed behind him without anyone else exiting, and Maddie's eyes narrowed. "Where's Will?" she asked.

Torix shrugged. "I had another task for him."

Maddie's shield was suddenly shoved aside and Jake's house filled her mind. Through the window, she could see Jake dancing with baby Amber in the living room. As she watched, Will crept around the corner with a gas can, splashing liquid along the outside of the house. He smiled with empty eyes.

Adrenaline surged through Maddie, providing a burst of energy, but she controlled it, taking a moment to examine the image. Daytime, and relatively recent judging by Amber's size, but she couldn't get any more context. Maddie thrust another shield between them to stop the vision. She wasn't a stranger to Torix's manipulation techniques. He couldn't lie, but he twisted the truth consistently.

In her few seconds of inattention, he'd edged closer to the center of the clearing. Maddie glared at him. He wanted her scared and panicking. Even if the vision happened in real time, she couldn't do anything about it. She'd have to trust Jake and Sera to protect themselves. Something she probably should have done from the beginning.

Maddie straightened. "Your tricks don't work on me."

Torix appeared in front of her in an instant, and Maddie barely had time to sidestep his grab. She'd assumed he wouldn't be as fast as before, but she'd been wrong. He lunged for her again, and Maddie stepped back as she conjured a blade of silver magic. She carefully circled away from him as he paused and stared at her sword.

"You'd use my own magic against me? Perhaps you learned more from me than you let on." His glittering eyes stayed on the blade as he shifted toward her. When she swung it, he blocked with an open hand, a small layer of muddled magic between him and her weapon. His eyes tracked up to her face, and his smile widened. The magic began to bend toward her painfully, and Maddie had to release it while flinging herself away from him.

His other hand came up while she backpedaled, and a blast of magic knocked her airborne. Maddie hit the ground hard, and the wind exploded out of her. She scrambled to a sitting position and scooted back as he approached, trying to suck in air.

Torix frowned for a moment, and his eyes lost focus as he studied her. "Something in you has changed."

Maddie finally took a full breath, but she wasn't about to waste her precious oxygen giving him ideas.

His eyes narrowed as he moved closer. "That blast should have knocked you unconscious. Your measly shield is no protection, so how did you—" Understanding dawned on his face, and his smile returned, filling Maddie with dread.

"An immunity. How delightful. I'll enjoy that new ability of yours."

Maddie's muscles relaxed a little, but she was careful not to let it show outwardly. She'd been afraid he'd be able to sense her connection with Aiden, but Torix couldn't recognize their bond. Now if only he'd reveal the source of his new power.

"This would all have been so much easier if you'd just returned what you stole. Unfortunately, I'm going to have to make this painful." Torix crouched down, and Maddie dug her fingers into the dirt, pulling a jolt of elemental magic into her palm. She needed him closer to have the best shot at his face.

"Get away from her." Aiden's voice came from nowhere for a second before a trod opened up next to them, and he sprinted into the clearing.

Relief washed over Maddie, along with a hefty dose of doubled-up magic. Now that they were together, she could feel the real depth of their power. Before, she'd only had access to a small sampling of their capabilities. Maddie released the elemental magic in favor of the blend that felt as natural to her as breathing.

Aiden skidded to a stop in front of Maddie and threw an explosion of magic at Torix, knocking him away from her. She couldn't see it, but she felt its reverberation. Torix went flying in an entirely satisfying manner. Unlike Maddie, he got up right away and dusted himself off as if nothing had happened. *Note to self: work on superhero landing.*

Torix sniffed in disdain. "A noble effort, but useless I'm afraid. You can't hurt me with your paltry magic tricks."

Aiden ignored him and glanced at her over his shoulder. "You okay?"

Seeing him here, determined to protect her, choked her

with emotion, so she nodded. Aiden returned his focus to the Dark Fae now across the clearing from them. A subtle glow drew her attention to the hand Aiden had positioned slightly behind him. The golden necklace slipped from his palm and fell to the forest floor with a quiet thud.

Maddie's eyes widened. What was that idiot doing? She surreptitiously palmed the necklace before standing up. Aiden had no protection against compulsion if Torix chose to use it, unlike the asshole Fae who seemed able to shrug off any magic attack.

Torix's eyes flicked back and forth between them, and he laughed dryly. "I see you've shared your magic with our girl, wolf." So much for him not figuring it out. "I'd be careful if I were you. She's in the habit of keeping what's not hers." His smile dropped a little, and his gaze slid past Aiden to land on Maddie mostly hidden behind him. "Magic is treacherous, dear. I thought you'd have learned that by now."

He raised a hand toward her and crooked his finger. Maddie gasped and involuntarily took a step past Aiden. She clenched her teeth and forced her legs to stop moving, but the compulsion grew. Aiden wrapped his arm around her and called his magic to shield them. The forward movement stopped, but she could still feel the pull. *What the actual hell?* The necklace was supposed to stop Torix from using his magic against the wearer.

"What's our plan?" Aiden whispered.

"Don't let him touch us and don't die."

"Got it."

Aiden raised his hand, palm toward Torix, and swept it sideways. Maddie felt a sucking pull from her center, and the tug disappeared. Torix frowned, and sweat popped out on Aiden's brow. He'd disrupted Torix's spell, but the interference took a lot of power for him to maintain. They needed a better strategy than 'don't get hit'.

The necklace warmed in her palm, and she remembered what Cassie had said. She had to be *wearing* it to be protected from magic. Maddie twined the chain around her wrist, and the warmth from her palm spread up her arm and through the rest of her.

Luckily, Torix stayed focused on Aiden. He seemed to be searching for something, then his smile returned, and Maddie's mouth went dry.

"Oh, I'm going to enjoy this," Torix muttered as he stepped to the side.

A brightly-colored lovebird flew out of the trees to land at his feet. In an instant, the bird changed form into a beautiful blonde woman with bright blue eyes wearing a simple sheath dress. Her tiny frame, maybe five feet tall, stood unsteadily on bare feet.

"Lexi." The name was torn from Aiden as his hand dropped to his side. Maddie felt his shock and surprise.

Aiden paused, his eyes on his wife, and Maddie's strength crumbled. Emotion moved freely between them, and after his shock came remorse...then longing. Hurt sliced through her.

Aiden longed for *Lexi*?

He missed the wife who'd betrayed him? Maddie understood in a twisted way. He'd loved Lexi. People could forgive anything for love. Do anything. Look at her brother and Sera. Look at Ryan. Hell, look at Zee.

Look at yourself.

Maddie silenced the quiet voice inside her. The small woman in front of them looked lost and afraid. She'd been in Lexi's position as Torix's slave. Maddie knew she'd use everything in her power to save Lexi from Torix, no one deserved that fate, but she wouldn't give up the man she loved without a fight. *Loved.* Maddie blinked in surprise, but it felt right. Real. *Well, that explained a lot.*

Her heart clenched painfully. What if Aiden wanted Lexi? What if in the end, Maddie still wasn't good enough? He'd chosen her. He *belonged* with her. But maybe now he'd make a different choice.

She blinked away tears. No. Hell, no. If Aiden chose Lexi, she'd been wrong about him, and he'd never been worthy of her.

Before Maddie could do something stupid, Aiden's arm tightened around her. That small motion made Maddie realize she'd erected an icy wall between her and Aiden as soon as she'd seen Lexi change. With a grunt of pain, she tore it down again.

Aiden's affection and warmth filled her, pushing out the last of her doubts. She chanced a peek at his face. He watched Lexi, but his jaw ticked and a tightly controlled ball of anger grew inside him. The bond made it clear that there *was* no choice for him. Only Maddie.

Lexi blinked at Aiden a few times, then smiled, ignoring Maddie completely. "Did you miss me, husband?"

Aiden shifted his hold on Maddie, subtly putting himself between the two women. "I want a divorce."

"But Aiden..." She stumbled forward, reaching for him with one hand. Maddie started to pull away, but Aiden shoved her fully behind him. A split second later, Lexi lunged and swiped with her other hand, her fingers transformed into sharp-looking talons.

Aiden easily dodged her, circling her further away from Maddie. He tilted his head. "Looks like *you* missed *me*."

Lexi growled and lunged again. Aiden danced back, well out of her reach. Her jerky movements made it look as if she hadn't used those muscles in a while. Out of the corner of her eye, Maddie noticed Torix watching them with a satisfied grin. Was he hoping to torture Aiden by bringing out his clearly not-dead wife? Torix's attention shifted to Maddie, and she realized that the torture wasn't for Aiden. It was for her.

"How do you like my pet? Beautiful, deadly, obedient. Everything you aren't." Torix's mind pushed at the edges of hers, but she still had the single shield between them. He liked it better when he could judge how well-aimed his barbs were. *Too bad.* For once, his manipulations had missed their desired effect. Maddie knew what Aiden thought of Lexi.

The other woman's growls and grunts echoed from the far side of the clearing. Controlling another creature, especially a demi-goddess, required a huge amount of magical power. Maddie narrowed her eyes and started using her brain. She revved her senses and examined Torix, then Lexi. A thin coating of magic should have completely covered Lexi, like Maddie had endured. Instead, only a braided cord connected them.

Lexi wasn't under his power; she *was* his power.

Maddie gasped. "Lexi's been feeding you this whole time."

Torix chuckled, low and dangerous. "I fill her needs, and she fills mine. The delicate fear that comes off of her when I've taken more than she can handle..." He shuddered, but his eyes stayed on Maddie.

Her skin crawled. "Why would she bind herself to you?"

He spread his hands, taking slow, deliberate steps toward her. "Why did you? Power. She accepted her role underneath me, and came to covet the domination. Every time she wakes from the brink of death, she craves more. You'll see."

The hell she would.

The beginning of a plan started to form. Now that Maddie knew his source, she needed to take Lexi out of the equation. Purposefully, she shifted and yelled toward where Aiden and Lexi were having a stand-off. "Aiden, take her out. Torix has decided on a new consort."

That got Lexi's attention. Anger warped her beautiful face.

"I will not be replaced by a lowly human." Lexi turned on her heel and raised both hands at Maddie. Aiden dove between them, pulling a large sword out of the air. A real sword, not one made of magic like Maddie's. It was sexy as hell, and Maddie again wished she had her own pocket trod.

Lexi either didn't notice or didn't care. She gathered a large torrent of magic between her hands and thrust it at Maddie. In one motion, Aiden swung the sword up and slashed across Lexi's abdomen. She folded at the waist and crumpled to the ground, blood soaking the bottom half of her dress. His action was too late to stop the spell though.

Maddie's eyes widened. She pulled hard on their shared power and threw a shield up as Lexi's magic struck her. As a precautionary measure, it would have been really effective, except in her need to defend herself from Lexi, she'd turned her back on Torix.

An arm wrapped around her throat and pulled her backwards. Maddie lost her balance and landed against a hard chest. Her hands came up to pull Torix's arm away from her neck, but he was immoveable.

Aiden jerked toward them, and Torix shook his head.

"Don't move or I *will* snap her neck." Torix held Maddie in front of him with a hand around her throat, his face next to hers. "That wasn't very nice, but I happen to know from experience she'll heal. It's refreshing having a creature that enjoys the pain almost as much as I do. On the other hand, I don't like other people playing with what's mine."

Maddie's heart thundered, and Torix breathed in her fear, dragging his open mouth across her cheek. She held herself still as he whispered in her ear.

"I like your taste best when you struggle."

Maddie shuddered at the familiar feel of him against her skin and pried her mind away from the litany of what-ifs cycling through it. Now wasn't the time for doubts.

"Let her go," Aiden growled.

"We've been here before, you and I. Would you make the same bargain, wolf? Your freedom for hers?"

Maddie knew Aiden could feel her fear, but she was determined to keep it off her face. She met his golden eyes, and felt his relief at the assurance in hers. She had a plan. Torix maintained his vice-like grip on her throat, but she could breathe for the time being. Maddie kept one hand on Torix's arm and held the other in front of her chest. As Aiden watched, she let the medallion of the necklace fall from her fist with the chain tangled around her wrist.

Aiden's face didn't change, but his confidence filled her. He trusted her to handle herself. *Also, he'd make a great poker player.*

His attention shifted to Torix, but his gaze didn't move from Maddie. "I'd do anything for her."

The sincerity in his voice and his eyes momentarily distracted her. He wasn't just telling Torix; he was telling her too.

Exhilaration bubbled in her chest, but Torix's fingers tightened on her throat. Now was probably not the time.

She loved a good romantic gesture, but a distraction would have been a tad more helpful.

Torix shrugged, oblivious to the undercurrent between them. "You were mediocre as an underling, always finding ways around my orders. I don't think I'm currently on the market for a new shifter as I already have one. I do believe I'll keep your mate as my new consort though."

Maddie recognized her moment. Torix intended to kill Aiden in front of her. He'd sworn years ago that if Maddie ever gave herself to anyone else, he'd destroy them. A punishment and a promise.

Her nails curled into Torix's forearm. At this distance, he'd have to use magic, and with or without the protection of the necklace, Maddie would put herself between Aiden and Torix's magic every time. Magic Torix still had access to. Her eyes darted to Lexi's crumpled body, and she realized Torix was right. Lexi would heal, and in the meantime, Torix hadn't weakened.

Now or never.

Maddie whimpered and slumped against him. The move forced Torix to hold her weight with only a hand at her throat, knocking him off balance. He stumbled back a step, and Maddie yanked her thread of magic to her. The Fae dagger flew in from behind them. As it approached, she gathered as much magic as she could from the nexus and Aiden and anywhere else she could reach.

A trickle of power from the trods that felt like her family and Oskar and Cassie, and even Seth, passed through her in an intoxicating rush, along her magic strand, and into the dagger. Connections she'd made and cherished. Maddie took all the separate magics and infused the blade with the will to penetrate and sever his twisted bond to Lexi.

Torix jerked to the side, narrowly dodging the dagger as

it flew past him, but the hilt landed securely in Maddie's hand. She immediately thrust the pointy end back into Torix. The blade sliced cleanly through his shields and into his flesh, sinking into his abdomen all the way to the hilt. Blood covered her hand, and the warmth surprised Maddie for a moment. He'd never felt warm to her.

Aiden darted forward as Torix's grip on her loosened. His hand fell away from her neck as she turned to face him. Maddie maintained her grasp on the dagger and made sure her spell finished. He slid backward off the blade, leaving a surprisingly large, oozing hole in the front of him.

The sense of magic from Torix vanished completely. Aiden halted beside her, but he made no move to stop Torix when he reached a bloody hand toward Maddie with a grunt. She simply side-stepped him and let him fall face-first into the dirt. He slowly shriveled until only a disgusting-looking husk remained. Without his magic, or Lexi's, he'd had no way to maintain his human form.

Neither of them made any move to help. Torix had brought this result on himself, and for once, Maddie was totally okay with her decision. She stared down at the dagger in her hand and released the magic she'd gathered. It let go reluctantly, and Maddie pursed her lips at the smugness coming from the weapon. One day soon, she'd have to ask Zee some pointed questions about the dagger, but that could wait.

A thud and some inventive cursing had them both swiveling with their weapons up to face the opposite side of the nexus. A tall man with dark red hair and familiar golden eyes rolled into the clearing, then stood and brushed dirt off his chest with a grimace and an oath. She'd never seen him before, but the word choice sounded familiar.

Aiden lowered his sword and put his arm out to do the

same for her dagger. "What the hell? You were right behind me."

Maddie squinted at him. "Seth?"

He looked up from cleaning himself. "Maddie." Seth straightened and ran his hands through his chin-length hair. "One second you were ahead of me, the next I was alone in the trod. I felt Maddie's call for power, so I sent what I could, but the Wood adamantly refused to let me be involved in this fight."

Aiden glanced over at her, and she shrugged. "I wasn't sure it would work."

Seth finally looked around the clearing and noticed Lexi's still body and Torix's husk. "Looks like you didn't need me after all."

"She didn't even need *me*," Aiden muttered. "Talk about a badass."

Seth approached Lexi and held a palm out several inches over her back. "She's injured."

"She's a bad guy," Maddie pointed out.

Seth looked at Maddie, then over to Aiden.

Aiden sighed. "We need to take her home. There are policies in place for people like her."

"Crazy, narcissistic demi-goddesses? I would hope so. She's lucky she's not dead." Now that the adrenaline and fear were returning to normal levels, Maddie remembered how pissed she was at both of these men for locking her away while they tried to save the world alone.

Maddie shook her head and crouched to wipe the bloody dagger on Torix's shirt. He wouldn't be needing it anymore. "You'd better take her before she heals enough to wake up. Aiden incapacitated her, but I won't be so generous to someone who voluntarily fed Torix all this time."

Aiden cocked his head. "How'd you know she was the source of his power?"

"Something Cassie said. 'The pretty ones always look out for themselves.' It gave me the idea to check."

Seth nodded and lifted Lexi into his arms. "I can get her back, but I'll have to leave her at the doorway for Keris."

"She's going to love this," Aiden mumbled.

Maddie stored the dagger in her pack and joined Aiden in the center of the clearing. "How binding is your marriage anyway?"

Aiden waved the question away. "Marriages among my people aren't particularly lasting unless accompanied by a bond of some sort. It would have been dissolved when Lexi was assumed dead. It won't be reapplied now that she's revealed to be alive after all."

Maddie jerked her chin at Lexi. "I hope she finds the help she needs." Both men stared at her. "I may not be a good person, but I'm not a bad one either." Maddie sucked in a ragged breath and stared down at Torix's body. She spoke to herself as much as to them, finally starting to believe the words. Torix's power—*her power*—didn't make her evil; *she* controlled how she used it.

Seth took a couple of steps, then turned back to them. "I'm calling in my favor."

Aiden nodded and slid his arm around her waist. "Anything but Maddie."

Warmth from his touch spread through her, concentrating around her heart. Maddie rested her head on his shoulder and waited to hear what Seth demanded.

"The artifact she's holding. I want it." He stood with his spine straight, shoulders back even with the weight of Lexi in his arms.

Maddie had the distinct feeling he hated asking for

anything. She lifted her arm. The necklace dangled from the chain wrapped around her wrist, spinning idly. The weight of the magic inside it seemed lighter than before, and Maddie wondered how much of it she'd used to get through Torix's protections.

She had no doubt it had saved her. In the split second between Torix dodging the dagger and Maddie stabbing him with it, she'd felt a pull. He'd tried to drain her, but the necklace stopped him. With Torix dead, she had no more use for it.

Aiden raised a brow as she untangled the chain and left his side to drape it over Seth's head. "I hope this path doesn't involve so much bloodshed."

Seth bowed his head to her. "Me too. The terms are met and the bargain fulfilled."

A tingle of magic danced over her skin then disappeared. Maddie wondered what would have happened if she'd said no. Could Seth have called off the deal without his favor or would the magic have enforced it whether he wanted it to or not? She had a lot to learn about demi-gods and their power. Especially now that she contained some of it.

Seth turned without another word and left. Maddie hadn't forgotten his role in trapping her, but she decided she'd rather pay him back once he'd forgotten his transgression. It would be more fun that way. Aiden, though, she'd deal with now.

Before she could accuse him of crimes against her freedom, he pulled her roughly into his arms for a tight hug. "That was terrifying. Can we please avoid any life or death battles in the future?"

Maddie softened against him, wrapping her arms around his waist, but she deserved an explanation. "What was that all about with Lexi? When she first showed up, I felt your longing."

Aiden grunted and pulled back to look at her face. "It wasn't Lexi I was longing for. It was all the time I spent searching for vengeance for a woman who wasn't dead."

"Not to mention a woman who tricked you into slavery."

He shook his head. "She's still clan."

"That's noble, but stupid."

A smile flitted across his features. "It seems I've done several stupid things today. I'm sorry I had Seth lock you inside the wards. I couldn't face the idea of losing you in a battle with Torix." He laughed dryly. "I should've known you'd find a way out. I should have trusted you."

Maddie smacked him in the shoulder, but his words soothed the hurt part of her. "Yeah, you should've. And I don't like waking up alone." The connection between them flared with heat. Aiden's golden eyes dropped to her lips and back up. A move Maddie felt like a physical touch.

"Do I get bonus points for figuring it out on my own?" His voice rasped over her skin, and Maddie had to concentrate on why she was upset at him.

"Depends. What exactly did you figure out?"

"That you're more important to me than anything in this or any other world. That I can't blame it on magic or the challenge ring. Take everything else away, and still, all I want is you. That I love you, *marenkya*."

Maddie sniffled, but couldn't look away from his mesmerizing eyes. "It nearly killed me when I thought you still wanted Lexi."

Aiden cupped her face, caressing her cheek with his thumb. "Never. I'll always choose you."

Maddie leaned into his hand. "I love you too, and I

demand you teach me how to make wards and a pocket trod first thing."

His head lowered to hers, speaking words across her lips. "First thing?"

Maddie raised onto her toes to bring them into contact. "Maybe second thing."

The deep kiss drugged her, and Maddie easily forgot she stood in a clearing with Torix's body and a magical dagger that may or may not be blood-thirsty. "Definitely second thing…"

EPILOGUE

MADDIE

MADDIE WASN'T NERVOUS, but she could feel the waves of Aiden's anxiety pushing against her from the bond. They stood on the porch of Jake and Sera's place, noticeably without any of Will's fire damage.

Sera had told her that they'd caught Will splashing gasoline around the outside of the house and called the police. She'd been about to go out and take care of it herself when Will had suddenly collapsed, covering himself in the liquid. The police had found him there with several lighters in his pockets. Once he'd regained consciousness, he'd been babbling about magic and killing the Fae with fire. He currently resided in a mental ward awaiting enough lucidity to stand trial.

And as promised, Maddie had brought Aiden to family dinner.

Aiden feigned nonchalance, but his grip on her hand tightened painfully as he tilted his head toward her.

"Are you sure you want me here?" Aiden whispered.

"Yes. Stop asking."

"I tried to kill Ryan...and Sera, for that matter." His brow furrowed. "I think I might have tried to eat Zee once too when she was small and flying around."

Maddie grinned. "I was going to say join the club, but I've never had the pleasure of eating Zee."

Aiden raised a brow at her.

"You heard me." Maddie knocked again, and from inside, Sera yelled something unintelligible.

"Remember, you can't tell them about Aecantha."

Maddie stifled a long-suffering sigh. At least he wasn't crushing her hand anymore. "I promise not to mention your stolen pocket dimension. I have some experience keeping secrets from my family, remember?"

He nuzzled her neck and inhaled with a growl. "You don't keep secrets from me, *marenkya*."

Tingles raced across her skin, and she wished for the hundredth time in the last fifteen minutes that they'd just stayed at home. "You're more than family."

Jake chose that moment to open the door. Aiden took his sweet time straightening up, and Maddie flushed a deeper color than she already was. Her brother's smile transformed into a scowl. "Is this why you didn't just burst in like normal? Needed a little extra time on the porch?" He sounded disgruntled, but Maddie knew better than to take it seriously.

She raised her chin. "I'm trying this new thing where I respect Sera's privacy."

"Just Sera's?"

"I like her more than you."

His hand gripped his chest as if she'd maimed him. "Ouch, that hurts. I thought I was your favorite brother."

"Your dad jokes are getting worse now that you're actually a dad."

Aiden had stood silently next to her up to that point, but he shifted when she mentioned baby Amber. The movement garnered Jake's attention.

Jake sobered, and his eyes dropped to their linked hands. He lingered on the ring Aiden had given her the night before, then moved back up to Aiden's otherworldly golden eyes. "I know you."

Aiden grinned slowly, danger in his smile.

Maddie rolled her eyes. *Enough with the macho crap.* "Jake, this is my mate, Aiden. Aiden, my brother, Jake. We've all tried to kill each other at some point because of an asshole I don't want to talk about. There, now you've met for real."

The tension in the air dissipated, and Jake chuckled as he held out his hand. "Nice to meet you for real."

Aiden released Maddie to shake it. "Likewise."

She threw her hands in the air. "Great. Can we come inside or are we having dinner on the front lawn?"

Jake muttered something about sassy females and opened the door wider. They joined the throng, and Maddie squealed when Sera came around the corner carrying a gorgeous dark-haired toddler.

"Amber! Come to Aunt Maddie." She made grabby hands until Sera handed the kid over with a smile.

"I could use a break. No matter where we hide the C-O-O-K-I-E-S, she finds them and magics them to her." Amber giggled as her mom tickled her feet, then settled against Maddie's shoulder to stare up at her adoringly.

Maddie felt Aiden's gaze on her and looked up to see him watching her across the room. He was talking with Zee, probably about what they'd done with Torix, but his focus never wavered from her. He liked the way she looked with a child in her arms. She could feel it through the bond, which had gotten stronger and more concentrated the more they used it.

Ryan walked out of the kitchen, a beer in his hand, and Jake called everyone to the table to eat. Maddie didn't remember a big dining table in the house, but then, a lot had changed in the last year. She handed Amber back to Jake and took a seat between Sera and Aiden. Around the table, people passed lasagna and garlic bread, told terrible jokes, and sent each other silent glances.

Her heart swelled with happiness at being surrounded by the people she loved safe and whole. A simple dream she'd thought she didn't deserve. Aiden had changed that. He rubbed her thigh under the table. Maddie grabbed his hand, then sent him a big grin. He understood her joy.

Ryan cleared his throat, then spoke over the dinner chatter. "We have enough magical firepower around this table to fight a shit-ton of bad guys. Oww—" He glared as Sera, who nodded at the baby sitting in a high chair between her and Ryan. "Right. Sorry. A whole lot of bad guys. We need a name."

Jake rolled his eyes. "Not this again. We're not the Avengers. We don't need a name."

"Well the Avengers is taken, obviously. But I was thinking—"

Maddie tuned Ryan out and squeezed Aiden's hand. They'd been through a hell of a journey, but she'd do it all again to end up here with these weirdos.

Aiden leaned over, oblivious to Jake's scowl, and whispered in her ear, "I love you, *marenkya*."

Maddie turned her head and brushed her lips against his. "I love you too."

Across the table, Zee snorted. "No. Absolutely not. It sounds like a crime-fighting octopus, and tentacles are creepy." She shuddered, and everyone laughed.

Aiden stretched his arm across her shoulders, and Maddie settled back into him, making a face at Amber. The others could battle it out for a group name they'd never use. She had no need to look for more trouble.

Maddie had everything she wanted right here.

Continue the adventure with Keely and Seth in Impulsive Magic!

If you loved Treacherous Magic, please take a moment to leave a review on Amazon, Goodreads, or Bookbub.

Can't get enough of snarky magical heroines? Get a fun short story with all new characters set in the Modern Magic world when you sign up for my newsletter, Muse Interrupted!

A NOTE FROM NICOLE

To my readers, you are why I love this job. It's always been my dream to spread some happiness in the world, so thank you from the bottom of my heart for taking your precious time to read Treacherous Magic. Maddie and Aiden have been my favorite to write so far. I hope you had a satisfactory amount of sass, magic, and romance as we ended the story arc with Torix. The Fae are only a small part of the diversity in the Modern Magic series, and I hope you'll come with me to explore new fantastic stories with familiar magical characters.

Want to learn more about Seth, the mysterious demi-god banished from his clan? His story continues in Impulsive Magic. Buy it on Amazon.

Join Muse Interrupted Romance, my Facebook group, for daily shenanigans and sexy man chest pictures. Sign up for Muse Interrupted, my newsletter, for first access to new releases plus extra content, giveaways, sneak peeks, and first look at new covers.

If you have time, would you mind leaving a review on Amazon? Goodreads or Bookbub would be amazing too! Readers help other readers like you find new books they love.

I appreciate you, and because I do, I've included an excerpt from the next book, Impulsive Magic right here for your reading pleasure. Turn the page to get started on Keely and Seth's adventure.

~Nicole

IMPULSIVE MAGIC

MODERN MAGIC - BOOK FOUR

I

KEELY

MEN WERE a pox on the Earth and nothing would convince Keely Cole otherwise. Her head ached from the tight chignon pulling on her scalp, and her skinny jeans were slowly becoming a second skin in the unseasonably warm April sun. New York City, and Manhattan specifically, was supposed to be a bastion of cool sophistication; the promised land after unpaid internships and grueling graduate work. But all Keely had to show for it was a box of her meager belongings, a mediocre reference letter, and a pair of ridiculous stilettos that weren't meant for actually walking.

Her asshole of a boss had fired her because the company was *going in a different direction*. What he meant was *I'm giving your job to my nephew*. It was a shit job to begin with.

Assistant editor at a no-name publisher that she suspected of being a glorified front for the owner. As far as she knew, they'd only published two books in the last year, and both had tanked. Keely hadn't worked on either. She'd been too busy getting coffee and finding new, inventive excuses to avoid paying the authors.

Mid-afternoon on a Tuesday meant a relatively empty street. Everyone else had jobs to do. Fine by Keely, the space gave her more room to stomp. She normally enjoyed the fifteen-minute walk from her office to her house, but unlike most afternoons, she hadn't brought her sneakers for the commute.

The day was rife with poor decisions.

A crack in the uneven sidewalk grabbed Keely's heel, and she lurched forward, dumping her box all over 3rd Avenue. She caught herself before hitting the ground, but her reflexes hadn't saved the special coffee mug Charlotte had given her when Keely had gotten the job. Shards of the last year of her life littered the sidewalk, forcing other pedestrians to tread carefully through her mess.

Keely braced herself in the middle of the concrete and yanked the offending shoe off her foot. The heel dangled uselessly, held on by a thin strip of fabric. She'd splurged on those shoes because she'd thought her meeting with her boss today meant she was getting a promotion. Ha! Let that be a lesson for future splurges.

Her job was toast, her savings were anemic, rent was due, and her sexy new shoes were ruined. Anger and frustration blurred her vision. Keely pulled off the still intact stiletto and tossed both as hard as she could down the alley next to her. One clattered against a metal dumpster, but the other hit something soft with a thud that elicited a quiet curse.

Keely's eyebrows shot up. The low, rough voice caused a weird little tingle to shiver its way down her spine. She'd most likely just pegged a homeless guy trying to get some sleep, but her Southern upbringing demanded she apologize. Her pathetic finances demanded she retrieve the shoes in the hopes that she could get them fixed.

She collected the rest of her office stuff from the sidewalk, set everything down carefully at the entrance to the alley, and pulled out her pepper spray. No New Yorker worth her salt went anywhere without pepper spray, and though Keely had only lived there six years, she tried her best to follow smart advice.

Like don't go down shady, deserted alleys to investigate a possible shoe maiming?

Keely told her inner voice to shut up. Barefoot and frazzled, she crept into the shadows cast by the red brick buildings lining the street. A large blue dumpster took up most of the alley. Almost taller than her, it smelled horrifically like rotting fish and oranges. After the first whiff, she tried to breathe shallowly through her mouth, but the smell lingered in the back of her throat.

The first shoe had landed at the base of the dumpster. Keely picked it up and tucked it under her free arm. The heel wouldn't even make a reasonable weapon. Piles of cardboard boxes mostly blocked the rest of the alley, but a rustling noise behind them clued Keely in to the location of her other shoe.

She peered around the boxes, and a long, dark snout with a tuft of brownish-red hair on top popped up from the other side. Keely squealed and jumped back a step. The animal tilted its head at her and stepped out from behind the mess.

A llama. There was a llama in the alley. Was that what she'd hit with her shoe?

No one else appeared at her shriek, but she'd definitely heard a man's voice. Keely leaned over and spotted her shoe near the llama's feet. A few metal doors opened into the alley, could she have scared off the owner?

Keely lifted her hand and reached for the llama's soft-looking nose. It didn't move as she approached, and Keely searched for any kind of collar or tag that would identify it. Did they even make collars big enough for llamas? She took a step closer, and her foot landed in a slimy puddle before she could make contact with fur.

Her eyes closed for a second, and her head dropped. Of course. *Of course.* There were any number of disgusting options for what she'd just stepped in, and she had no intention of looking to see what it was. Llama or no, she'd hit her limit. The shoes could rot with the rest of her future.

Keely shook her head, pulled her shoulders back, and turned to walk the rest of the way home barefoot. Hopefully, it would scrape off whatever clung to her toes.

As an afterthought, she spoke over her shoulder. "Sorry, llama. Let your owner know I didn't mean to assault him."

Apology accepted.

Keely spun around again at the same male voice she'd heard before. The llama had come out past the boxes, but the alley remained empty of other people. Unless someone was hiding in the dumpster. The dingy metal sides reached up past her head, so she couldn't look inside. Also, anyone willing to hide in that god-awful stench was clearly insane and not someone she wanted to mess with.

"Hello?" Perfect. She sounded exactly like a stupid heroine about to get murdered.

No one answered, but the llama came closer, stepping

through the puddles in the alley on dainty feet. Not a word she ever thought she'd use to describe a llama, but it was a day for firsts as well as poor decisions. The animal had clean fur and seemed docile, but Keely didn't feel like taking any more chances as it approached her. She backed away from the animal in favor of the open street.

Male laughter filled her mind. Not the alley. Not the street. Her mind.

Holy shit, the llama was telepathic. The laughter got louder, and Keely had the urge to kick the llama in the shins. Did llamas have shins?

Her eyes narrowed. There was a better than nothing chance that she'd finally snapped under the stress, but Keely suspected the weirdness happening right now had nothing to do with how crappy her life had suddenly become.

"You're not really a llama, are you?"

Good guess. The llama—she needed something better to call him than that—stopped before forcing her out of the alley. *As entertaining as this meeting has been, I need your help before you run away.*

Keely placed her hand firmly on the trigger for the pepper spray and her weight on her toes just in case. She was no stranger to weirdness. Her brother and sister-in-law had an imp that they thought they kept secret, and her twin nephews definitely had magical tendencies. It hadn't come from her side of the family though. All her relatives exemplified mundane and boring. At least, the ones she knew about. Her parents weren't exactly forthcoming with family information.

The llama tilted his head. *You have some experience with magical creatures, right?*

The disconnect between the sexy voice drifting across

her mind and the furry figure in front of her messed with her head. "No. You'd be my first. What do you need help with?"

He sighed. *I need you to kiss me.*

Keely winced. "That's a little cliché, don't you think?"

It wasn't my idea.

A tinge of embarrassment came across with the words, and Keely wondered whose idea it had been. Then she decided it didn't matter. As long as he didn't try to bite her, it wouldn't kill her to kiss a cute animal. Maybe the fairy tales were true and he'd turn into a handsome prince.

Keely leaned forward, but the llama jerked his head out of the way. The sense of embarrassment thickened.

Not...on my face.

She stared at him for a second, uncomprehending. "Where else would I..." Both eyebrows shot up. Nope. Hard nope. "I'm not kissing your ass. Good luck on your quest."

Barefoot and completely done with the day, Keely turned, grabbed her box, and marched back into the flow of pedestrians.

Wait...

The loud voice echoed a bit, but she didn't hear the sound of llama hooves behind her. Keely forced her mind back to her lost job and resolved to ignore any future telepathic llamas. She hadn't even gotten his name.

The rest of the trip home passed in a blessedly uneventful blur. Keely shook her head as she strode up the steps to the small row house she shared with her roommates. Three of them lived in two bedrooms, and they all shared a single bath. The lack of space sucked, but her roommates were nice. Not nice enough to let her live there rent-free, though.

For once, there wasn't a cacophony of noise the second

she opened the door. The place seemed bigger in the silence. She carried her box up the steps to the bedroom she shared with Dru. As usual, Dru's side of the room disappeared under clothes strewn about like confetti. She lived her life the same way. One big party.

Keely sighed and sank down on her bed, the box in her lap. She didn't even have time to start panicking before Samantha tapped on her door. Samantha—always Samantha, never Sam—was the alpha roommate; the one whose name actually appeared on the lease. Perfectly made up, her hair in a sleek ponytail, Samantha towered over Keely, physically and emotionally.

She loved rules, as long as they were *her* rules, and woe to anyone who broke them. Despite the staid veneer, she'd be a vicious enemy to anyone who'd cause harm to her friends. And her frown made Keely search her mind for any infractions she may have inadvertently caused.

Samantha leaned against the doorframe without waiting for Keely to invite her in. "Why aren't you at work?"

Keely lifted the box a couple of inches. "I got fired."

"I thought you were expecting a promotion."

"I was." Keely let the box drop back onto her lap.

Samantha's frown deepened, etching dark furrows into her forehead. "That's problematic. I need to talk to you about your rooming situation."

"I'll be able to pay my rent." Keely just didn't know *how* quite yet.

"I'm not worried about that right now. Dru's best friend is moving to New York."

Sadness and exhaustion swept through Keely, as her shoulders fell a little further. She liked Dru. The woman made a mean margarita. The prospect of losing a great roommate and a better friend hurt, but worse, she didn't think she could afford a larger slice of the rent.

Samantha cleared her throat, and Keely realized she'd been staring down into her box, wallowing. She schooled her face and met Samantha's hazel eyes.

"How long do we have before Dru leaves?"

The frown disappeared. "Oh, Dru isn't leaving. She wants Nick to move in here."

Keely sputtered. "Here? With us? Why didn't she tell me?"

"She felt, appropriately, that she should consult me first. I have no problem with a man living here, but you'd all have to share this room. I was going to wait until you were both home tonight, but an opportunity presented itself."

"Are you serious?"

Samantha's brow furrowed. "Yes. Dru agreed to cover the cost of a bunk bed for them, but you'll need to move some of your things to make space. Your rent will go down a small amount, which I guess is good timing considering your job."

Keely stared at Samantha in horror. Four of them, one a dude, sharing one bathroom. They'd already maximized their room for storage. How were they supposed to fit in another whole person worth of stuff?

"I'm moving out." The words left Keely's mouth before her brain had a chance to weigh-in.

Surprise flashed across Samantha's face. "Since Nick is moving in, if that's what you want, we can make it happen. You're paid through the end of April, so you'll have a couple of weeks to look for a new place." She shook her head. "I don't think now is the best time to make rash decisions, but you're an adult so I'll mind my own business."

Keely blew out a breath she'd been holding. "Thanks,

Samantha. You're a fantastic landlord. I just need something new."

"Dru will be sad, but I think Nick will help alleviate that." Her lips tipped up in a half smile. "She'll miss you. We both will."

Panic threatened to overtake Keely. Samantha had a point, but this rash decision felt right. That didn't stop her chest from getting tight. Keely smiled through the free fall, but judging by Samantha's worried look, her eyes still appeared wild.

"It's not like I'm leaving the planet. There's more to New York than Manhattan."

Samantha gasped. "Blasphemy. Bite your tongue, foul wench."

Keely rolled her eyes, but gave her a real grin. "Take your bastardized Shakespeare elsewhere."

"That's better. Now that you don't look like you're going to chew through your own arm, I have work to finish up. Dinner at six, if you're interested."

Samantha pulled the door closed behind her, and Keely's good mood evaporated. She'd have to decline dinner at six. Samantha and Dru always wanted to eat out, and her money had suddenly become a lot more precious. Peanut butter and jam would do.

Before then, Keely needed to get ahold of herself. Rash decisions hadn't been her thing for a long time, and lately, she'd jumped from one to the next like stepping stones. If she'd learned anything from her disastrous last year of college, she needed to haul herself to a stop and let her common sense catch up.

A couple of deep breaths relaxed her shoulders and reminded Keely that the scented plug-in needed to be replaced. The smell leaned more toward burnt apple than summer bounty. She kept track of those things for Dru, and in exchange, Dru talked her into the occasional flamboyant color when Keely went too far with the beige.

They'd both have to learn to deal on their own now.

One foot in front of the other, a motto her mom said often when faced with hardship. A pang of homesickness threatened to knot her back up again, but she shrugged it off. Texas wasn't the answer. She intended to follow through with her future plans even if they were slightly delayed, but the doubt planted years before choked out most of her optimism. What was the point in chasing a dream that made her miserable?

For a short moment, Keely gave in to despair and let the tears come. They flowed down her face in hot streaks until she angrily wiped them away. Enough. Tears had never helped her achieve her goals, and they wouldn't now.

Keely set her jaw. She'd worked hard to build the life in New York she'd always wanted, and no amount of homelessness or poverty would stop her. She got shit done. Period. Which meant she'd better start with finding a new job. Landlords frowned on renting a place to someone without any income.

Her laptop sat on the side table she used for a nightstand, dresser, and desk, the only piece of furniture she owned besides her bed. Keely finally dropped the box onto the floor near her feet and took stock. Sweaty, dirty, morose, and potentially hallucinating magical llamas with butt fetishes.

Her emotions fluctuated wildly, so any decisions she made would be questionable at best. Better to take a break and come back to it with full power.

Keely took advantage of the uninterrupted bathroom time in the middle of the day. She stayed in the shower until the hot water ran out, then dressed in her favorite jeans and tee shirt. The one that said *book nerd* in big letters across the front. Her afternoon stretched before her, suddenly empty, and Keely needed some time in the sun. Maybe a walk to the park where she could obsess about how her future might be going down in flames.

She shoved a sack of stale bread in her bag and grabbed one of her secret ice cream bars from the back of the freezer. Keely hid them in a box of frozen okra, a trick she'd learned in her teen years when her brother repeatedly stole all the good popsicles. Why did they even put grape ones in there? No one wanted grape.

Keely ate the ice cream while standing at the window staring into their backyard. If not for Dru, it would probably be a jungle of weeds, but the wild greenery looked like something from a magazine. A fairy garden with a flagstone path running through the middle, though the path only led to a rickety table by the back fence. She remembered when Dru had come home with a stack of uneven, flat stones and refused to say where she got them.

A purloined flagstone path. It sounded like a cozy mystery that her former company would pretend to publish. Bitter thoughts fought for dominance, but Keely only wanted to feel sad for a bit. The job may have sucked, but it had been her dream once upon a time. A dream she'd almost given up and had fought desperately to keep.

Without the solid foundation Samantha and Dru provided at the beginning, she might have lost it anyway. The row house had been her home for more than a year, and now she'd chosen to leave that too. Compounding bad luck with bad decisions? Who could tell?

All her carefully laid plans were crumbling, and Keely didn't know how to shore them up.

Find a job. Find a place to live. Adjust her dreams. It didn't sound hard, but it had taken her close to six months to find that first job. She had three weeks.

First, the park. Keely licked her fingers, grabbed the messenger bag she'd dropped on the counter, and turned away from Dru's urban paradise. She'd take one day to think and mourn, then she'd get to work.

The front door slammed behind her, but for once Keely didn't care about staying on Samantha's good side. She pulled up short half-way down the steps when she noticed the large reddish-brown llama standing on the sidewalk outside their wrought iron fence. She looked around, but none of the other pedestrians paid him any mind. What were the chances there were two llamas wandering around the east side of Manhattan?

Two identical llamas?

Fancy meeting you here.

Keely dropped her head, pushing her fingers through her hair to let her palms rest at her temples. There was no mistaking that husky voice. The alley llama had followed her home.

My name is Seth.

She looked up, but kept her hands in her hair. "Why are you haunting me?"

I told you. I need your help.

"There's something like one point five million people in Manhattan. Why not ask one of them?"

Seth didn't answer, and it occurred to her that she was essentially talking aloud to herself. Luckily, most people were desensitized to crazy in New York. Keely lived on a fairly quiet street, but traffic started to pick up as the work day ended. A steady throng of people walked by, and exactly none of them noticed Seth, let alone at her.

As she watched, a man in a blue suit walked right into Seth's butt. The man bounced back and looked in confusion at the sidewalk in front of him. He glanced back and forth, then glared at her when she made eye contact.

"Sorry," Keely called as he edged closer to the street and kept walking. She didn't know why she'd apologized. Seth was the one blocking the sidewalk. For that matter, why hadn't the guy just gone around the giant-ass llama in his way?

They can't see me.

Keely glowered at him. "I'm special then?"

An older woman nearly collided with him, but he side-stepped at the last second. Keely sighed and opened the gate so he could come into their tiny courtyard area.

Evidently.

Keely leaned against the brick and lowered her voice. "Why can I see you if they can't?"

It's part of the spell.

She waited, but he didn't explain. He sniffed at the potted plant Dru must have put there; she always brought home sad looking plants. Nothing about him said anything other than llama to her, and a seed of doubt started growing a little at a time.

"Do I get a better explanation than that?"

Nope. Also part of the spell. I can't talk about the details.

She couldn't deny his voice in her head, but she'd heard hallucinations could be vivid.

Hallucination or not, she knew an easy solution that didn't involve grilling a reluctant fake llama. Charlotte, her sister-in-law/best friend well-versed in the hidden magical world, was only a phone call away.

Seth nibbled on a broad leaf of the plant while Keely pulled out her cell phone. *Who are you calling?*

"My best friend."

Need reassurance you're not crazy?

Keely ignored him, and Charlotte answered on the third ring, breathless. "Yes?"

"Is that how we're answering the phone now?"

"It is when I know who's calling and I was busy doing *something else*." Keely winced. She didn't want to think about Charlotte and her brother getting naked.

"Gross. Isn't it the middle of the day there? Who's watching the twins?"

A low grumble in the background preceded a door closing, and Charlotte sighed. "Well, now you have my full attention. Rav is with the boys."

"Your imp is babysitting the twins?"

"It's fine. She does it all the time. Honestly, she's better with them than we are."

"They're four times her size!"

Charlotte was silent for a moment. "How big do you think the twins *are*?"

Keely shrugged even though Charlotte couldn't see her. What did she know about babies? Seth pulled on the leaf and almost knocked the plant over. Keely swatted at him, and he huffed warm air across her arm.

"New topic. I'm going to ask a question, and it's going to sound crazy. Remember when you called me about Rav and I totally believed you right from the start? I'm going to need some of that faith." Keely took a deep breath. "What do you know about invisible, telepathic llamas?"

Charlotte laughed so hard on the other end that Keely considered hanging up and calling her brother instead.

"It didn't seem that funny to me."

Charlotte gasped for breath and finally calmed down enough to respond. "You're right. I'm sorry. I've never heard of an invisible llama. I know telepathy is possible but rare among magical types. I'm afraid I can't help you."

Keely deflated. "That's what I thought you'd say."

Charlotte sobered. "Are you in trouble?"

"No. Just having a hard day."

"Okay, but be careful. Llama or not, magical creatures are tricky. There's always more to it than what they're telling you." A high-pitched squeal echoed in the background, and Charlotte sighed. "That was Jax. I have to go. Love you. Be careful."

"I will. Love you too."

Keely hung up and shoved her phone back in her bag. Seth hadn't moved, but the plant was missing a couple of leaves. "If I do this, you'll leave me alone? There's no fine print involved in this magic?"

He tilted his head at her. *Spent some time with the Fae, have you?*

"No. And you didn't answer the question."

There's no fine print. You kiss me. I change back. Done.

It still felt dangerous to simply do as asked. Complicated magic often didn't take free will into account. Or so she'd heard from Charlotte. Keely's experience with magic was limited to second-hand accounts and meeting Rav the one time she'd gone home when the twins were born.

Frustration leaked into his voice. *All I need is one little kiss. It won't cost you anything, and I can go back to my life. That seems like a pretty good trade-off to me.*

She looked away with a frown. He was right. One stupid kiss wouldn't kill her, so what if he needed it on his backside instead of his front. What could possibly happen that would be worse than the day she'd already had?

"Okay. Fine. Turn around or whatever before I change my mind."

Relief came off him in waves. *Thank you.*

A second later, she was face to butt with a llama and really questioning her life choices. At least he didn't smell bad.

Keely pressed a kiss to his flank, making sure she pushed hard enough to get past the fur and connect with muscle. The surprisingly soft hair tickled her cheek, but when she pulled back, nothing had changed. Seth was still a llama.

Fuck.

Yeah. That seemed about right.

Impulsive Magic

ALSO BY NICOLE HALL

Modern Magic

Accidental Magic

Insidious Magic

Treacherous Magic

Impulsive Magic

Rebellious Magic

Chaotic Magic

ABOUT THE AUTHOR

Nicole Hall is a smart-ass with a Ph.D. and a potty mouth. She writes stories that have magic, sass, and romance because she believes that everyone deserves a little happiness. Coffee makes her happy, messes make her stabby, and she'd sell one of her children for a second season of Firefly. Her paranormal romance series, Modern Magic, is available now.

Let Nicole know what you thought about her sassy, magical world because she really does love hearing from readers. Find her at www.nicolehallbooks.com or Muse Interrupted Romance on Facebook!

Want to find out when the newest Nicole Hall book hits the shelves? Sign up for the weekly Muse Interrupted newsletter on her website. You'll get a welcome gift, the *Modern Magic* ebook, plus new release info, giveaways, exclusive content, and previews of the new books especially for fans.

f facebook.com/nicolehallbooks

o instagram.com/nicolehallbooks

a amazon.com/author/nicole_hall

BB bookbub.com/authors/nicole-hall